Phyllis looked toward the living room, and the first thing she noticed was that the cookies she had left on the end table were now scattered across the floor. Some of them were crushed as if they had been stepped on.

Phyllis took an instinctive step backward, then stopped as she saw a couple of feet in fuzzy slippers sticking out between the sofa and a coffee table. She spotted one of the legs of a walker, too, and she could tell from its position that it was overturned.

Her heart pounding, Phyllis rushed into the living room, crying out, "Agnes!" She came around the sofa and saw the elderly woman lying on her side, unmoving. Agnes's robe had fallen open.

Phyllis recoiled as she realized why the robe was open. The belt was wrapped around Agnes's neck and pulled so tight, it was sunk into the flesh. . . .

MORE PRAISE FOR THE FRESH-BAKED MYSTERIES

"The whodunit is fun and the recipes [are] mouthwatering."
—The Best Reviews

"Washburn has a refreshing way with words and knows how to tell an exciting story." —*Midwest Book Review*

"Delightful, [with a] realistic small-town vibe [and a] vibrant narrative . . . *A Peach of a Murder* runs the full range of emotions, so be prepared to laugh and cry with this one!"
—The Romance Readers Connection

"I really enjoyed *Murder by the Slice*. . . . It's got a nice plot with lots of twists." —James Reasoner

Other Fresh-Baked Mysteries
by Livia J. Washburn

A Peach of a Murder

Murder by the Slice

The Christmas Cookie Killer

A Fresh-Baked Mystery

LIVIA J. WASHBURN

AN OBSIDIAN MYSTERY

OBSIDIAN
Published by New American Library,
a division of Penguin Group (USA) Inc.,
375 Hudson Street, New York, New York 10014, USA
Penguin Group (Canada), 90 Eglinton Avenue East, Suite 700, Toronto,
Ontario M4P 2Y3, Canada (a division of Pearson Penguin Canada Inc.)
Penguin Books Ltd., 80 Strand, London WC2R 0RL, England
Penguin Ireland, 25 St. Stephen's Green, Dublin 2,
Ireland (a division of Penguin Books Ltd.)
Penguin Group (Australia), 250 Camberwell Road, Camberwell, Victoria 3124,
Australia (a division of Pearson Australia Group Pty. Ltd.)
Penguin Books India Pvt. Ltd., 11 Community Centre,
Panchsheel Park, New Delhi - 110 017, India
Penguin Group (NZ), 67 Apollo Drive, Rosedale, North Shore 0632,
New Zealand (a division of Pearson New Zealand Ltd.)
Penguin Books (South Africa) (Pty.) Ltd., 24 Sturdee Avenue,
Rosebank, Johannesburg 2196, South Africa

Penguin Books Ltd., Registered Offices:
80 Strand, London WC2R 0RL, England

First published by Obsidian, an imprint of New American Library,
a division of Penguin Group (USA) Inc.

First Printing, October 2008
1   3   5   7   9   10   8   6   4   2

OBSIDIAN and logo are trademarks of Penguin Group (USA) Inc.

LIBRARY OF CONGRESS CATALOGING-IN-PUBLICATION DATA

Washburn, L. J.
The Christmas cookie killer: a fresh-baked mystery/Livia J. Washburn.
p.   cm.
"An Obsidian mystery"—T.p. verso.
ISBN 978-0-451-22534-4
1. Newsom, Phyllis (Fictitious character)—Fiction. 2. Retired teachers—Fiction 3. Baking—
Fiction. 4. Weatherford (Tex.)—Fiction. 5. Murder—Investigation—Fiction. I. Title.
PS3573.A787C48   2008
813'.54—dc22   2008016304

Set in New Caledonia   •   Designed by Elke Sigal
Printed in the United States of America

This book is dedicated to my husband, James Reasoner,

and my two daughters, Shayna and Joanna,
who helped make this book possible.

And to my brother Bruce
for his tasty ham recipe.

Chapter 1

*T*here were probably a few things in the world that smelled better than freshly baked cookies, but right now, for the life of her, Phyllis Newsom couldn't think of what they might be.

Throw in the scent of pine from the Christmas tree in the corner of the living room, and this had to be what heaven smelled like, Phyllis thought. The only thing that might improve it would be if she asked Sam Fletcher to start a fire in the big stone fireplace. Since this was Texas, where the winters were mild except for the occasional blue norther that came roaring down out of the Panhandle, the fireplace didn't get much use. Phyllis's late husband, Kenny, had gotten a fire going in it once or twice a year, on average, but it hadn't been used since he passed away.

Phyllis felt a mental twinge and wondered if it would be disloyal to Kenny's memory to have Sam build a fire. She decided that it wouldn't. The hearth was there to be used, after all. And with a cold front blowing through, by tonight the heat from some flames would feel awfully good in this drafty old house.

Of course, there was a central heating and cooling unit humming away, but that wasn't the same thing. It just wasn't the same thing at all.

Phyllis stood in the big, arched opening between the living room and dining room and watched with a smile on her face as most of her neighbors milled around the dining table, which was covered with platters of cookies—all kinds of cookies: plain, fancy, some with frosting, some not. Holiday decorations abounded. Phyllis was sure the cookies tasted as good as they looked, too, but for now, no one was sampling them. This was the time to just admire them.

On a day like today, with so many guests, having a big house came in handy. Quite a few people lived in this neighborhood of older homes a few blocks from the downtown square of Weatherford, Texas, and most of them had come over on this Saturday afternoon for the annual Christmas cookie exchange. As busy and hectic as life was these days, folks didn't see their neighbors as much as they used to. It was good to catch up on what had been going on in everybody's life. The get-together also served as an unofficial welcome party for people who had moved into the neighborhood since the previous Christmas.

Sam Fletcher moved up beside Phyllis and asked in a quiet voice, "Is there always this big a turnout?"

That reminded Phyllis that this was Sam's first Christmas in the house. He was a relative newcomer, too. He had moved in only during the summer, although he fit in so well with Phyllis and her other boarders that it seemed as if he had always been here. Even Carolyn Wilbarger, who had been leery of the idea of having a man living in the house with three women, had accepted him.

Phyllis had started taking in boarders after Kenny's death, when it became obvious that the house was too big for her alone. It wasn't so much a matter of money. It was more that she couldn't stand rattling around by herself in it. As a retired teacher, she had extended the offer to friends of hers who were also longtime educators and found themselves in need of a place to live. There had been other boarders along the way, but at the moment the inhabitants of the house consisted of herself; Carolyn Wilbarger, who was widowed like Phyllis; Eve Turner, who was divorced—or between marriages, as she liked to put it; and Sam Fletcher, who had lost his wife to cancer a couple of years earlier—all former teachers, and now all good friends. One of the rooms upstairs was vacant, but Phyllis hadn't gone out of her way to look for another boarder. She didn't want to disrupt the chemistry that had developed in the house. She knew from the years she had spent in a classroom that once a group of people got along well, you didn't want to go messing with it too much.

"Yes, there's usually a big crowd," she said to Sam, tilting her head back a little so she could look up at the lanky, raw-boned former basketball coach and history teacher. Phyllis had taught eighth-grade history, so she had a love of the past in common with Sam. "People like to socialize at this time of year, and they'll always come out for cookies, even on a chilly afternoon like this."

A grin creased Sam's rugged face. "Can't argue with that. I'm a mite fond of cookies myself. When can we dig in?"

"In a little while. Just be patient."

Sam shook his head. "I'll try. But it won't be easy." He paused, then added, "When are you supposed to find out who won the contest?"

"The winner will be announced in the paper next week, a couple of days before Christmas."

"Think you've got a shot at winnin'?"

"I *always* think I have a chance to win. Otherwise I wouldn't enter."

Carolyn had come up behind Phyllis in time to hear that comment. She said, "Yes, you have to get credit for perseverance. It's a shame it hasn't paid off for you very often."

Phyllis turned her head to glare over her shoulder, but she didn't really mean it. It was true that she and Carolyn had a long history of competing against each other in various baking contests, and it was also true that Carolyn won considerably more often than she lost, but Phyllis didn't take the rivalry all that seriously. She didn't really care who won as long as she had a good time coming up with the recipes.

At least, that was what she tried to believe. . . .

"We'll see what the judges think next week."

Phyllis and Carolyn had both entered recipes in the local newspaper's annual Christmas cookie contest. The rules were simple: bake a batch of cookies and take them to the newspaper office along with the recipe, and a panel of expert judges would select the best cookies. The recipe would be published in the paper. Phyllis wasn't exactly sure who those expert judges were—she suspected they were all the people who worked at the newspaper and that the contest was at least partially a way to get people to give them free cookies—but she didn't care. What she enjoyed was creating the recipes and baking the cookies.

This year she had baked lime sugar cookies sprinkled with sugar and cut with a special set of snowflake cookie cutters so that each cookie was shaped a little bit differently from all the others. The cookies were unusual, looked good, and tasted great, so Phyllis thought she had at least a decent shot at winning.

Eve joined Phyllis, Carolyn, and Sam in the archway and

scanned the crowd with avid interest, reminding Phyllis a little of a hunting falcon.

"If you're looking for eligible men who have moved in since last year, you're out of luck," Carolyn said. "You'll have to find husband number five—or is it six?—somewhere else."

Eve smiled and took Sam's arm. "Why, the most eligible man in the neighborhood is right here, don't you think, dear?"

Carolyn snorted and Sam looked uncomfortable, and to change the subject Phyllis said, "I suppose I'd better put a plate of cookies together for Agnes."

"I hadn't noticed that she's not here," Eve said. "She's always so quiet, you hardly notice when she's there, let alone when she's not."

"She called and said she wasn't coming," Phyllis explained. "She's getting around a little these days, but she still has to use a walker, and it's not easy for her. I went over earlier and picked up her plate of gingerdoodle cookies, and I promised her I'd bring her a sampler of everyone else's."

"What in the world are gingerdoodle cookies?" Carolyn asked. "I've never heard of those."

"I asked Agnes that same question when I picked up the cookies. She said that they were like snickerdoodles, but they have ginger in the coating."

Agnes Simmons had lived next door to Phyllis for more than thirty years. They were friends but had never been close. Agnes was in her late eighties, more than twenty years older than Phyllis, and they had little in common besides being neighbors and attending the same church.

A month earlier, when Agnes had fallen and broken her hip, Phyllis had pitched in to help her because that was what neighbors did, whether they were close friends or not. Once Agnes returned home from the rehab hospital, Phyllis visited often, bringing food, cleaning up around the place, running any errands that needed doing. Sam had gone with her a time or two to do some carpentry and yard work.

Phyllis went into the kitchen and got a large plate from the cabinet. She had made a big bowl of punch and had it sitting on the kitchen counter along with a stack of plastic cups so that people could help themselves. Young people would probably be horrified at the thought of visitors milling around unattended in their houses, some of them almost strangers. But Phyllis had been raised in a more hospitable time, a more innocent time, she supposed, and despite her own brushes with violent crime over the past six months, she liked to think that she maintained some of that bygone innocence—mixed with a healthy dose of reasonable caution, of course.

She returned to the dining room and filled the plate with cookies from the various platters, taking two or three of each kind for Agnes Simmons. When the plate was full, she covered it with plastic wrap. Catching Carolyn's eye, she said, "I'll be right back."

"Would you like some company?"

"No, that's all right. I'll be fine." It would take only a couple of minutes to walk next door.

Phyllis felt the chilly wind on her face as she stepped out onto the porch. The cold front that had come through wasn't strong enough to be considered a blue norther, but it would drop temperatures to a respectable December level. The sky was thick with clouds.

She followed the walk to the sidewalk by the street and turned right, preferring to follow the concrete path rather than cutting across her own lawn and Agnes's yard. That was another vestige of her upbringing. You didn't walk on the grass if you could avoid it.

Agnes's two-story house had a large front porch, like Phyllis's, with a big picture window that had the curtains pulled back, but unlike Phyllis's, it had no swing hanging from chains attached to the porch roof. The porch had a rather bare look to it, in fact. Agnes had been widowed for fifteen years. She had children and grandchildren, but they seldom visited. Knowing that made Phyllis's heart go out to the older woman. She had only one son herself, but Mike stopped by nearly every day, and Phyllis saw her daughter-in-law, Sarah, and her grandson, Bobby, fairly often, too. Whenever she stopped to think about it, although she missed Kenny, she still considered herself to be a lucky woman, surrounded as she was by family and friends.

Phyllis rang the bell, and a moment later she heard the clumping of Agnes's walker as the woman approached the door. "It's just me, Agnes," she called.

The clumping stopped as Agnes replied, "Come on in."

Phyllis opened the screen door and then the wooden door and stepped into the house. Heat washed out at her in waves. Agnes liked to keep the place warm—more than warm, actually. It was stifling in there a lot of the time. Phyllis had learned to put up with it, though. She herself was more prone to getting chilled than she had once been, and Agnes was considerably older. Age thinned the blood, one of many drawbacks to getting on in years.

If only the alternative hadn't been so much worse.

Phyllis saw that Agnes had sat down in an armchair in the living room, next to the big window. The room was well furnished, with a thick rug on the hardwood floor and heavy, plush upholstered furniture. The chairs had lace doilies on the backs. Sitting in a corner by itself was an old-fashioned console TV in a cabinet of dark wood, the top of which held a lace doily, along with several framed pictures of children and grandchildren and a layer of dust. Nothing in the room was less than thirty or forty years old, but that suited Agnes. The television, for example, still had vacuum tubes, but she insisted that it worked just fine and she wasn't going to get a new one until it didn't.

Agnes grasped her walker and pushed herself to her feet again as her gaze landed on the plate of cookies.

"Oh, my," Agnes said. "Don't those look good! You're a dear to bring them over to me like this, Phyllis."

"I just wish you felt good enough to attend the cookie exchange," Phyllis said. "Maybe next year."

"Yes, next year," Agnes said with that dry irony of the elderly, as if the thought of her still being around next year was almost too far-fetched to contemplate.

"Would you like me to put them in the kitchen for you?"

"Bring them over here first. I'd like to take a look at them and maybe try one."

Agnes was a small woman; not birdlike and frail, as so many elderly women are, but compact, with no wasted flesh on her. She wore a quilted pale blue robe. The cloth belt that went with the robe was decorated with fancy silver stitching that matched the stitching on the collar.

Phyllis held the plate where Agnes could see all the cookies. The woman's face, which bore the marks of the strain she had been under since her injury, lit up with a smile.

"They all look wonderful," she said. "I'm sure my grandchildren will love them."

"Oh? Your grandchildren are coming for a visit?"

"They're already here," Agnes said. "Well, not *here*, exactly. Not right at the moment. Frank, Ted, and Billie, and all their families, came in earlier today. I'm not surprised you didn't notice, since you were busy getting ready for the cookie exchange and all."

"Where are they now?" Phyllis asked.

"They drove over to Fort Worth to go to the mall. They'll be back later."

Phyllis nodded. She wasn't convinced that Agnes's sons and daughter and their families had actually arrived to visit her. Agnes might be saying that just so that Phyllis wouldn't think she was going to be alone again on the holidays. But questioning her wouldn't serve any purpose.

"Well, I hope everyone enjoys the cookies."

"I'm sure they will." Agnes took one hand off the walker and reached for the plate. "Look at these snowflakes! They're so pretty!"

"I made those," Phyllis said, not trying to keep the pride out of her voice. When it came to baking, she didn't believe in false modesty.

Agnes broke off a piece, took a bite of the cookie, and exclaimed over how good it was. "How in the world did you get them cut in different shapes?" she wanted to know.

"I have a special set of snowflake cookie cutters," Phyllis explained.

"Would you mind if I borrowed them, dear? I plan to do some baking with my granddaughters while they're here, and they would love to make some cookies like that."

"Of course," Phyllis said. "I'll run next door and get them."

"You're sure you don't mind?"

"Not at all."

"Thank you. That's awfully nice of you, Phyllis."

Phyllis set the plate of cookies on an end table. "I'll be right back."

She left the house and headed back toward her own, tugging her thick sweater tighter around her as she went. She cut across the yards this time, not wanting to be away from her house and the cookie exchange any longer than she had to. Being neighborly to Agnes was one thing, but she had a houseful of guests, and it wasn't right to make Carolyn and Eve look after them for any longer than necessary.

"How's Agnes?" Carolyn asked when Phyllis went inside.

"All right. I'm going to loan my snowflake cookie cutters to her."

Carolyn frowned. "Right now?"

"Her granddaughters are visiting, and she wants to do some baking with them."

Carolyn's eyebrows rose. She was as surprised as Phyllis had been by the idea that Agnes's family had come to spend even part of the Christmas holiday with her.

Before Phyllis could find the cookie cutters, Eve came into the kitchen. "There you are," she said. "Joyce Portwood has to leave early, but she wanted to speak to you before she goes, Phyllis."

"Oh, all right," Phyllis said as she started toward the living room. It wouldn't hurt anything if it took her a few more minutes to get those cookie cutters over to Agnes. After all, it wasn't like Agnes was going anywhere.

Phyllis spent about ten minutes chatting with Joyce, who lived across the street on the next block to the north. She was effusive in her thanks to Phyllis for hosting the cookie exchange, but that was nothing unusual. Joyce was always effusive, no matter what the circumstances. She was apologetic, too, for having to leave early. Phyllis told her not to worry about it.

Once she was finished talking to Joyce, Phyllis got the set of cookie cutters from the kitchen, although it took her longer than she expected to find them because during all the preparation for today's get-together, they had been moved and put in a different drawer from the one where she usually kept them. She'd been gone long enough that she hoped Agnes hadn't started to worry about her.

When she left, she went out the back door this time, walking between the houses to the front yards again. A hedge divided the properties, and she heard a door shut somewhere on the other side of it, in Agnes's house. Maybe the kids and grandkids were back from the mall.

No strange cars were in the driveway, though, Phyllis noted as she reached the front of the house and climbed to the porch again. She planned to just knock and go on in, since Agnes was expecting her back, but she noticed that the wooden door was ajar behind the screen. She felt the heat coming out of the house before she even reached the door. That was odd, to say the least. Agnes never liked to let hot air out or cold air in.

Phyllis pulled the screen door open and leaned toward the wooden door. "Agnes?" she called. "It's just me again. I've got the cookie cutters. Sorry it took me so long."

No response came from inside. Phyllis supposed that Agnes could have gone into the kitchen or somewhere else in the rear of the house. She had heard that door shut, after all.

"Agnes?" Phyllis stepped inside. "Are you still here?"

She looked toward the living room, and the first thing she noticed was that the cookies she had left on the end table were now scattered across the floor. Some of them were crushed as if they had been stepped on. The plate lay upside down on the floor next to the table.

Phyllis gasped in surprise at the sight. She took an instinctive step backward, then stopped as she saw a couple of feet in fuzzy slippers sticking out between the sofa and a coffee table. She spotted one of the legs of the walker, too, and she could tell from its position that it was overturned.

She knew in that moment what had happened. Agnes, none

too steady even on the walker, had fallen again. She had probably reached out as she was toppling over, trying to catch herself, and hit the plate of cookies with her hand, sending it flying. Those slippered feet weren't moving, so it was likely Agnes had either passed out or knocked herself out when she fell.

With her heart pounding, Phyllis rushed into the living room, crying out, "Agnes!" She came around the sofa and saw the elderly woman lying on her side, unmoving. Agnes's robe had fallen open, revealing a pink flannel nightgown under it.

Phyllis recoiled as she realized why the robe was open. The belt that had been around Agnes's waist was no longer there to hold it closed.

That was because the belt was wrapped around Agnes's neck and pulled so tight, it was sunk into the flesh. Agnes's eyes were wide-open, staring sightlessly from her twisted, lifeless face.

Chapter 2

For a moment, the enormity of what she was looking at failed to register in Phyllis's stunned brain. She had seen dead bodies before—too many of them, in fact—but she would never become accustomed to making such grisly discoveries. It would have been bad enough to have come in and found that Agnes had fallen and injured herself again—worse still if the fall had knocked her out or even killed her.

But this was no accident. Someone had taken the belt from Agnes's robe, wrapped it around her neck, knotted it, and used it to choke the life out of her.

This was murder.

And remembering that shutting door she had heard a few minutes earlier, Phyllis suddenly realized that the killer could still be right here in the house.

But maybe Agnes wasn't dead, Phyllis thought as she fought down the panic that tried to well up inside her. She didn't know how long it had been since the attack had taken place. Maybe Agnes could still be revived. Phyllis had been trained in CPR.

She couldn't let her own fear make her abandon Agnes if there was even the slightest chance the woman was still alive.

Phyllis hurried forward, dropped to a knee at Agnes's side, and struggled to loosen the belt around her neck. She was barely able to get her fingers under it, and even then she couldn't budge the knot. She tugged at it for a moment, then realized she needed to get something to cut it.

Her gaze darted around the room, searching for a sewing basket or something else that might have some scissors in it. But there was nothing. Agnes wasn't much for sewing or knitting or anything like that. Mainly, Phyllis knew, she liked to sit by the picture window and watch everything that was going on in the neighborhood.

There might be some scissors in the kitchen, Phyllis realized. Nearly every kitchen had a "junk" drawer, and among assorted screwdrivers, keys, loose change, little jars of screws and nuts and bolts, and all the other assorted clutter of everyday life, there was usually a pair of scissors. If not, there would be a knife.

The thought took only a second to flash through her brain, and then she was up and hurrying into the short hallway that led from the living room to the kitchen. Phyllis walked quickly along it and turned to her left, stepping through an open door into Agnes's simply furnished kitchen. She saw cabinets on both sides of her and had no idea which one contained Agnes's junk drawer. She was about to start opening them at random when she heard a slight noise behind her.

Then something struck her on the back of the head, hard enough to send her stumbling forward. She took a couple of steps and fell to her knees. Pain shot up her thighs, rivaling the pain in her head, as her knees cracked against the linoleum floor. She sobbed and clutched at the kitchen counter, trying to keep from collapsing.

But her fingers slipped, and she stretched out full-length on the floor. Her head twisted to the side as her cheek pressed against the cool linoleum. Blackness closed in around her.

Later, Phyllis knew she had passed out for only a few moments, but at the time she had no idea how long the spell lasted. It could have been mere minutes, or an hour, for all she knew. All she could really be certain of, all she could think about at first, was that her head and her knees hurt like the dickens.

Then she remembered Agnes Simmons, and the belt knotted so tightly around the old woman's neck.

With a groan, Phyllis pushed herself to her hands and knees. She wondered how she had managed to hit her head so hard, and what she had hit it on. She remembered how Kenny had run into an open door one time, hitting his head on the edge of it with such force that it opened up a gash through one of his eyebrows and gave him a concussion. People always joked about running into a door, but he'd actually done it. Phyllis wondered if she had hit her head on a cabinet door—

Then the memory of the sound she'd heard came back to her, and she gasped as she realized that it hadn't been an accident. Someone had come up behind her and hit her. They had followed her into the kitchen. . . .

Or they'd been hiding behind that open door.

She jerked around, eyes wide as she looked for her attacker. The kitchen was empty, though, except for her. The house was quiet—so quiet, Phyllis heard the ticking of the grandfather clock in the hallway and the pounding of her own pulse inside her head.

Whoever had struck her had fled, she told herself. And Agnes was still lying out there in the living room with that robe belt around her throat. With one hand on the counter to steady herself, and wincing from the pain in her head and knees, Phyllis started jerking open drawers as she searched for a pair of scissors.

She found one in the third drawer she opened and turned to start back to the living room. As she did, the floor seemed to tilt and the world spun crazily around her, as if it had started revolving the wrong way on its axis. She slapped her free hand on the counter to catch herself. She didn't want to fall again, especially while holding scissors.

Phyllis's balance began to come back to her as she forced herself to draw in several deep breaths. When she thought she could move without getting too dizzy, she tried again to reach the living room. She was successful this time, making it all the way to Agnes's side. Using the sofa to brace herself, Phyllis knelt and started trying to work one side of the scissors under the belt around the older woman's throat.

Phyllis couldn't have said how she knew, but she felt that the person responsible for this—undoubtedly the same person who had hit her—was gone. The house just had an empty feel to it. Phyllis was scared, but not for herself. Time was running out for Agnes.

If only that belt hadn't been so blasted *tight*!

Tears began to roll down Phyllis's cheeks as she realized that her efforts were being wasted. She stopped trying to cut the belt and laid a hand against Agnes's cheek instead. It was cool. The warmth of life was gone. Phyllis had known, deep down, that Agnes was dead, as soon as she saw those horribly staring eyes. She just hadn't wanted to admit it, even to herself. That was the reason for her stubborn determination to do something for Agnes—even though there was really nothing she could do.

She dropped the scissors on the floor next to Agnes and covered her face with both hands for a moment. A shudder ran through her. This was not the first time death, even violent death, had struck someone close to her. But that was something no one ever got used to, either. At least, Phyllis hoped she would never grow accustomed to it.

When her emotions were a little more under control, she got to her feet. She was still shaky, and she discovered that if she tried to move too fast, she got dizzy again. So she moved slowly and deliberately across the living room, touching a piece of furniture now and then to steady herself. She wanted to get home. She wanted to be back in her own house, where she would be warm and safe.

She left through the front door, thinking as she did so that she was forgetting something. The porch steps were difficult. Every time she brought her foot down, a fresh surge of pain went through her head. Turning to her left, she went toward her house.

But she didn't go to the front door. She couldn't go in the front door like this, with her face red from crying and her clothes rumpled from lying on the floor of Agnes's kitchen. She had a house full of guests, after all. It wouldn't do for them to see her in this condition. She had to straighten herself up.

A small part of her brain told her that she shouldn't be worried about such things. It was much more important that Agnes was dead and that someone had killed her—murdered her. Phyllis realized she needed to call the police. She would do that, she vowed, once she was back in her own kitchen.

Sam was standing beside the punch bowl, using the dipper to fill a cup with the bright red liquid, when Phyllis opened the back door and came in. He turned his head to look at her as she weaved first one way and then the other. The dipper splashed into the punch as he dropped it and said, "What the hell!"

Then, in the blink of an eye, he was beside her, and one hand gripped her arm while his arm went around her waist and steered her toward one of the chairs by the kitchen table. He was very strong, Phyllis thought. Instead of sitting down, she wished she could lean against him and rest her head against his chest. Maybe then it wouldn't hurt so bad.

"Carolyn!" Sam shouted. "Eve! I need some help out here!"

Phyllis gazed up at him as he lowered her onto the chair. The memory of how Agnes had looked crowded back into her mind, and she said, "Oh, Sam. She's dead. She's dead, and some-body killed her. . . ." He touched the back of her head, carefully. It hurt anyway, and she said, "Ouch!" When he took his hand away, she saw something red smeared on his fingertips. "Is that . . . blood? My blood?"

Then she moaned and slumped over onto the table, and that was all she knew for a while.

Mike Newsom took the corner too fast, the wheels of the cruiser sliding a little. He warned himself to slow down. As a deputy in the Parker County Sheriff's Department, he didn't really have any jurisdiction here in the city limits of Weatherford, didn't have any reason to be rolling on this call—other than the fact that his mother had been hurt . . . attacked . . . right there next door to her own home, the house where Mike had grown up.

He'd been out on the interstate, south of town, working radar, when he'd heard the ambulance call on the scanner and recognized the address immediately. That was enough right there to start him racing toward his mother's house.

But then the first call had been followed by several more, including a summons for the chief of police, detectives, and the crime scene team. Then Mike had known that something was *really* wrong, and he could only pray that his mother was all right.

On the way across town, he'd listened to all the follow-up

chatter on the radio and breathed a little easier when he heard that the suspected homicide victim was next door, a woman in her eighties. That would be Agnes Simmons, Mike knew, and although he felt a pang of sympathy at her passing, he couldn't help but be relieved that his mother hadn't been killed.

Then he'd heard the report about the attack on the woman who had discovered the body, and he knew from the age given that it was Phyllis. Carolyn Wilbarger was two years older than her, Eve Turner a year younger. Mike's foot had gotten even heavier on the gas after that.

But he eased off the accelerator as he turned the last corner onto the street where he had grown up. He saw the flashing lights of the emergency vehicles parked in front of the houses a couple of blocks away. He brought his cruiser to a halt behind one from the Weatherford PD. Not taking the time to grab his Stetson from the seat beside him, he threw the door open and ran across the yards toward his mother's house.

A lot of people were crowded into the front yard, with police officers standing around as if to keep them there. Some of them were shivering in the chilly air and didn't look happy about being detained. As they parted to let Mike through, he vaguely recognized a few of them as Phyllis's neighbors.

He touched only one of the steps as he bounded up onto the porch.

An officer Mike didn't know stood at the front door. "We got this, Deputy," he began, jealously guarding the crime scene from any unwanted incursion by the sheriff's department.

Mike forced down an angry response, telling himself that the officer was just doing his job. But if the guy didn't get the hell out of the way—!

"I'm Mike Newsom. It was my mother who was attacked." His voice sounded a lot calmer than he felt.

Understanding dawned on the officer's face. He stepped aside and said, "Oh. Sorry, Deputy. I didn't know. Chief Whitmire's already inside."

Mike's instincts as a lawman came to the fore for a second. "What about the crime scene?"

The officer nodded toward Agnes Simmons's house and said, "Over there. Don't worry; you won't mess up anything by going in here."

That was good, because Mike was going in, one way or another. Nothing was going to keep him from getting to his mom.

Mike opened the door and went inside. Chief Ralph Whitmire, a stocky veteran cop, stood in the living room talking to Sam Fletcher. Mike couldn't stop himself from interrupting.

"Sam! Is my mom okay?"

Sam and Whitmire turned to face Mike. It was the police chief who answered the anxious son's question. "I think she'll be fine, Mike," he said.

Sam's craggy features bore a worried look, though. "She got hit on the head pretty hard," he said. "I reckon she'll probably need to go to the hospital."

Mike's eyes widened. "The hospital!"

"Just as a precaution," Whitmire said. "There's always the danger of concussion with a head injury."

"Or worse," Mike said.

"Better not go borrowin' trouble," Sam advised. "Gettin' walloped like that is nothin' to take chances with, but your mama's a strong lady." He managed a faint smile, even though he was obviously concerned. "Some might even say hardheaded, which comes in handy at a time like this."

Mike felt a flash of irritation that Sam could be making jokes like that, but he eased off the angry response he almost made when he realized that Sam was just trying to get him to settle down a little.

"Where is she?"

"In the kitchen," Whitmire said. "The EMTs are still examining her. When they're done, I hope I can ask her a few questions before they take her to the hospital."

That reminded Mike of the other bulletins he'd heard on the radio while he was driving over here. "Is it true?" he asked. "Somebody killed Agnes Simmons?"

Whitmire nodded. "It's true. Someone choked her to death with the belt from her housecoat. At least, that's what it looks like. The medical examiner will have to confirm that."

"Phyllis found her," Sam said. "It was right after that, somebody hit her on the back of the head."

"The killer." A shudder went through Mike at the thought. "She was right there in the house with the killer."

"Looks like it," Whitmire said. He frowned. "I don't have to tell you to keep all this to yourself, do I, son?"

"No, sir," Mike said. "I understand." This was the Weatherford PD's case, and while Chief Whitmire and Sheriff Royce Haney were friends and had a long history of cooperation, both men could be a little territorial at times. Whitmire had opened up to him more because he was Phyllis's son, not because he was a deputy.

One of the emergency medical technicians came out of the kitchen and started for the front door. Whitmire intercepted him before Mike could and asked, "How's Mrs. Newsom?"

"Her vital signs are good and the bleeding from that laceration on her scalp has stopped. She'll need a couple of stitches, but we'll let them take care of that at the hospital."

"You *are* taking her to the hospital, then?" Mike asked.

The EMT nodded. Mike didn't know him, but that wasn't

unusual. Parker County was growing so fast that he didn't know a lot of the public safety personnel. "Yeah," the man said, "I'm on my way to get the gurney. I'm sure the ER doc will want to admit her for observation overnight."

"Just as a precaution?" Sam said.

"That's right. Now, if you'll excuse me, sir . . ."

"Can I ask her a few questions?" Whitmire asked.

The EMT nodded on his way out the door. "Sure. She's conscious and coherent now."

"Now?" Mike repeated as he, Sam, and the chief started toward the kitchen. "What did he mean by that?"

"She was pretty shook up when she got back over here," Sam explained. "I could tell somethin' was wrong as soon as I saw her. I got her sittin' down at the kitchen table and she started talkin' about somebody bein' dead. Then I saw the blood on her head and hollered for Carolyn and Eve to come take care of her. That's when Phyllis passed out cold. While I called the cops and an ambulance, she regained consciousness, so she wasn't out long. By the time the first officers got here, Phyllis had told us about Agnes Simmons bein' dead. She didn't know exactly what had happened, but she was clear enough about that."

Whitmire stopped them just outside the kitchen. "I know you're gonna be glad to see your mom, Mike, but after you've given her a hug, you let me ask the questions, okay?"

Mike nodded. Normally some of the detectives would handle the interview with a witness in a homicide case, but there was nothing that unusual about the chief taking a hand in the investigation himself, especially in a case like this that might turn out to be rather high profile.

"All right," Whitmire said. "Let's see what the lady has to say."

Chapter 3

*P*hyllis was still seated at the kitchen table when she looked up and saw her son come into the room, followed by Sam and Chief Ralph Whitmire. "Mike!" she said.

He hurried over to her and bent down to put his arms around her. "Are you all right?" he asked in a strained, worried voice.

"I'm fine," she told him. "My head hurts a little, that's all. Oh, and my knees are bruised, I think."

Mike looked at the EMT who had stayed with Phyllis, a tall woman with long blond hair pulled back into a ponytail. "What's wrong with her knees?"

"From what she said, she banged them pretty hard when she fell on the floor, over there in the kitchen next door," the EMT said.

Phyllis nodded. "That's right. I probably would have skinned them up if I'd been wearing a dress, but since I had on jeans . . ."

"They can check that out at the hospital."

"I told them I don't need to go to the hospital," Phyllis said with a sigh. "All I need is some aspirin for this headache—"

"That might be the worst thing in the world for you, Mrs. Newsom. If you've got a bleeder in your brain, aspirin would just make it worse. You need an MRI to make sure there's no serious damage."

Phyllis made a face. She didn't like all this fuss, didn't like putting people to so much trouble. But she supposed she didn't have much choice. And it *was* better to be sure nothing serious was wrong.

Chief Whitmire said, "I need to ask you a few questions, Mrs. Newsom, if you think you're up to it."

"About the murder, you mean?"

"You're sure it was murder?"

"Agnes didn't tie that belt around her own neck like that," Phyllis said. "For one thing, I don't believe she was strong enough to pull it that tight."

Whitmire nodded. "Understand, I've just barely glanced at the scene, but is it possible she could've tied the belt around her neck and used it to hang herself? Her weight could have drawn it tight."

Phyllis frowned as she thought about the question, and that made the wound on the back of her head twinge a little, or maybe it was the thinking that did that. Either way, after a moment Phyllis said, "No, I don't think that's possible. There was nothing right above her where she could have tied the belt, like a light fixture or something like that, and also it would have had to have broken in order for her to fall where she was lying. I saw both ends, and it wasn't broken."

"That's pretty observant of you," Whitmire said with a smile, "especially considering how scared and shocked you must have been."

"I wasn't really all that scared. Not then. I was just worried about Agnes."

"What did you do after you found her? Tell me everything you can remember about it."

Quickly, Phyllis told him about her actions, about trying to untie the belt and then going to the kitchen to look for some scissors when that failed.

The other technician rolled the portable gurney from the ambulance into the kitchen and said, "All right, Mrs. Newsom, let's get you on here and take you to the hospital."

"Wait just a minute," Whitmire said. "I'm not finished talking to her."

"Well, no offense, Chief, but you'd better make it fast. This lady needs some more medical attention."

Phyllis wanted to tell the man that she didn't, either, but she knew it wouldn't do any good. "I heard something behind me," she told the chief. "Maybe it was a footstep; I don't know. Then something hit me. I fell on my knees and then went the rest of the way to the floor. I guess I passed out then."

"There was just one blow?"

"That's right, as far as I know."

"You didn't see your assailant?"

"No, not at all. He was behind me the whole time."

The female EMT edged forward. "Chief . . ."

"All right." Whitmire nodded and stepped back. "Thank you, Mrs. Newsom. You've been a big help."

"Not really," Phyllis said. She sighed. "And I was no help at all to poor Agnes, I'm afraid."

Mike rode with her in the ambulance, holding her hand the whole way. That made Phyllis feel better. It wasn't like Mike had been a clingy little mama's boy growing up; far from it, in fact. But they were close and she was glad to have him with her now.

She was glad, too, that as she was being wheeled out of the house on the gurney, Sam had patted her on the shoulder and said, "Carolyn and Eve and I will be right behind the ambulance, and we'll see you at the hospital."

The neighbors who had been at the cookie exchange were gathered on the lawn, and several of them called out encouraging words to her as she was being brought out and loaded into the ambulance. Since there were quite a few police officers also standing around, Phyllis wondered briefly if everyone had stayed because they were worried about her—or because they weren't being allowed to leave just yet. She knew from experience how the police liked to question everyone who had been in the vicinity of a crime. Canvassing, they called it.

She summoned up a smile and lifted a hand, waving at Lois and Blake Horton, who lived directly across the street, and Monte and Vickie Kimbrough, who lived next to the Hortons, opposite Agnes. Oscar Gunderson, the widower who lived to the left of Phyllis's house, was there, as were the Chadwicks, the Ralstons, the Stephensons, the Paynes, and half a dozen other couples from up and down the block. You'd never know that divorce was so prevalent from the people who lived in this neighborhood; the only people with failed marriages behind them were Eve, and Helen Johannson, who lived in the next block with her two children. And it wasn't so much that Eve's marriages had really *failed*. It was just that, as she liked to say, they all had expiration dates.

Helen and her kids hadn't been at the cookie exchange, though they had been invited, so they weren't standing on Phyllis's lawn. Phyllis waved again at the others as she was lifted into the ambulance. Mike climbed in behind her, along with the female EMT; Sam called, "See you at the hospital," from just outside the emergency vehicle; and then the doors were closed.

Phyllis heard the driver's door open and then close with a solid sound, and a moment later the ambulance pulled away from the curb. Phyllis smiled and asked, "What, no siren?"

The EMT chuckled. "I don't think we need it, Mrs. Newsom. Even without it, it won't take long to get to the hospital."

That was true. Campbell Memorial was less than a mile away.

That was far enough for a frown to appear on Mike's face while they were getting there. He squeezed her hand and said, "You told the chief you never got a look at whoever hit you because he was behind you the whole time."

"That's right. He certainly was."

"Why 'he'?"

It was Phyllis's turn to frown. "What?"

"You keep saying *he* hit you; *he* was behind you. How do you know it was a man?"

"Well . . . I don't suppose I do. I just thought . . . well, it doesn't seem likely that a woman would have hit me like that." Phyllis paused. "But I suppose it's possible. It's just . . . I was so sure. . . ."

"I know," Mike said. "And it's not really like you to jump to conclusions. I think maybe you *did* see something, and you're just not remembering it yet. Something that convinced you your attacker was a man."

"His shoe," Phyllis said. The words just sort of popped out of her mouth and made her add, "Oh," in surprise.

Mike leaned forward. "You saw a man's shoe?"

"Not even the whole shoe. Just the heel. When I fell on the kitchen floor, my head twisted a little. From the corner of my eye, I saw the heel of a man's dress shoe, just for a second. Just a glimpse, really. And I had forgotten all about it until you reminded me, Mike."

"A black dress shoe?"

"The heel was black," Phyllis said. "I suppose the rest of the shoe could have been brown or some other color." She closed her eyes. "Let me think. . . ."

But no matter how hard she racked her brain, she couldn't come up with any more details. She opened her eyes, shook her head, and said as much.

"That's okay," Mike told her. "That cuts down on the number of suspects, anyway."

They arrived at the hospital then, and the next hour or so was a hectic blur that started off with a blizzard of paperwork to be filled out and signed. Mike took care of most of that, for which Phyllis was grateful. Then the emergency room doctor examined her, clipped off a little of her graying light brown hair so that he could get to the cut on her scalp, and took a couple of stitches to close it up. He sent her to X-ray for pictures of her skull and her knees; then she was taken for an MRI on her brain. Even over the music piped in through earphones, she could hear the clanging of the machine, and it didn't do much for her headache.

But it didn't last forever, and when the MRI was finished she was taken to a regular patient room, rather than back to the emergency room. Someone must have gone to the ER and gotten Mike, because he was there waiting for her when she was wheeled in. A couple of nurses shooed him out, got Phyllis into a hospital gown, and put her in the bed. She didn't have an IV, but they did attach a pulse, respiration, and blood oxygen monitor to her.

"All this bother really isn't necessary," she said when Mike was allowed back into the room.

"Until we know for sure that you're all right, it is," he insisted.

A moment later, Carolyn and Eve came into the room, followed by a clearly uncomfortable Sam. "What's wrong?" Phyllis asked him.

He glanced around the room, which was a semiprivate one with the other side unoccupied at the moment. "I don't care much for hospitals," he muttered.

"Oh!" Phyllis said as she remembered that Sam's wife, Victoria, had died of cancer. She wasn't sure how long and drawn out the ordeal had been—Sam didn't talk much about that part of his life, although he didn't mind telling stories about better times with the pretty, redheaded Vicky—but even if her passing had been relatively quick, Phyllis was sure Sam had spent more than enough bad times in hospitals—this very hospital, probably. "Oh, Sam, I'm sorry."

He waved a hand. "Don't worry about me. How are you doin'?"

"I'm fine," Phyllis said.

One of the nurses was still in the room. She said, "We'll know that once the doctor gets your test results back, Mrs. Newsom. Until then, you need to rest, which means you don't need a lot of company."

Carolyn fixed the woman with a glare. "This happens to be our best friend," she said.

"We won't tire her out," Eve added.

The nurse gave in. "All right, but y'all don't stay too long, hear?"

She left the room. Carolyn and Eve stood on one side of the bed, Mike on the other, and Sam stood at the foot with his hands awkwardly tucked into the hip pockets of his jeans.

"I'm sorry about ruining the cookie exchange," Phyllis said.

"It certainly wasn't your fault," Carolyn said. "You didn't have anything to do with poor Agnes being killed."

Phyllis sighed. "No, but the way things like this keep happening, I'm starting to think that I'm jinxed! Did everyone at least take some cookies home with them?"

"Don't worry about that, dear," Eve told her. "People managed to split them up before the police started questioning everyone."

Carolyn frowned. "I'm not sure why they were interrogating our guests. It's not like any of them could have had anything to do with Agnes's death. I swear, sometimes the authorities go overboard. . . ." She looked at Mike. "I mean—"

"That's all right, Miz Wilbarger," he told her with a smile. "I know what you mean. Chief Whitmire just wants to make sure the investigation doesn't overlook any important information. You never know where it'll turn up."

"I suppose." Carolyn had fallen under suspicion of being a murderer herself at one point in the past, so Phyllis understood why she was a little leery of the methods employed by the police. "Anyway," Carolyn went on, "it's obvious that Agnes was killed by a burglar. One of those home invaders, isn't that what they call them these days?"

"How do you figure that?"

"Well, who else would have had any reason to hurt her? She was just a harmless old woman. And with her hip trouble, she could barely get around, even with her walker."

"Which means a burglar wouldn't have had any reason to kill her," Phyllis said.

They all looked at her.

"Think about it," Phyllis continued. "Agnes was no physical threat to anybody. She couldn't go running out of the house and scream for the police. All a burglar would have to do was make sure she couldn't get to a phone. He could have tied her up easily and gone right on about his business without any interference."

"But if she saw him," Mike pointed out, "she might have been able to identify him later. Some criminals are pretty callous about not leaving any witnesses behind, I'm sorry to say."

"Well, that's true," Phyllis admitted. "The killer *might* have been a burglar. But he doesn't *have* to have been."

"Sounds to me like you're thinkin' a little too hard about it," Sam said. "The police'll find the fella, whoever he is. There'll be some fingerprints or some other sort of evidence that leads 'em to him. You don't have to worry about figurin' this one out, Phyllis."

Mike nodded. "Sam's right, Mom. No need for you to even think about it."

She looked back and forth between them and said with an exasperated frown, "For goodness' sake, you two are acting like I go out looking for murders to solve. I'd just as soon never be involved in another murder again."

"That sounds good to me," Sam said. "Huntin' killers is best left to the professionals."

"You're a fine one to talk," Phyllis said. "You were the one who nearly got a knife stuck in you not that long ago, not me."

But, of course, that incident had occurred while Sam was trying to keep someone whom *she* had identified as a killer from getting away, Phyllis reminded herself. So maybe her argument wasn't that strong after all.

"Anyway," she went on, "I'm in the hospital. I don't think I can do much investigating from here, now, can I?"

A few minutes later, the nurse came back in and insisted that everyone except Mike leave. "We'll go sit out in the waitin' room," Sam said.

"No, go on home," Phyllis said firmly. "There's no point in any of you wasting your time sitting around here. If I need you to do anything, I'll let you know."

"Are you sure?" Carolyn asked.

"I'm certain."

"Well, then . . . all right. I don't think you'll be here very long, anyway."

"Just overnight, probably," Eve said. She linked arms with Sam. "Come along, dear. Hospitals give me the willies."

She started to lead him out, but Sam reached back and patted one of Phyllis's feet through the sheet, even though he looked a little embarrassed about doing it. It was a simple gesture, but it made Phyllis feel better.

The visitors hadn't been gone long when Dr. Walt Lee came in. Walt was Phyllis's family doctor, and she hadn't really expected to see him. When she said as much, he smiled and replied, "When one of my patients shows up at the ER with a goose egg on her head and bad knees, they know to call me. I've checked the X-rays and your MRI results, and I don't see anything to be worried about."

Mike blew out his breath in a sigh of relief.

"Your knees are bruised, so don't try running any races for the next few days," Walt went on. He took a little flashlight from his pocket and shone it in her eyes, making her wince a little. "Possible slight concussion, but again, take it easy for a few days, and you'll be fine. There's no skull fracture and no bleeding in the brain, at least not that I can see. I want to run the X-rays and MRI past a radiologist and neurologist, just to be sure, but I'm confident they'll agree with me. It helps that you're as healthy as a horse to start with, Phyllis."

"Thanks . . . I think. So, when can I get out of here?"

Walt replaced the light in his pocket, took out a pen instead, and scribbled instructions on her chart. "Tomorrow," he said. "That'll be plenty soon enough. I want you to stay here tonight where they can keep an eye on you." He hung the chart back on the end of the bed and shook his head. "That was terrible about Agnes Simmons. She wasn't one of my patients, but I'd seen her here in the hospital after she broke her hip. Do the police have any idea who killed her?"

"We don't know," Mike answered. "They didn't when we left in the ambulance."

"Oh, well." Walt smiled again. "I'm sure they'll find the killer. And if they don't . . ." He looked at her and raised his eyebrows meaningfully.

"Good grief," Phyllis said. "Not you, too."

Chapter 4

*B*ecause of the risk of concussion, the nurses didn't want Phyllis to go to sleep for a while. So Mike stayed there talking to her, long enough that she started to worry.

"Weren't you working today?" she asked. "That was why you couldn't come to the cookie exchange, you said."

"Yeah, I was on duty," he admitted, "but after I heard the emergency calls on the radio and recognized the address, I called in to the dispatcher to let her know what was going on. Sheriff Haney himself called back while I was on my way across town and told me not to worry about finishing my shift if you were hurt. He was going to send somebody to your house to pick up the cruiser."

"Then, how will you get home?"

Mike thought it over and said, "Well, I guess I ought to call Sarah. She can come and get me and take me back to the sheriff's department so I can get my car."

"She doesn't know what happened yet?"

Mike shook his head. "I guess not. Not unless somebody else called her, like Miz Wilbarger or Miz Turner."

Phyllis and her daughter-in-law had a close relationship. How could she not love Sarah when Sarah so obviously made Mike happy? And Sarah had given Phyllis her first and so far only grandchild, the adorable toddler Bobby.

"You'd better call her now," Phyllis advised her son. "She's not going to be happy that you didn't let her know what's going on."

"You're probably right about that," Mike admitted as he took his cell phone from his pocket. After a moment of fiddling with it, he made a face. "No signal in here. I'll have to walk down the hall to get through to her. You'll stay awake, won't you? The nurses said it was important that you not go to sleep just yet."

"Well, I don't see why not, but I guess I'll do what they say. You go ahead and make your call."

Mike nodded and left the room. Phyllis sighed and leaned back against the pillows propped behind her, getting comfortable . . . but not *too* comfortable. She didn't want to do anything to make her condition worse.

Despite that resolve, she felt her eyelids getting heavy and blinked several times, fighting the lassitude that was trying to steal over her. She was grateful when she heard the door of the room swing open. Either Mike was back already, or someone else had come to visit her.

A man's voice said, "Knock-knock. Are you awake, Phyllis?"

A handsome, dark-haired man around forty put his head around the corner of the short hallway that led from the door past the closet and bathroom to the room itself. She smiled as she recognized him and said, "Come in, Brother Dwight. It's good to see you."

Dwight Gresham was the pastor of the local Baptist church Phyllis attended, just a few blocks from her house. He returned her smile as he stepped over to the bed and took her right hand in both of his.

"I heard about what happened. Are you all right?"

"Oh, I'm fine," she said. "Just a bump on my noggin, basically. Nothing to worry about."

"I don't know about that," the preacher said, growing more serious. "A head injury is nothing to mess around with."

"Well, they're being careful with me here; you can count on that."

"I'm glad to hear it. How long do you think you'll be in the hospital?"

"Just overnight, according to Dr. Lee. For observation, you know."

Dwight nodded. "I was here calling on some of the other folks from church who're in the hospital, and when I heard you'd been admitted, I knew I had to come see you. What happened?"

Phyllis gestured toward the chairs and said, "Sit down and I'll tell you all about it." She was grateful to have somebody here to occupy her mind and keep her awake until Mike got back.

For the next few minutes, Phyllis gave him the details of the afternoon's events. Dwight shook his head and muttered, "Dear Lord in Heaven," several times during the story. "Poor Agnes," he said when Phyllis was finished. "I know she hadn't been to church lately because of her health issues, but she was still a faithful member. I took the videotapes of the services and dropped them off at her house on a pretty regular basis."

"I didn't know that."

"Oh, yes, we have a homebound ministry, if you ever need to take advantage of it," Dwight said. "In fact, given your current situation—"

"My current situation is that I'm going to be just fine," Phyllis said. "Don't worry, Dwight; I'll be there in church next Sunday morning, as usual. I don't think I'll get out of here in time tomorrow to make it."

He laughed. "All right. I know it'll take a lot to keep you from attending services. But being hit on the head might do it." He grew more serious again. "You didn't see the man who hit you?"

"No, not at all." Phyllis didn't say anything about that glimpse of the heel of a man's shoe, since she still wasn't completely sure she hadn't imagined it.

"Well, I hope they catch him, whoever he was." Dwight sighed and shook his head. "I know it's not very Christian of me, but when I think about how that man killed Agnes and tried to kill you . . . Well, I know the Lord says that vengeance is his, but I wouldn't mind being the instrument of that vengeance, maybe."

"Oh, goodness, don't say that! I'm sure the police will find him."

Phyllis wasn't really certain, however. She hadn't been able to give them much to go on, and if the killer hadn't left any physical evidence at the crime scene, there was a chance that he *would* get away with it.

Mike came in a moment later and looked a little surprised to find the preacher there. "Hello, Dwight," he said as they shook hands. "Word's already gotten to the church about what happened?"

"I don't know; I was here at the hospital already, visiting some other patients, when I heard about your mother being admitted."

Mike nodded. "Appreciate you stopping by."

"I was glad to. Why don't we have a word of prayer before I go?"

Phyllis and Mike bowed their heads, and Dwight said,

"Lord, we ask that you watch over Phyllis and guide the doctors and nurses in caring for her and restoring her to health, and we ask as well that you show mercy on the soul of Agnes Simmons and welcome her into your kingdom. Thank you for all the blessings you have bestowed upon us. We ask these things in Jesus's name . . . amen."

"Amen," Mike murmured.

Dwight took Phyllis's hand again and said, "If there's anything at all I can do for you . . ."

"I'm fine, Dwight, but thank you."

He smiled, nodded, and lifted a hand in farewell to Mike. "See you later," he said as he went out.

"Did you get hold of Sarah?" Phyllis asked her son.

Mike nodded. "Yeah, she's coming right over." He chuckled and added, "You were right; she wasn't very happy that I didn't call her until now. She said she would have been here sooner if she'd known."

"There wasn't any need for that. I swear, I don't know why everybody's making such a fuss over me."

"Well, it could be because we love you."

"Oh, go on with you," Phyllis said.

But inside, a nice warm feeling went through her. It was good to know that people cared. Sometimes life got so busy that nobody had time anymore to say things like that. You might know it anyway . . . but it was good to hear it, too.

She wondered how long it had been since somebody from Agnes Simmons's family had said, "I love you," to her. Phyllis hoped that it hadn't been too long. . . .

Now they'd never get that chance again.

Rather than bringing Bobby to the hospital, Sarah had left him with their friends next door, the parents of a toddler who often shared playdates with him. Mike wasn't surprised that Sarah was still a little cool toward him when she came into his mother's room. She visited with Phyllis for a while, asked if there was anything she could do to help, and promised to come back early the next morning so that she could help when Phyllis was released and ready to go home.

"You two go on now. I'll be fine," Phyllis told them. "Goodness, it must be past suppertime already. You need to go eat."

"What about you?" Mike asked.

"I'm sure they'll bring me something."

He made a face. "Hospital food."

"Oh, it's not that bad. Of course, it's not like my own cooking. . . ."

Mike was reluctant to leave, but when she threatened to get up from the bed and shoo him out, he finally agreed to go. As they left the room and started down the hall, he took Sarah's hand.

"I'm still a little put out with you," she said. "I can't believe you didn't think to call me sooner." Her voice softened as she went on, "But you must've been really scared, huh?"

"Yeah," he said. "I didn't know what was going on at first, only that my mom had been hurt somehow. And then after I got to the house, everything was kind of hectic. It was the same way here, what with all the tests they were doing. . . . Anyway, I'm sorry."

"Apology accepted." As they reached the parking lot, Sarah went on, "Bobby's all right where he is for a while. You want to stop and get something to eat, like your mom said?"

"Sure. But I want to make a stop somewhere else first."

Sarah looked over at him. "And where would that be?"

"The police station. I want to see if Chief Whitmire's found out anything yet about the killer."

Sarah hesitated for a second and then nodded, as if she knew it wasn't going to do any good to argue with Mike right now.

The headquarters of the Weatherford Police Department was on the opposite side of the street that ran by the hospital, just a few blocks away. It took Mike and Sarah only a couple of minutes to get there. When they went inside and he asked at the main desk for Chief Whitmire, the officer on duty said, "The chief's gone home. What did you want to see him about, Deputy?"

Mike was still wearing his uniform, of course. Sarah was in jeans and a denim jacket, with her blond hair pulled back in a ponytail, looking more like a teenager than a mom in her middle twenties.

Mike explained about his connection with the Simmons case, and said, "I was just hoping that the chief could tell me if the investigation has turned up anything yet."

"Detective Largo is in charge of that case. She's here." The officer picked up a phone, talked on it for a moment, then said to Mike, "She'll be right out."

Mike nodded his thanks, then walked over to some chairs with Sarah. They didn't sit down, just stood there waiting. Sarah asked, "Do you know this Detective Largo?"

Mike shook his head. "Nope. But the PD's grown so much, I don't know all the officers anymore. Shoot, I don't hardly know all the deputies these days."

"The curse of progress."

"Tell me about it."

A Hispanic woman with short dark hair came through a door into the lobby of the police department. She looked at Mike and asked, "Deputy Newsom? I'm Isabel Largo."

Mike shook hands with her and introduced Sarah. Mike

said, "I was hoping you could tell me something about the investigation into the murder of Agnes Simmons and the attack on my mother."

Largo frowned. "I'm fairly new to the department, Deputy, so I'm not sure about the protocol here. I know that Chief Whitmire and Sheriff Haney like to cooperate, but you have no official standing in this case. You're just a relative of one of the victims, as far as the police department is concerned."

Mike kept a tight rein on his temper. "I appreciate that, Detective, but I'm not trying to poach your case for the sheriff's department."

After a moment of considering the matter, Largo nodded. "Come on back. Both of you," she added with a smile for Sarah.

She took them down a hallway and into a cramped office with a single window that looked out on the brush-choked creek running behind the police department building. Not much was visible, though, since a thick December dusk had settled over Weatherford.

Largo nodded Mike and Sarah into straight-backed metal chairs in front of the paper-cluttered desk. The only personal touch in the office was a small photo cube on top of a filing cabinet. It was turned so that the only picture Mike could see was of a grinning, round-cheeked baby.

Largo sat down and opened a file folder that was already on the desk. "We're still waiting on the report from Crime Scene," she said, "so all we've got so far are the interviews from the canvass. We talked to everyone who was at your mother's house for that Christmas party—"

"It was a cookie exchange," Mike said. "Not really a party."

"People milling around, talking, eating cookies, and drinking punch . . . sounds like a party to me," Largo said. "Not a very exciting one, mind you, but still . . . Anyway, we interviewed them and everyone else we could find at home for a couple of blocks either way. Some of them didn't even know Mrs. Simmons. The ones who did told us that she was just a harmless old lady and couldn't imagine why anybody would want to hurt her."

"Did anybody who wasn't at my mother's house see anything suspicious going on in the neighborhood? Anybody sneaking around the Simmons house or something like that?"

Largo shook her head. "Not that they'd admit to, anyway. I checked the records to see if there have been any burglaries or anything else like that in the neighborhood recently, but I came up empty." She smiled. "Weatherford seems to be a nice peaceful town most of the time . . . not like where I come from."

"Where's that?"

"Corpus Christi."

Mike nodded. The city down on the Gulf Coast was beautiful, but it also had a reputation among law enforcement agencies as a violent, dangerous place.

"You were thinking that if there was a pattern of break-ins in the area, then this was likely just another burglary gone bad?" he asked.

"That's right," Largo said. "As for the victim's family . . ."

That was going to be Mike's next question, so he was glad Largo had brought it up.

"We weren't able to contact them until they returned to Mrs. Simmons's house," the detective went on. "They'd gone to Fort Worth to shop and had no idea something had happened to Mrs. Simmons." She checked the file in front of her. "Two sons, Frank and Ted Simmons, and one daughter, Billie Hargrove, plus their spouses and assorted children. Naturally, they were all quite upset."

"You believe them?" Mike asked.

Beside him, Sarah said, "What do you mean by that? Of course they were upset!"

"In any murder, you always look at the family first," Mike said with a shrug. "A spouse if there is one, children if there's not. Statistics will bear out that they're the most likely suspects."

Sarah shook her head, as if she didn't like to see her husband being so cynical.

"We're looking into the family," Largo said. "In fact, I'm going back over there this evening to do more extensive interviews with all of them. Under the circumstances, I figure they'll all alibi one another . . . but you never know." She picked up a pen and toyed with it. "I'd invite you to come along with me, Deputy, but I'm afraid that *would* be pushing the bounds of protocol."

"That's all right. Like I said, I don't want to horn in on your investigation." Mike got to his feet. "Thanks for talking to us—"

"One thing," Largo cut in as she got to her feet, too. "Can *you* tell me of anyone who might want to harm Mrs. Simmons?"

"Me?" Mike frowned. "I never even knew her that well. She was just the old lady next door when I was growing up, that's all."

"What about her children? Did you know them?"

"Yeah, some, but not well. They're all older than I am. The boys got married and moved out a long time ago, and Billie's been gone for quite a while, too."

"What about your mother?"

Mike's frown deepened. "What about her?"

"Is it possible the attack on her wasn't connected to Mrs. Simmons's murder?"

"I don't see how. Nobody would want to hurt my mother. Everybody loves her."

"Everybody has enemies," Largo pointed out quietly.

Mike shook his head. "You're on the wrong track there, Detective. My mom got hit on the head because she walked in on the killer. That's the only thing that makes any sense."

"I think you're probably right," Largo said with a shrug. "I'm just covering the bases, that's all."

"Yeah, of course. I understand." They all shook hands again, and Mike added, "I'll be in touch."

As they left the building, Sarah said, "Well, I believe that you never met Detective Largo before."

"Why's that?" Mike asked.

"As attractive as she is, I'm sure that if you'd met her, you would have remembered her."

"Is she that attractive? I didn't really notice."

And why was it, Mike wondered, that guys always lied about things like that? Of course he had noticed that Isabel Largo was attractive. He knew it, Sarah knew it, and he knew she knew it. And yet he played dumb despite that.

He took his wife's arm and said, "Come on; let's go get something to eat. What are you in the mood for, anyway?"

Chapter 5

*S*am, Carolyn, and Eve came back to the hospital that evening for a visit, but the nurses didn't let them stay long. Carolyn brought Phyllis a change of clothes in case she was released the next day as planned. Dr. Lee dropped by again and told her that the neurologist believed she didn't have a concussion, so it was all right for her to get some rest.

Phyllis was glad to hear that, since she had been fighting off drowsiness all evening.

But despite her being so tired, her sleep was troubled and not particularly restful. She kept seeing Agnes Simmons's face and the way that tightly drawn belt had buried itself in the stringy flesh of her neck. . . .

As usual, it seemed to take forever for the orders to be written and the paperwork to be drawn up for Phyllis to be discharged from the hospital on Sunday morning. Sarah showed up to help in any way she could, and so did Carolyn. Mike had to work, since he had taken off the previous afternoon during his shift. The sheriff was fairly lenient about personal emergencies, but Mike hadn't wanted to push Royce Haney's generous nature, Sarah explained.

"Sam said to tell you that he'd see you at home," Carolyn told Phyllis. "I don't think he likes hospitals very much."

"I don't blame him. Neither do I." Phyllis frowned as a thought occurred to her. "That means he's there alone with Eve."

Carolyn smiled. "Why, Phyllis, you actually sound a little jealous."

"Not at all," Phyllis answered instantly. "Sam's a grown man. He can take care of himself. I just don't think it's a good idea to throw too much temptation in Eve's path."

"You're just afraid that *she'll* throw something in Sam's path."

"I just hope she's not like one of those spiders that devours the male afterward."

Both of them laughed.

Sarah looked back and forth between the two older women and frowned a little. "No offense, ladies," she said, "but I thought you two used to teach school. I didn't realize you were still in junior high."

"When you get older, you'll find out for yourself that a part of you will always be in junior high," Phyllis said.

"Anyway," Carolyn said, "don't tell me you wouldn't be jealous if some good-looking woman was flitting around Mike like a butterfly."

Sarah's mouth tightened, and Phyllis thought that Carolyn's comment might have unwittingly hit a target. She wondered about that, but she didn't want to press Sarah on the matter right now.

A nurse finally arrived with a wheelchair. She didn't have a chance to help Phyllis get dressed, since she had dressed herself at six o'clock that morning, right after the last time someone had woken her up to check her vital signs. The nurse did insist that she ride out in the chair—hospital regulations, she explained.

Phyllis knew that already, so she didn't put up a fuss. She just sat in the chair and allowed the nurse to wheel her out through the main entrance to the driveway, where Sarah had pulled up her car after hurrying out ahead of them.

"Now, don't forget that Dr. Lee wants you to come in to his office in a couple of days for a follow-up appointment," the nurse said as Phyllis got into Sarah's car.

"I won't," Phyllis assured the woman. "I'll call his office tomorrow."

The ache in her knees wouldn't let her forget. The wound on her scalp was still tender to the touch, but the actual headache had gone away, proving what she'd been saying all along about having a hard head, she thought.

When Sarah pulled into the street where Phyllis lived, with Carolyn following in her own car, Phyllis saw that a couple of strange cars were parked in Agnes Simmons's driveway, and another vehicle was parked at the curb in front of the house. "I guess it wasn't just wishful thinking," she murmured.

"What?" Sarah asked.

"Those cars at Agnes's house. Her family really did come to visit her."

That visit had turned tragic, though. A stray piece of yellow crime scene tape that hadn't been removed from the porch was a mute reminder of that.

"I'll need to go over and see them," Phyllis went on. "Let them know that if there's anything I can do . . ."

"I think you should be more worried about taking care of yourself," Sarah said. "It hasn't been twenty-four hours yet since you were brutally attacked."

"Yes, I know. I just want to be neighborly, that's all."

Sarah pulled into the driveway, stopped the engine, and got out to hurry around the car and open Phyllis's door. Carolyn parked beside Sarah's car. Sam's pickup was in its usual spot at the curb in front of the house.

Sam himself came out of the house. He must have been watching and waiting for them to arrive, Phyllis thought. Eve followed him, and Phyllis couldn't help but wonder how much flirting had gone on while those two were alone in the house. Not that it was any of her business whom Sam flirted with, or even if he flirted with anyone. But Phyllis had known Eve for a long time, and she was confident that the former high school English teacher had relished the opportunity to spend some time alone with Sam.

"Let me give you a hand," Sarah said, and Phyllis didn't argue. She still had a little dizzy spell every now and then, so she was glad to have Sarah's hand on her arm steadying her as she went to the porch and climbed the steps.

"Welcome home, dear," Eve said with a smile.

"How're you feelin'?" Sam asked.

Phyllis nodded as she came up the steps. "I'm fine. My knees are a little sore, but that's all. No headache or anything like that."

"You're lucky that monster didn't bust your skull wide-open," Carolyn said from behind her. "I hope the police catch him soon."

Sam nodded toward the house next door. "That little gal who's the police detective was back over there a while ago. She stopped by here when she left and said to tell you that she wants to talk to you, Phyllis."

"I'll be glad to answer any questions she might have, but I don't know if I can tell her anything I didn't already tell Chief Whitmire. You say she's a female detective?"

Sarah answered before Sam could. "Her name is Isabel Largo," she said. "Mike and I stopped by the police department and spoke with her yesterday evening after we left the hospital."

"Oh." Phyllis thought she heard a little tension in her daughter-in-law's voice, as if Sarah didn't care much for Detective Isabel Largo. "Well, I'll be happy to talk to her whenever she'd like."

"Let's get you inside, out of this cold air," Sam said as he opened the front door.

It was still chilly and overcast this morning, with the temperature in the thirties, Phyllis guessed. In less than a week it would be Christmas, so it was appropriate that the weather was cold. Chances were that it wouldn't be a white Christmas, though. Those were rare in this part of Texas. In her more than sixty years of life, she could remember seeing only a handful of Christmases on which it had snowed. Even then, any snowfall was usually just flurries that didn't stick, but melted when they hit the ground.

The warmth inside the house felt good as it closed around her. The tree in the corner of the living room with the colorfully wrapped presents underneath it was another reminder of the season. This was the time of the year to celebrate birth—one birth in particular—instead of death.

And yet Agnes Simmons's death was inescapable. So far, Phyllis hadn't been successful at putting it out of her mind for very long. She probably wouldn't be able to until she knew that the killer had been brought to justice.

"Why don't you sit down here in your chair and make yourself comfortable?" Sarah said as she led Phyllis to her favorite recliner.

"Can I get you something?" Carolyn asked.

"Got coffee in the kitchen," Sam put in.

"And there are plenty of cookies left from yesterday," Eve added.

Phyllis laughed. "It's a little early in the day for cookies, but I'd take a cup of coffee. They brought me some with my breakfast in the hospital this morning, but it wasn't very good."

"Comin' right up," Sam said. He hurried out to the kitchen.

"You know, I never did get to try your pecan pie cookies," she said to Carolyn. "I suppose one wouldn't hurt."

Carolyn smiled and brought one of the cookies from the kitchen. It was a round shortbread cookie with a depression in the center that was stuffed with pecan pie filling and topped with a pecan half.

"I have a feeling this will be the winning entry in the newspaper contest this year," Carolyn said as she gave the cookie to Phyllis, not even trying to conceal the pride in her voice.

Phyllis took a bite and said, "My, it *is* good. You may be right, Carolyn. But have you tried my lime snowflake cookies?"

"Yes, and they're fine, but you know how people feel about pecan pie, and these are like having little pecan pies in the shape of cookies."

Sam returned from the kitchen with a cup of coffee for Phyllis before the rivalry could get out of hand. She took a grateful sip of the hot liquid, finished off the pecan pie cookie, and was ready to sit there and rest for a while as she drank the rest of the coffee.

That plan might have worked if the doorbell hadn't rung just then.

"I'll get it," Eve volunteered. She went into the front hall and returned a moment later with a heavyset man following her. Phyllis recognized him right away, even though he was a lot beefier and his dark hair was a lot grayer than it had been when he was a young man living next door.

"Hello, Frank," she said. "I'm so sorry about your mother."

Frank Simmons nodded in acknowledgment of her sympathy. "How are you, Mrs. Newsom? I heard that you were attacked by the same person who . . . attacked my mother."

"I'll be just fine, Frank. Won't you sit down?"

He glanced around uneasily. None of the others in the room knew him very well, although like many people who had grown up in Weatherford over the past forty or so years, he had been in Eve's English class when he was in high school. He had missed having Phyllis or Carolyn for teachers.

Frank Simmons was in his midforties. Phyllis had lost track of him after he got married and moved away, but she seemed to remember that he lived in Dallas, which was about an hour to an hour and a half to the east, depending on which part of that sprawling city you were talking about. She had no idea what he did for a living. He sat down awkwardly in one of the armchairs and said, "I just wanted to tell you that I'm, uh, sorry about what happened to you."

"I appreciate that, Frank, but it wasn't your fault."

Unless he had something to do with his mother's death, Phyllis thought suddenly, then felt a little ashamed of herself for even thinking such a thing. She had been around murder too much lately, she told herself. It was making her overly suspicious of everybody.

Frank clasped his hands together between his knees. "Yeah, but you wouldn't have gotten hit if you hadn't been trying to help my mother. The cops said you were trying to find something to . . . to get that belt off of Mama's neck when that guy attacked you."

"That did seem to be the way it was," Phyllis said with a nod. "But it was just bad luck. It wasn't anyone's fault."

Sam grunted. "I'd say it was the fault o' the no-good rascal who did it."

"Well, yes, of course," Phyllis agreed.

"Have y'all heard anything about whether or not the cops have any leads?" Frank asked. "Your boy's a policeman, isn't he, Mrs. Newsom?"

"Mike's a deputy sheriff. The police department's in charge of the investigation." Phyllis looked over at Sarah. "I believe he talked to the detective last night. . . ."

Sarah shook her head. "We didn't really find out anything. You've talked to Detective Largo since the last time any of us have, Mr. Simmons."

Frank sighed and said, "I know. I just thought she might've said something, told you something that she wouldn't tell the family. . . ."

"I'm sure the police will keep you up-to-date on any new developments," Sarah told him.

"Yeah." Frank put his hands on his knees and pushed himself to his feet. His face was red, and he seemed to be short of breath. Phyllis wondered what sort of shape his heart was in. "I guess I'd better be running along. . . ."

"Are all of you going to be staying next door?" Phyllis asked.

"Well . . . for a while, I suppose. We'd planned to visit for a week or so. Now, of course, we have to arrange for the funeral and . . . and take care of all that." Frank grimaced at the thought, causing Phyllis to feel another pang of sympathy for him and the other members of the family.

"Let me know if there's anything I can do to help," she said.

"That goes for the rest of us, as well," Carolyn added.

Frank nodded. "Thanks." He moved toward the front door. "I'll be seein' you."

"I'll walk you out," Sam said.

Frank stopped before he reached the hallway. He looked back and said, "You know my boy Randall, don't you, Mrs. Newsom?"

"I remember hearing Agnes talk about him, and I'm sure I've seen pictures of him," Phyllis said, "but I don't recall that I ever met him, Frank."

"Well, if you see him . . . if he happens to come by while we're not around . . . I'd appreciate it if you'd tell him we're looking for him. We, uh, haven't seen him for a while."

Sam frowned and said, "You don't know how to get in touch with him?"

"No, I'm afraid not. He moves around a lot."

"All right," Phyllis said, her voice gentle. "I really don't think it's very likely I'll be seeing him, Frank, but if I do, I'll be sure to tell him to talk to you."

"Thanks." Frank Simmons lifted a hand and this time left the house.

When Sam came back from closing the front door behind the visitor, he asked, "What the heck was that last bit about? You know anything about the guy's kid, Phyllis?"

She cast her mind back over conversations she'd had with Agnes in the past and then said, "I think Randall Simmons was sort of the black sheep of the family. From things that Agnes said, I think Frank had a lot of trouble with the boy when he was growing up. They never got along very well. I didn't know that Randall had disappeared, though."

"I can't imagine a child going off like that so his family doesn't have any idea where he is," Carolyn said. "That must be a terrible feeling."

"Randall would be a grown man by now. He must be Mike's age, at least." Phyllis paused, then went on. "But I know what you mean. It doesn't matter how old your child is; he's still your child. And you still worry about him."

Sarah smiled and said, "You mean I'm never going to stop worrying about Bobby?"

Phyllis shook her head. "No, dear, I'm afraid you won't. That's just part of being a parent. You worry about your kids, and your grandkids, and your *great*-grandkids. . . ."

She knew that Agnes Simmons had worried about her grandson Randall. Phyllis could remember hearing the concern in the older woman's voice when she talked about the troubles between Frank and Randall. It was unusual for Agnes to open up that much about family matters, especially since she and Phyllis hadn't really been all that close. But that was a good indication of just how upset she was about the subject.

Sarah stood up and said, "Speaking of my kid, I've got to go pick him up. Is there anything I can do for you before I go, Phyllis? Or anything you need from the store?"

Phyllis shook her head and said for what seemed like the hundredth time, "No, I'm fine. And if there's anything I need, I have these three here to help me." She smiled at Sam and Carolyn and Eve.

"And we're not goin' anywhere," Sam said. "I reckon you can count on that."

Phyllis did. She had come to count on their friendship every day of her life.

Chapter 6

Later that morning, Phyllis dozed off in the recliner, and that sleep was actually more restful than what she had gotten in the hospital the night before. She supposed it had something to do with being home again.

When she woke up, the smell of good food cooking filled the house. She smiled without opening her eyes. All rivalries aside, Carolyn really was an excellent cook, and Phyllis didn't mind admitting that.

She stood up and went to the kitchen, pausing just inside the doorway in surprise when she saw Sam standing at the counter with a saucepan in one hand and a spoon in the other. He was placing dollops of some sort of caramel mixture from the saucepan into the center of what looked like chocolate oatmeal cookies arranged on a long sheet of waxed paper. On the other side of the kitchen, Carolyn tended to food that was cooking on the stove.

"Why, Sam Fletcher," Phyllis said, "I didn't know you could bake cookies."

Sam started a little and looked around, almost guiltily, like a little boy caught doing something he shouldn't, Phyllis thought. "Well, you, uh, don't have to bake these," he said. "You just mix 'em up in a saucepan and cook 'em on the stove. Actually, I've made these before, and I think they're pretty good. Just about the only thing I *can* make, except sandwiches."

From the other side of the kitchen, Carolyn said, "I know; you could have knocked me over with a feather, too, when he came in here and started rummaging around. But I didn't think it would do any harm."

"No, of course not," Phyllis agreed. She went over to where Sam was working. "What are you making?"

"I call 'em fudgy peanut butter cookies," he explained as he spooned the mixture from the saucepan into the depression in the center of the last cookie. "They're sort of like oatmeal cookies. You mix up milk, sugar, cocoa, and butter in a saucepan, boil it a little, take it off the fire, and blend in some oatmeal and a little vanilla. Then you put 'em on the wax paper, gouge out a little place in the center while they're still soft, and fill it with a mixture of peanut butter and corn syrup." He hefted the saucepan in his hand. "This stuff here."

Phyllis looked over at Carolyn and said, "That's sort of like your pecan pie cookies, isn't it, only with peanut butter instead of pie filling."

Carolyn shook her head. "I've never *gouged* anything in my life."

Phyllis let that go and turned back to Sam. "If you knew how to make these, why didn't you make some for the cookie exchange?"

"Oh, I didn't figure they'd be good enough for somethin' like that, what with you ladies almost bein' professionals at bakin' cookies and all."

"Nonsense," Phyllis said. "You should have entered them in the newspaper contest, too." She patted him on the shoulder. "Well, maybe next year."

"Better wait and see how they taste first." He paused. "My wife liked 'em. I made 'em for her when she was sick, sort of a treat for her since I couldn't make anything else, and, well, since you got hurt and were in the hospital . . ." His voice trailed away and he shrugged.

Phyllis tried not to show how touched she was, but there was a lump in her throat. She managed to say, "I'm sure they'll be very good, Sam."

And they were. She ate three of them for dessert after lunch, and of course Eve exclaimed over how good they were, too. Even Carolyn ate a couple of the cookies and grudgingly admitted that they were tasty. "Maybe you *should* enter the recipe in the contest next Christmas," she told Sam.

Still feeling a little tired, Phyllis went upstairs to her room to read for a while. Sam and Eve started watching a football game on the big-screen TV in the living room. Phyllis figured Eve was more interested in sitting on the sofa with Sam than she was in watching the game, but she also thought it was unlikely that Eve would be able to distract Sam very much from the Dallas Cowboys.

The sound of car doors slamming caught her attention. She got up from the comfortable chair in her bedroom and went to the window, which looked out over the front yard. From here she could see the Simmons driveway and the street in front of the house. She saw people coming from the house and getting into the various parked cars. She thought she recognized Ted Simmons, who was taller and balder than his older brother, Frank. Billie, who was the baby of the family, had sandy brown hair, a slender figure, and the nervous mannerisms of a constant dieter.

Phyllis saw a couple of women and a man she didn't know and supposed they were the spouses of the Simmons siblings. Several children, a mixture of teenagers and adolescents, got into the cars, too. Then all three vehicles pulled out and drove off.

The family was all going somewhere, Phyllis thought. The funeral home? Possibly. It wasn't really any of her business, although she *was* curious about when Agnes's funeral would be. She wanted to attend, even though she knew her presence might be a distraction, depending on how much the news reports played up her part in the older woman's murder.

An hour or so later, Carolyn came upstairs and appeared in the open doorway of Phyllis's room. "Dwight Gresham is downstairs to see you," she said.

Phyllis set her book aside on the table beside her chair. "Dwight visited me in the hospital yesterday," she said. "I wonder what he's doing here today."

"I guess he wanted to make sure you were all right. And he has some sort of tape for you, I think."

"Tape?" Phyllis repeated with a frown.

"A videotape."

The only way to find out what this was about was to go downstairs, Phyllis told herself. She followed Carolyn to the stairs and went down to the front hall. The preacher was waiting in the living room with Sam and Eve. Sam had muted the sound on the football game, but he hadn't turned it off. Phyllis couldn't help but notice that the Cowboys were leading the Washington Redskins 24 to 20 in the fourth quarter.

Dwight stood up from the armchair where he'd been sitting—the same armchair where Frank Simmons had sat earlier, Phyllis noted—and extended a hand to her. As she took it, he said, "Well, you're looking a lot better than the last time I saw you, Phyllis."

"Being out of the hospital will do that," she said with a laugh. "Please sit down, Brother Dwight. Did you come by just to check on me?"

"And to give you this," he said as he picked up a videotape box from the little table beside the chair. "It's the tape of this morning's service, since you weren't able to be there. I told you we have a homebound videotape ministry, so I moved you to the top of the list."

"Oh, goodness, you didn't have to do that! I'm sure the Lord would understand why I wasn't able to attend today."

"Well, it's just for this week, since I'm certain you'll be back in church next Sunday morning." He held out the tape. "Go ahead and take it, and when you've had a chance to watch it, just call the church. I'll come back by and pick it up to take to the next person, or one of the deacons will."

"That's very nice of you," Phyllis said as she took the tape from him. "Thank you, Dwight."

Sam sat forward suddenly on the sofa, drawing her attention. A sheepish grin appeared on his face as he said, "Cowboys just kicked a field goal. Now it's gonna take a touchdown and an extra point to tie, or a touchdown and a two-point conversion to win."

"Yes, but it's still a one-possession game," Dwight pointed out.

"Yeah," Sam admitted. "Up to the defense now."

Dwight turned back to Phyllis. "Well, I'd better be going. Got the sermon for the evening service to work on, you know, and Jada said something about some other chore she wanted me to take care of this afternoon."

Jada was Dwight's wife, a pretty redhead of about thirty who worked at one of the local insurance agencies. She'd always struck Phyllis as being a little high-strung, but that wasn't unusual for a preacher's spouse. The same held true, or even more so, for children of ministers. Having a preacher in the family seemed to put a lot of pressure on people. They felt like they had to be shining examples of just about everything. Jada Gresham, for example, kept about the cleanest house Phyllis had ever seen.

"Nice fella," Sam said when Dwight was gone.

"Yes, he is," Phyllis agreed as she looked down at the videotape in her hand. "I sort of wish he hadn't gone to so much trouble, though. Now I feel like I have to go ahead and watch this tape right away so that it can go on to somebody who's really homebound."

Sam gestured toward the big screen, where time was ticking down as the Redskins drove toward the Cowboys' goal line. "You want to use the TV?"

Phyllis laughed. "I wouldn't do that to the two of you," she said. "The game's almost over, isn't it?"

"That's all right, dear," Eve said. "We don't mind, do we, Sam? We could go watch the rest of it on the TV in my room."

"No, you can finish it up right here," Phyllis said. "I insist. And I hope the Cowboys win."

"Well, okay," Sam said as he settled back against the sofa cushions and turned his attention to the game again.

Phyllis left the room with the videotape before Eve had a chance to glare at her.

Despite what she'd said about it not being necessary, Phyllis enjoyed watching the church service on the videotape. She didn't think anybody would want to come back and get it today, but she told herself she would call the church office the first thing in the morning and let them know she was done with it.

She went downstairs in the late afternoon and looked around

the kitchen for a snack. No one ate a formal dinner on Sunday evening in her house. The custom was for everyone to sort of fend for themselves.

Phyllis was surprised when she saw the half dozen round plastic containers on the kitchen counters. They were full of cookies, all of which she recognized from the cookie exchange the day before. It looked like more than half of them had been left from the get-together.

She found Carolyn in the living room, working on some knitting. The whine of power tools from the garage that had been audible in the kitchen had told her where Sam was. There was no sign of Eve, who was probably upstairs.

"I thought you said people took cookies home with them yesterday," Phyllis said.

"They did," Carolyn replied as she looked up from her knitting.

"Then, what are all those in the kitchen?"

"Well . . . after what happened to Agnes . . . and after everyone had been questioned by the police . . . I guess people didn't feel as festive as they would have otherwise. Not everybody took cookies with them, and some of the ones who did probably didn't get as many as they might have if all that hadn't happened."

Phyllis supposed that made sense, but even so, she couldn't help but be disappointed. The cookie exchange was one of the highlights of the Christmas season for her, and it bothered her that people hadn't enjoyed it as much as they should have.

"I wonder if the Simmonses would like some of them, since we have plenty left," she said.

"You already took cookies over there, remember?" Carolyn asked. "I mean, I know you remember. You'd have to."

"What with finding Agnes's body and all, right after that." Phyllis nodded. "Yes, I'm not likely to forget that. But those cookies were knocked off the table and stepped on and ruined. I'm sure someone cleaned them all up and threw them away. But I could take a nice fresh batch over there."

"You're supposed to be resting," Carolyn pointed out.

"I feel fine. Goodness, I'm getting tired of saying that! But it's true. I'm sure it won't hurt me just to walk next door. My knees don't even hurt that much anymore."

Carolyn set her knitting aside. "All right, but I'm coming with you, just in case."

"Just in case what? Do you think I'm going to pass out or something?"

"Well, I certainly hope not, but you never know."

Phyllis didn't waste time or energy arguing with her. Besides, she wouldn't mind having Carolyn's company.

She went to the kitchen, put an assortment of the leftover cookies on a paper plate, then slid it into a plastic Ziploc bag and sealed the bag. The two women put on their coats and left by the kitchen door, walking up the shrub-bordered space between the houses. A chilly north wind whistled through the opening, rattling the bare branches of the post oak trees. Phyllis heard a scraping sound and glanced up to see that one of the branches was rubbing against the shingles on the roof of the Simmons house.

At the same time, someone pushed back a curtain in one of the second-floor windows, looked down at her and Carolyn, and then disappeared. In that brief glimpse, Phyllis wasn't able to tell who the person was, but she supposed it had been one of Agnes's children, in-laws, or grandchildren.

When they reached the front yard, Phyllis saw that none of the cars that had left earlier had returned. "I guess they're not back yet from wherever they went," she said, "but I know someone's here. I just saw somebody at one of the second-floor windows."

"Well, we can give them the cookies," Carolyn said as she went up the steps to the porch. "Maybe they won't eat all of them before the rest of the family gets back."

She rang the doorbell while Phyllis held the plate of cookies. Moments went by, but no one came to the door. Carolyn rang the bell again but still got no answer.

"Are you sure you saw somebody?" she asked with a frown.

"Yes, I'm sure," Phyllis said, although as a matter of fact she was starting to doubt herself. "At least, I saw the curtain move. I know that."

"Maybe it was the cat."

"Agnes didn't have a cat."

"Maybe one of the others brought a cat with them."

"It wasn't a cat," Phyllis said, a little exasperated. "I think I saw somebody look out at us. I just couldn't tell who it was. Ring the bell again."

Carolyn pushed the button for the bell several times, then shook her head when there was still no answer to the summons. "Whoever it was doesn't want to come to the door. Maybe the person's sick, and that's why they didn't go with the rest of the family."

"I suppose that's possible."

"You could leave the cookies here on the porch. They'd see them when they came back in."

"Then a cat *would* come along and get them," Phyllis said.

Carolyn shrugged. "We'll have to bring them back later, then, I suppose."

"Agnes hardly ever locked her door. Try it and see if it's unlocked."

Carolyn turned toward her and frowned. "I don't like the idea of going into someone's house uninvited."

"We wouldn't actually go in," Phyllis said. "All we'd have to do is just set the cookies inside. There's a little table in the hall I could put them on."

"Well . . . all right." Carolyn opened the storm door and tried the knob of the wooden door. It wouldn't turn, and she sounded relieved when she said, "Agnes might not have kept things locked up, but her family obviously does."

"Let's go around back and try the kitchen door," Phyllis said.

"Why are you so obsessed with taking those cookies inside? If somebody *is* here, you're going to disturb them." Carolyn's eyes suddenly widened as she must have thought about what she'd just said. "If somebody's here, it could be . . . Oh, my goodness! It could be the person who killed Agnes and hit you!"

Phyllis hadn't thought about that—but then she wondered if that suspicion had been lurking in the back of her brain all along, ever since she'd seen the curtain flick aside in that upstairs window.

"I'm sure that's not the case," she said. "That business about the killer returning to the scene of the crime only happens in books and TV shows."

"And in real life, too, sometimes," Carolyn insisted. "I've read about just such things happening."

"Well, it's not like we're going to search the house or anything like that. If the back door's open, we'll just put the cookies on the counter and leave."

Carolyn shook her head. "Absolutely not. You should call Mike right now, if you think there's really somebody in there who shouldn't be. Either him or that Detective Largo."

"I don't want to be any bother—"

"No, you'd rather barge in there and confront a killer!"

Phyllis couldn't bring herself to believe that a murderer could be skulking around the Simmons house . . . but she wouldn't have believed that such a brutal murder could take place right next door to her own home, either, if she hadn't learned that death could strike just about anywhere, from a peach orchard to an elementary school carnival.

When Phyllis hesitated, Carolyn said, "At least go and get Sam if you're bound and determined to go in there."

That comment struck Phyllis as ironic. When Sam had first moved in, back in the summer, Carolyn had been adamantly opposed to the idea of a man living in the house with the rest of them. Now she was ready to turn to him at the first sign of potential trouble.

But to tell the truth, it sounded like a pretty good idea to her, too, Phyllis thought. She nodded and said, "All right. I think he's still in the garage."

"Let's go see."

They walked over to the front of the two-car garage attached to Phyllis's house and looked through the narrow window in one of the doors. The lights were on in the garage, and Sam stood at the workbench that had once been Kenny's with his back turned toward them. Carolyn rapped sharply on the window glass.

Sam didn't have any of the power tools going, and when he turned around in response to the knock, Phyllis saw why. He had a length of wood in one hand and a piece of sandpaper in the other. He'd been sanding the wood manually. Phyllis had seen enough of his work to know what a delicate touch he had with such things.

He set the wood and sandpaper aside, then thumbed one of the buttons by the kitchen door that activated the garage door openers. The door where Phyllis and Carolyn waited rumbled upward.

Sam walked between the cars toward them. "What're you two ladies doin' out in the cold?" he asked. "You didn't lock yourselves out of the house, did you?"

"Of course we didn't lock ourselves out," Carolyn said. "Phyllis decided to take some more cookies over to the Simmonses."

Sam nodded at the plate in Phyllis's hands. "I can see that. Mighty nice of you."

"No one answered the door," Phyllis said, "and I saw Frank and Ted and Billie and their families leave earlier."

"Then I reckon nobody's home."

"Yes, but I saw someone at a second-floor window. I'm sure of it."

"She made me try the front door," Carolyn said. "When it was locked, she wanted to go around back and try that door."

Sam frowned. "I'm not sure that's such a good idea."

"That's what *I* told her. For goodness' sake, if there's really somebody in there, it could be the person who murdered Agnes!"

Sam nodded. "Yep. Could be. Or maybe it's just one of those folks who're visitin', who doesn't want to come to the door for some reason."

"All I want to do is set these cookies on the kitchen counter," Phyllis said. "I'll just step in and step right back out . . . if the door's even unlocked. But Carolyn thought we should get you to go with us while we see."

Sam nodded without hesitation and reached for the plate of cookies, taking it out of Phyllis's hands before she knew what was going on.

"All right. But I'll take the cookies in. Just in case."

"I didn't ask you to do that—" Phyllis began.

"I know. I'm volunteerin'." Sam turned and walked toward the back of the Simmons house, carrying the cookies.

Phyllis and Carolyn hurried after him. The three of them went through an opening in the hedge that led them into the backyard. There was a screened-in porch on the rear of the house. Sam went to the door and opened it. He looked over his shoulder at the women and said, "You ladies wait here. I'll be right back."

Phyllis caught her upper lip between her teeth. She wanted to follow Sam right up to the back door, but she did as he requested. He held the plate of cookies in one hand and used the other to open the screen door and then try the back door knob.

This one turned. The door swung open. Sam stepped inside.

He hadn't been in there more than a heartbeat when he let out a startled yell, which was followed by a crash of some sort.

Chapter 7

Phyllis hesitated, but only for a second. Then she ignored the fear that shot through her and plunged toward the porch door of the Simmons house. Behind her, Carolyn called, "Phyllis! Phyllis, wait!"

Phyllis didn't slow down. Sam was in there, possibly in danger. She wasn't going to wait.

The back door was still partially open, although the screen had closed behind Sam. Phyllis yanked it toward her and shoved the wooden door so hard that it flew back and crashed against the wall inside the kitchen. She stumbled a little on the threshold as she entered the room. Catching herself, she looked with wide eyes at Sam and the young man who stood tensely on the other side of the kitchen.

The young man was a little wide-eyed himself. In fact, he looked like a trapped animal, his gaze darting back and forth frantically. Sam lifted a hand, held it out to him, and said in a calm voice, "Take it easy, son. Nobody's gonna hurt you."

"Who . . . who are you?" the young man asked. His voice cracked a little with strain. "What are you doing here?"

"Just bringin' over a plate of cookies for the folks who're stayin' here," Sam explained. "I live next door." He glanced over his shoulder and added, "Phyllis, go on back outside. Everything's fine."

Phyllis wasn't so sure of that. She knew that Sam wanted her to leave because he was worried about her safety. But she was worried about him, too.

The intruder, if that's what he was, looked just about as scared as Sam and Phyllis were, if not more so. He could still be dangerous, though. A broken glass lay in pieces at his feet. Phyllis thought he must have come into the kitchen just as Sam was stepping in through the back door, and he'd dropped the glass he was carrying, causing it to shatter on the floor. Phyllis didn't see any puddles of liquid, so the glass must have been empty.

Something about the young man was familiar. He was slender, stood a little below medium height, and had close-cropped dark hair. His face was a little gaunt, as if he hadn't been eating well. He wore a maroon Texas A&M sweatshirt and blue jeans.

Suddenly Phyllis knew why he seemed familiar. He bore a resemblance not only to Frank Simmons, but to Agnes as well. Remembering what Frank had said earlier, Phyllis took a guess. "Randall? Is that you?"

His eyes widened even more, though that hardly seemed possible. "How do you know who I am?"

"I remember you visiting your grandmother when you were little. And your father mentioned you earlier today. I guess he found you after all."

Randall Simmons shook his head and started to back away.

"Sorry I startled you, son," Sam said. "We didn't know anybody was here. I was just gonna put these cookies down and then leave—"

"You didn't see me," Randall interrupted. "Please. You can't tell anybody I'm here."

Phyllis and Sam both frowned. "But surely your family already knows—" Phyllis began.

"No. They don't." Randall suddenly turned around and took a step toward the door that led into the rest of the house, as if he were about to run away. But then he stopped short, hung his head low, and said in a half moan, "What's the use?"

He sounded so despairing that Phyllis couldn't help but move forward a step and ask, "Randall, what's wrong? Don't your parents know you're here?"

Without looking around, he shook his head. "No. My grandma's been letting me stay up in the attic. I don't come out except when nobody's here, and I don't move around and make any noise."

"You're hidin' out?" Sam asked.

"I have to," Randall replied in a tortured voice. "If they find me, they'll kill me."

The words were like a physical shock to Phyllis. She couldn't imagine why anyone would want to kill Randall Simmons.

But the fear that he felt at such a possibility was obviously why he had been hiding out in the attic of his grandmother's house.

Sam was still holding the plate of cookies in the plastic bag. He finally set them on the counter and then said to Randall, "Who'll kill you?"

The young man just shook his head mutely. He looked like he was afraid that he had already said too much.

"Phyllis!" Carolyn called from outside, causing Randall to jump in fear again. "Phyllis, are you all right? Sam, are you in there?"

"Who . . . who . . . ," Randall choked out.

"Don't worry. It's just a friend of ours," Phyllis said.

Carolyn's next words provoked an even more violent reaction from Randall. "I've already called the police!" she shouted.

Randall gave an inarticulate cry and turned to plunge out of the kitchen. He had barely gotten the swinging door open when Sam tackled him from behind.

They didn't fall, but the impact of their collision made both men stagger on through the doorway out of sight. Phyllis cried, "Sam!" as she hurried after them.

Agnes Simmons's house had a formal dining room, and that was where Sam and Randall wound up struggling. Randall tried to twist away, but Sam had his long arms wrapped around the young man and hung on. Phyllis moved skittishly around them as they swayed back and forth, wondering whether there was anything she could do to help Sam. She was afraid that if she picked anything up, like the empty crystal punch bowl that was sitting on a sideboard, and tried to hit Randall over the head with it, she would accidentally strike Sam instead. Anyway, she didn't want to hurt Randall. She just wanted him to stop trying to get away.

That was when the front door opened, people started to troop in, and Frank Simmons's startled voice yelled, "Randall! What the hell are you doing here?"

Randall groaned and stopped struggling as his father and several other members of the family crowded into the doorway between the living room and the dining room. Sam let go of him, and the young man simply sank to the floor and put his head in his hands as if he were overwhelmed, as if everything in the world was just too much for him.

"Phyllis!" Carolyn called as she stepped through the back door into the kitchen. "Phyllis, what's going on here?"

Phyllis had no real idea, but as she looked at the clearly devastated Randall Simmons and then heard the wail of a siren in the distance, she thought it was likely that things were about to get even worse.

. . .

A fortyish woman with dyed blond hair pushed past Frank and knelt beside Randall to throw her arms around him. "Randy!" she said. "What are you doing here? I hoped you'd come, but it's been so long since we've heard from you. . . ."

"Mom," Randall managed to say. "Mom, you don't understand—"

"What none of us understand is how you could just disappear like that and worry the hell out of us," Frank said in a loud, angry voice. He stepped forward and reached down to take hold of the blond woman's arm. "Come on, Claire. Leave him alone. He doesn't deserve you fawning over him like that."

The woman had to be Frank's wife and Randall's mother, Phyllis thought. She remembered seeing her a few times in the past, but she didn't think they'd ever met.

And she was struck by the hundred-and-eighty-degree turn in Frank's attitude. Earlier in the afternoon, when he was over at her house and had asked about Randall, she had seen and heard the anguish he was feeling over not knowing where his son was. Now he was just angry. Phyllis wondered if something had happened to change the way Frank felt, or if such bluster just came naturally to him when he was confronted by an emotional situation.

Frank pulled his wife away from Randall, who remained slumped on the floor with his back against one of the legs of the dining table. Frank seemed to notice then that Phyllis, Sam, and Carolyn were inside his mother's house. "What are you folks doing here?" he asked, his tone a blend of curiosity and anger at the intrusion by relative strangers.

"We brought some cookies over," Phyllis explained as she stepped forward. "I knew Agnes usually left the back door unlocked, so I thought we'd just set them in on the kitchen counter. I'm sorry, Frank; I know we had no right to just let ourselves in like that—"

"And Randall was here?" Frank still sounded baffled by that.

"I'm sure he'd just gotten here, too," Claire said.

Phyllis and Sam glanced at each other. They knew that wasn't the case. From what Randall had said, he'd been here for a while, hiding in the attic. But had he arrived today, or—

Phyllis suddenly wondered whether he had been here when Agnes was murdered. In fact, was it possible that he'd had something to do with his grandmother's death? Phyllis didn't want to think that could be true . . . but what was it Mike always said?

In nearly every murder, family members are the most likely suspects. . . .

"Well?" Frank demanded. "Was the boy here when you came in?"

Randall had to be in his midtwenties and probably didn't care much for being called *the boy*. Young men could be foolishly prideful about such things.

"He was here," Sam said. "Don't know who was more spooked when we ran into each other in the kitchen, him or me. But he dropped the glass he was carryin' and it busted all to pieces, so you'd better be careful if y'all go in there. Somebody'll need to clean up that broken glass."

"I'll do it," Billie Hargrove said as she circled around Frank, Claire, and Randall. Frank and Ted's younger sister gave Phyllis a nod as she passed by. Phyllis hadn't seen Billie, or any of the Simmons children, for quite a while until this weekend, and hadn't spoken to her for years.

The living room was crowded with people. Ted Simmons stood there swallowing nervously, his prominent Adam's apple bobbing up and down. Next to him stood his wife, a tall woman with short dark hair and glasses. Billie's husband, a heavyset man with a toupee, looked like he wanted a drink. He licked his lips every few seconds. There were six or eight children in there, too; Phyllis couldn't see well enough to get an accurate count of them, but their ages ranged from about ten to sixteen or seventeen. The house felt crowded.

"All right, Randall," Frank said. "Where have you been? It's been months since you called."

Randall shook his head without looking up. "I don't have to answer your questions."

Frank reached down to grab his arm and haul him to his feet. "Blast it, boy, you can't talk to me like that!"

The sound of an approaching siren had been getting progressively louder. Now it was right outside, and it came to an abrupt stop. Randall was trying to pull away from his father's grip when a sharp knocking came from the front door. "Police!" a man's voice called. "Open up!"

"Now you've done it," Frank snapped at his son. "Now we have to deal with the cops."

Phyllis saw that wild fear flare in Randall's eyes again. She had an idea of what was about to happen, but before she could call out a warning to Frank, Randall hauled off and hit him. The blow was an awkward one and not particularly powerful, but Frank appeared to be so stunned that his own son had punched him that he let go of Randall's arm and took a step backward.

Randall turned and tried to run toward the kitchen, but Sam was blocking his way. At the same time, Ted Simmons jerked the front door open and said to the two police officers there, "Help! My nephew's gone crazy!"

The cops rushed in as various members of the Simmons family hurriedly got out of their way. Both officers were young but probably experienced enough to know how dangerous domestic disturbance calls could be, and this incident gave the appearance of falling into that category. They were wary as they closed in on Randall.

"Get down on the floor!" one of them shouted at him. "Down on the floor now!"

Randall darted back and forth, obviously still looking for a way out. One of the cops suddenly leaped at him, clamped a choke hold on him, and rode him to the floor. Claire Simmons screamed, "Oh, my God! Don't hurt him! Randall, don't fight them!"

But it was too late for that. Randall was thrashing around in the grip of the officer. The second cop joined in the struggle. He managed to get a knee in the small of Randall's back and pin him to the floor long enough for the other officer to grab one of Randall's wrists, slip a plastic restraint around it, and then jerk Randall's other arm behind his back as well. A second later both wrists were caught in the restraints. Randall groaned and stopped struggling.

One of the cops climbed to his feet while the other knelt on top of Randall and started patting him down. "Listen to me, pardner," he said. "You got anything in your pockets I need to know about? Any weapons or needles? I'm not gonna be happy if I stick myself on something."

Randall started to sob. "N-no. Nothing."

"You better be tellin' me the truth," the officer warned as he continued the search.

The other cop turned to the rest of the people in the crowded dining room and said, "All right; somebody tell me what's going on here." He pointed to Frank. "You."

Frank ran a hand over his pale, suddenly haggard face and said, "That's my son, Officer."

"Is he drunk? Or on drugs?"

Frank shook his head. "I have no idea. I didn't smell any alcohol on him. I . . . I just don't know about the drugs. Today is the first time I've seen him in seven or eight months."

"How old is he?"

"Twenty-four."

"Too old to be considered a runaway, then. He got a history of erratic behavior? Mental disorders or anything like that?"

Claire said, "He's not crazy, and he's not drunk or on drugs! He's just scared; can't you see that?"

Phyllis had to agree. Even though she was shaken by the violent behavior she had just witnessed from Randall, she had seen the fear in his eyes. Terror was more like it, she thought. That was what had motivated him to try to get away from Sam in the first place and what had caused him to strike his father. Randall was just plain scared out of his wits, and Phyllis had no idea why.

It was none of her business—unless Randall was the one who had choked the life out of Agnes and then hit Phyllis on the back of the head. She glanced down at his feet, remembering that shoe she had caught a glimpse of. Randall wasn't wearing dress shoes with black heels at the moment. He had on a worn pair of running shoes. But that didn't mean he couldn't have been wearing different shoes the day before, at the time of the murder.

The second cop stood up, then reached down and grasped Randall's arms to pull him to his feet. That looked to Phyllis like it must have hurt, but Randall didn't cry out or say anything.

"What happened? Did he just start causing trouble suddenly?" the first cop asked Frank. "Is he not supposed to be here? Did he break in?"

Before Frank could answer, the second cop said, "Wait a

minute. Is this the house where that old woman was killed yesterday? It is, isn't it?"

"That old woman was my mother," Frank said stiffly. "And yes, this is where she was killed."

Phyllis's attention went back to Frank. She glanced down at his shoes. They were black shoes, but they were worn and scuffed. Quickly she did a survey of the other feet in the room. None of them wore the heel she was looking for.

"Does this business with your son have anything to do with the murder?" the second cop asked.

"No!" Claire cried. "That's insane. Randall loved his grandmother. He never would have hurt her."

The officers looked at each other and seemed to come to the same conclusion at the same time. "We better call this in," one of them said.

"Yeah," the other agreed. He reached for the radio clipped to his belt.

Before he could use it, an attractive Hispanic woman in a long black coat strode into the living room. A badge was attached to the belt around her waist. The two uniformed officers looked at her, and one of them said, "We were about to call you, Detective."

Phyllis figured the newcomer was the detective Mike and Sarah had mentioned. Isabel Largo—that was her name, Phyllis recalled. She was a rather severe-looking woman, but she had an undeniable air of competence about her.

"I heard the call and recognized the address, so I came right over. What's this about?" she asked the officers.

"We got a call that there was a possible burglary in progress at this residence," one of the cops answered. "But when we got here it shaped up to be a domestic disturbance instead." He pointed to Ted Simmons, who looked uneasy. "This guy said his nephew was going crazy. We came into the dining room and saw the suspect here jumping around like he was trying to get away. We had to subdue him in order to place him in custody."

"Did you see him actually do anything other than try to flee?"

The cops glanced at each other and then shook their heads. "Not after we got here."

Phyllis looked at Frank Simmons. Randall had punched him, and she imagined that Frank could swear out an assault complaint and make it stick. But if nobody said anything about the punch, the police might not have enough to hold Randall, unless they tried to make a case for resisting an officer.

Claire glared at her husband, and Phyllis would have been willing to bet that Frank wasn't going to say anything about Randall hitting him. In fact, Frank said to Isabel Largo, "Detective, this is all just a big misunderstanding. This is my son Randall. He has just as much right to be here as any of the rest of us. It's just that we hadn't seen him for a while and we didn't know he was coming, so we were surprised when we walked in and found him here." Frank swallowed. "We, uh, haven't always gotten along that well, so there may have been a little yelling going on, but it didn't mean anything."

Detective Largo nodded slowly as she considered Frank's statement. Then she looked at Phyllis, Sam, and Carolyn and asked, "What about you folks? Are you members of the Simmons family, too?"

"No, ma'am," Sam said. "We live next door. I'm Sam Fletcher, and this is Mrs. Phyllis Newsom and Mrs. Carolyn Wilbarger."

Recognition showed in Detective Largo's dark eyes. "Ah. You're Deputy Newsom's mother," she said to Phyllis. "The one who was attacked by Mrs. Simmons's murderer."

"That's right," Phyllis said with a nod.

"How are you feeling? No aftereffects from the assault?"

"No, I'm fine," Phyllis told the detective. "We were bringing some cookies over for the family, and we sort of . . . walked into things."

She was aware that Claire Simmons was watching her nervously. Claire and Frank hadn't said anything about that punch Randall had thrown—but Phyllis, Sam, or Carolyn still could.

"I'd planned to come by and ask you a few questions about the attack on you, Mrs. Newsom," Detective Largo said. "I'd do that now, but I'm afraid it's going to have to wait." She turned to the officers and told them, "Take him out and put him in your car. Be sure and read him his rights. I'll meet you at the station."

"What . . . what are you doing?" Claire gasped.

"I'm placing your son under arrest, ma'am."

"But why?" Frank demanded. "I told you; this was all just a misunderstanding. A family argument. We don't want to press any charges against Randall, for God's sake!"

Detective Largo shook her head. "This isn't about that, sir. Your son already has outstanding warrants against him for failure to appear and possession with intent."

"Wha . . . what?"

"He skipped out on his bail and didn't show up in court to be tried on charges of dealing drugs," Largo said. She motioned with her head to the officers. "Take him."

The cops flanked Randall, each of them gripping an arm, and marched him out of the house, past the dumbfounded members of his family. Claire began to weep. Frank looked almost too shocked to comprehend what the detective had just told him, but after a moment he awkwardly put an arm around his wife's shoulders and tried to comfort her.

Randall hadn't said a word in response to Detective Largo's accusation. He hadn't claimed it was all a mistake or cried out that he was innocent. Instead his head had hung forward and his gaze had been directed at the floor like that of a defeated, guilty man, Phyllis thought. She understood now why he had tried so desperately to get away.

It appeared that Randall Simmons had a lot to run from.

Chapter 8

*B*efore leaving to head for the police station, Detective Largo turned to Frank, Claire, and the other members of the Simmons family and said, "It's your claim that you didn't know Randall was going to be here?"

"It's not *our claim*," Frank said. "It's true. We had no idea."

The detective nodded. "I suppose there's no need to bring up charges of aiding and abetting a fugitive, then. But if I find out differently . . ."

"There's no need to take that tone, Detective. We've told you the truth. And I don't believe for a minute that my son is . . . is a drug dealer. I'm going to get him a lawyer—"

"You do that, Mr. Simmons. He's going to need one."

With that, Detective Largo turned toward the door. She paused and added over her shoulder, "We're going to need to get fingerprints from all of you." She glanced at Phyllis. "That goes for you, too, Mrs. Newsom. We lifted quite a few prints from the house, and we need to match up as many of them as we can."

"We'll ask the lawyer about that," Frank snapped.

"I'll be in touch." The detective left the house.

Claire turned, buried her face against her husband's chest, and wailed. Frank told her, "At least we know where he is now," but that didn't seem to help much.

Phyllis approached them and said, "Frank, I'm sorry about all this. If we hadn't come over here, the police might not have found Randall."

Frank shook his head. "No need to apologize, Mrs. Newsom. The cops would have caught up to him sooner or later. You saw how he was. He was like a wild animal. He would have fought back when they tried to arrest him and might've gotten hurt really bad. As bad as it is, this is better."

"He . . . he's innocent," Claire got out between sobs. "I know he is."

Phyllis wasn't surprised that she felt that way; she was Randall's mother, after all. But Phyllis couldn't help but think again about how Randall hadn't denied the charges.

And she couldn't help but remember how Agnes's face had looked with that belt knotted around her neck, choking out her life. If Randall was responsible for that, then he deserved whatever happened to him. Phyllis didn't care as much about the attack on her. The effects of that weren't going to last very long. But Agnes was always going to be dead.

"We'd better be gettin' back," Sam said. "We've intruded on you folks for long enough." He hesitated, then added, "The, uh, cookies are on the counter in the kitchen, for whatever that's worth."

Frank nodded. The bleak look on his face made it clear that nobody was all that interested in cookies at the moment. The rest of the family looked just as stunned by everything that had happened.

Phyllis, Sam, and Carolyn left by the front door. The police cars that had been parked in front of the house had drawn plenty of attention. People were standing out in their yards all along the street, looking toward the house where, for the second day in a row, emergency vehicles had arrived with lights flashing and sirens wailing. Across the street, Monte and Vickie Kimbrough stood on their walk. Vickie turned and said something to her husband, then hurried across the street to intercept Phyllis.

Vickie Kimbrough was around thirty years old, a very pretty woman with medium-length blond hair. She wore jeans and a baggy, fuzzy pink sweater. She kept her hands in her pockets because the air was still chilly. "Hi, Phyllis," she said. "I hope you don't think I'm a terrible gossip, but what happened there today?"

The Kimbroughs had lived across the street for about four years, which meant that they weren't old-timers in the neighborhood. But they had been there long enough to be friendly with most of the people who lived along the street. Vickie was, anyway; Monte, a tall, dark man, always seemed a little stiff and standoffish to Phyllis. They attended the same church as Phyllis, so she thought she knew them about as well as anybody did. She didn't mind telling Vickie, "The police arrested Agnes's grandson Randall."

"Do they think he's the one who killed her?" Vickie sounded both surprised and horrified.

"I don't know. They didn't really say anything about that. Evidently he's been in trouble with the law before and jumped bail on some drug-dealing charges."

"Good Lord. To think that such a thing would happen here."

"It's a rough world," Sam said.

"Yes, I know, but . . . this street especially seems like it could still be back in a . . . a better time, when there weren't any murders or drugs or . . . or anything like that."

"I know what you mean," Phyllis agreed, "but I don't think things were ever really like that. The bad things used to just be better hidden than they are now."

Vickie nodded. "I suppose you're right. I ought to know that, given the line of work I'm in." She worked for a lawyer, Phyllis recalled, and probably saw all sorts of unpleasant things in her daily life. Vickie thrust her hands deeper in the pockets of the fuzzy sweater and went on. "I don't hardly know what to hope for. I hate to think that Agnes's own grandson could murder her, but I don't like the idea that the killer could still be on the loose, either. He could come back here to the neighborhood."

"Maybe he's someone who *lives* in the neighborhood," Carolyn suggested.

Vickie shook her head. "Now, *that* I refuse to believe. And I'm not even going to think about it." She glanced across the street and saw that her husband had gone into the house. "I'd better get back. Monte's probably wondering what's keeping me. He doesn't like it all that much when I stand around gabbing with people."

She took a hand out of a sweater pocket and lifted it in farewell, then turned and went back across the street.

Carolyn snorted and said quietly, "I wouldn't stay married to a man who didn't let me talk to people."

"Monte didn't try to stop Vickie from talking to us," Phyllis pointed out. "He just went in the house."

"Yes, but she looked a little worried, like he might be angry with her. That's the sort of man who's usually abusive."

Phyllis didn't really believe that Monte Kimbrough abused his wife. He just didn't seem like the type to her, despite what

Carolyn had said. But it was almost impossible to know what really went on in people's private lives, she reminded herself.

She had seen more evidence of that than she liked to think about.

Eve had to hear about everything that had happened next door and was disappointed that she had missed out on all the excitement.

"Not that I don't feel sorry for the family," she said. "It's terrible losing Agnes that way, and then having to deal with the possibility that her own grandson killed her."

"What do you think, Phyllis?" Sam asked as the four of them sat in the living room. "Do you reckon he could've done it?"

"I don't know Randall well enough to say either way. I really don't know him at all. But Agnes must have known he was hiding from the law when she agreed to let him stay in her attic. Maybe she got worried and tried to convince him to turn himself in. If he refused, she could have threatened to let the police know he was there, anyway. Or he might have believed that she would, whether that was true or not."

Carolyn said, "That's just pure speculation."

"That's about all we've got to go on," Sam said. "I'm glad it's not up to us to find out what really happened."

Phyllis wondered for a second if that comment was directed at her. She supposed it probably was. And considering the events of the fairly recent past, it was probably well deserved, too.

Through the front window, she saw a sheriff's department cruiser pull up at the curb in front of the house. A smile appeared on her face. Mike often stopped by on his way home after his shift was over. She saw him get out of the car, wearing his cream-colored Stetson and brown leather uniform jacket, looking like a cross between a modern policeman and an old-fashioned Western lawman. That was typical of Texas: the Old West was long since gone, the memories of it fading with each passing day of cable TV, broadband Internet access, and text messaging—all the technology that was doing its best to make every place like every other place—but a few vestiges of the past remained. Phyllis hoped they always would, at least as long as she was alive.

Mike came up the walk. She met him at the door and let him in. He had a worried look on his youthful face as he said, "I heard there was more trouble at the Simmons house. Were you mixed up in it, Mom?"

"Sam and Carolyn and I were all over there when it happened," Phyllis said.

"The cops have a suspect in custody in Mrs. Simmons's murder?"

"I don't know about that. They arrested Randall Simmons for jumping bail on drug-dealing charges. Sit down and we'll tell you about it."

Mike took a seat in one of the armchairs, and for the next few minutes, Phyllis and Sam filled him in on what had happened, with Carolyn adding the occasional semicaustic comment. When they were finished, Mike asked, "You don't know how long Randall had been hiding up there in the attic?"

"I have no idea," Phyllis said with a shake of her head. "And with Agnes dead, unless Randall provides an answer, I don't see how they'll ever know. I suppose he could have been up there for weeks. I don't think so, though, because I was over at Agnes's house quite a bit after she came home from the rehab hospital, and I never saw any signs of anyone else being there."

"Couldn't have been too comfortable, stayin' in an attic," Sam commented.

"Part of it was finished out as a little bedroom," Phyllis explained. "Agnes's husband did that years ago. I know because Kenny helped him a little with some of it. The quarters are a little cramped, but not too bad."

"Better than jail," Mike said. "That's where he'll be spending his time now. Since he already failed to appear on those other charges, I'm sure his bail was revoked, and if there are any new charges, he'll be considered a flight risk, and bail will probably be denied for those."

"It's such a shame," Eve said. "I hate to see anyone locked up."

"That's where some people belong, Mrs. Turner," Mike said. "I can promise you that." He reached for his hat, which he had placed on a little table beside his chair. "Maybe I'll stop by the police department and see if I can find out any more from that Detective Largo."

"She's sort of a hard-boiled character," Sam commented. "Likes to act like one, anyway."

"Yeah, but she seems to be good at her job." Mike stood up and put his hat on, then stepped over to the sofa and bent to give Phyllis a kiss. "See you later, Mom." He waved at the others on his way out. "So long, folks."

Phyllis was glad that Mike was going to try to find out the status of the case against Randall Simmons. She was curious, and there was no point in denying that.

But she recalled the way Sarah had reacted at the mention of Detective Largo's name, and she hoped that she hadn't detected too pronounced a note of eagerness in her son's voice when he mentioned stopping to talk to the woman again.

The door of Isabel Largo's office was open when Mike got there, but he paused in the hall and knocked on it anyway, out of courtesy. The cop on duty at the front desk today had known him and sent him on back without announcing him.

Largo was turned sideways at the desk, typing on a keyboard in a pull-out drawer under her computer monitor. She glanced at the doorway and said, "Deputy Newsom. Come on in. I'll be with you in a minute, soon as I finish entering these reports."

"Always plenty of paperwork, isn't there?" he said as he came in to the cramped office and sat down in one of the metal straight-back chairs.

"That's something about police work that'll never change." Largo clicked the mouse, and the hard drive purred as it saved her files. She swiveled her chair toward Mike and asked, "How come your mother makes a habit of showing up at crime scenes?"

The blunt question took him by surprise. He grunted and said, "Just lucky, I guess. Or unlucky, depending on how you look at it. I hear she came across something else related to the Simmons case today."

Largo nodded. "I figured that was why you were here. I don't have to share that information with you, you know."

"Of course not. I just thought—"

"Professional courtesy and all," she cut in.

"Well, yeah."

Largo picked up a pen and toyed with it for a second before she said, "I'll tell you what I know, Deputy, but I warn you . . . if you do anything to jeopardize my case, you'll never get anything else from me."

"Don't worry, Detective; I know how to be discreet." Mike knew his voice sounded a little stiff, but he couldn't help it. Isabel Largo seemed determined to rub him the wrong way.

"I already knew Randall Simmons had been in the house."

Mike's eyebrows rose in surprise.

"We sent off all the fingerprints we lifted, and earlier this afternoon some of them kicked back from the fugitive database as matching those of Randall Edward Simmons, who has warrants outstanding on him in Dallas County for flight to avoid prosecution and possession of narcotics with intent to distribute. He's a bad guy."

"What sort of narcotics?"

"Cocaine. Both the regular stuff and crack."

Mike nodded. "Once the fingerprint match came back, were you going to get a search warrant for the house?"

"That's right. I was about to get that process started when I heard the disturbance call at the same address." Largo smiled, which relieved the stern lines of her face a little. "That saved me some trouble. Randall Simmons was already in custody when I got there."

"Has he admitted to killing his grandmother?" Mike knew that was the main thing his mother would want to know.

"He hasn't admitted anything. His father showed up with a lawyer almost right away, and she told him to keep his mouth shut."

"Who's the lawyer?"

"Juliette Yorke."

Mike nodded. Juliette Yorke hadn't been in Weatherford for very long—she was from back east somewhere—but a while back she had represented one of the suspects in that murder out at Oliver Loving Elementary School. Now she had picked up another client who might be mixed up in a high-profile killing.

"What are you going to do if he won't talk?"

"We can hold him for a little while," Largo said with a shrug, "but Dallas County wants him, and I guess we'll have to give him to them unless we can come up with something tying him to the murder. If we can do that, we can hang on to him here. All I know to do is try."

"Yeah. At least he's in custody. If he *is* the killer, he won't be able to hurt anybody else."

"He'll go away on the drug-dealing charge," Largo agreed. "This day and age, he might get a stiffer sentence for that than for killing the old lady." She sighed. "Still, it would be nice to *know* that he's the killer."

"Yeah." Mike got to his feet. "Thanks, Detective. If I run across anything that might help your case, I'll let you know."

"I'd appreciate that."

Mike paused to look at the picture of the baby in the photo cube on top of the filing cabinet. "Your kid?"

"My son, Victor. He's fourteen months."

Mike smiled. "Cute kid. My son, Bobby, is almost three. You and your husband have any others?"

"No. And I'm not married."

Mike had noticed that she didn't wear a wedding band but had figured that didn't mean anything. A lot of cops wore little if any jewelry while they were on duty. Largo didn't offer any explanation for having a kid but no husband, and Mike wasn't about to ask, feeling he had already stuck his foot in his mouth. He knew he was being old-fashioned to even wonder about such a thing, but that was the way he'd been raised. Old-fashioned didn't necessarily mean bad, either.

"Well, I'll be in touch," he said into the somewhat awkward silence that had fallen.

"So long, Deputy."

Cold wind gusted in Mike's face as he walked from the building to his car. He wished he hadn't even said anything about the baby in the photo. Detective Largo was already doing him a favor by sharing information about the Simmons case with him. He shouldn't have put her on the spot by asking about her husband.

But it was too late to worry about that. Anyway, he told himself, it was possible he wouldn't ever cross paths with her again unless he went out of his way to do so.

And as he took a deep breath of the chilly air, he decided it would probably be a good idea not to do that.

Chapter 9

$\mathcal{F}$rom time to time during the rest of that day, Phyllis looked out one of the side windows in the living room that gave her a view of the Simmons house. She wondered what was going on in there, although she knew it was really none of her concern. She saw Frank leave and come back a short time later, and then leave again after that. She hoped he'd been able to find a lawyer for Randall. Getting someone to take on a case on a Sunday afternoon less than a week before Christmas might not be easy. But she supposed lawyers were probably used to being on call twenty-four hours a day, all year round, just like doctors.

Phyllis halfway expected that Isabel Largo would come back to question her and take her fingerprints, along with those of Sam and Carolyn. But the detective never showed up, so Phyllis went to bed that night with that interview still hanging over her head.

The next morning, Carolyn announced, "I think we need to get our minds off all that trouble next door and pay attention to something much more pleasant—Christmas dinner."

"It's less than a week away," Eve agreed. "We need to decide what we're going to make this year."

If Phyllis had wanted to be uncharitable, she could have pointed out that Eve never made anything in the kitchen. She claimed that her culinary skills were limited, usually adding that she made up for that with her talents in other rooms of the house.

Phyllis let Eve's comment pass without any reaction this time. Instead she said, "I was thinking about cooking a ham this year."

"Nothin' much better'n a good ham," Sam put in.

Carolyn frowned. "Christmas dinner is usually a turkey."

"But it doesn't have to be," Phyllis said. "Plenty of people cook hams for Christmas. And I was thinking about a special way to prepare it that might make it even better. Remember the roast we had that was cooked in cola?"

Sam smiled and licked his lips. "I sure do," he said. "It was mighty good."

"I was wondering if you couldn't cook a ham the same way."

"Basting it in cola the way you did the roast?" Carolyn asked.

"That's right. But I was also thinking that you could get one of those meat injectors and put the cola right in the ham. Baste it from the inside out, so to speak."

"Soundin' better all the time," Sam said.

"I don't know," Carolyn said with a dubious frown. "Injecting cola into a ham? It sounds pretty far-fetched to me." She paused. "What about stuffing? You have to have stuffing for Christmas, whether you cook a ham or a turkey. I have a recipe for some wild rice and cranberry stuffing that I've been wanting to try."

"You mean you combine the stuffing and the cranberry sauce?" Phyllis asked. "That's an interesting idea."

"It's settled, then. I'll make the stuffing."

"And I'll cook the cola ham."

Sam said, "And I'll do my part by eatin' both of 'em."

There was some more talk about other side dishes and desserts, although Phyllis thought they had so many cookies left, they might not need any extra desserts. Still, it wasn't really Christmas without a pie or two, was it?

Carolyn was right; the discussion about Christmas dinner took Phyllis's mind off of Agnes Simmons's murder, and she didn't really think about it again until that afternoon, when the doorbell rang and Phyllis opened the door to find Detective Isabel Largo standing there on the porch. The overcast had broken, but the temperature was still pretty cool. A chilly wind whipped Detective Largo's long black coat around her calves, and across the street Vickie Kimbrough was huddled in her heavy sweater again as she came outside to get the mail.

"Hello, Mrs. Newsom," the policewoman said. "How are you feeling today?"

"Not bad," Phyllis replied. She stepped back and ushered Detective Largo into the house.

"No problems from what happened to you a couple of days ago?"

Phyllis shook her head. "No, but I'm going to see the doctor again tomorrow, just to be sure." She had called Walt Lee's office and made the appointment like she was told to when she was released from the hospital.

"That's good. If you've got a few minutes, I'd like to talk to you."

"Of course. Let me take your coat."

Phyllis hung the coat in the hall closet and then took Detective Largo into the living room. The woman had a short-barreled revolver holstered on her right hip. She wore black slacks and a dark red silk shirt and looked more stylish than Phyllis expected a police officer to look. She also carried a small briefcase that she placed on the floor next to the coffee table as she sat down on the sofa.

"I'll need to take your fingerprints, too, as well as those of the other people who live here."

Phyllis nodded. "Of course. Anything we can do to help." She hesitated. "I assume that Randall Simmons hasn't confessed yet."

A faint smile touched Detective Largo's lips. "I'm afraid I can't discuss the case."

"Of course. That's fine. I didn't mean to pry."

Anyway, she would ask Mike about it later, Phyllis thought, then felt a little embarrassed at the idea—not enough to keep her from doing it, though.

"Now, I know you've been over all of this before," Detective Largo began, "but I'd like you to tell me again exactly what happened Saturday afternoon. Everything that you can remember. You never know what's going to turn out to be important, so if you can recall any details now that you didn't think about before, please don't hesitate to include them."

Phyllis nodded and said, "I understand." She launched into yet another recital of the facts, casting her mind back to the moment she had started gathering up a sampler of cookies to take next door to Agnes.

She didn't think there was anything new in her story this time. She laid out all the facts for Detective Largo, who nodded and made notes as she let Phyllis tell the story in her own way, at her own pace. The detective was a good listener, Phyllis thought. In her job, she probably got plenty of practice.

When Phyllis was finished, Detective Largo asked, "Can you tell me who was here at the party Saturday afternoon?"

"Oh, just people from the neighborhood. The cookie exchange is sort of a tradition. We always have it here on the last Saturday before Christmas."

"Do you send out invitations?"

"No, people just know to come and bring a plate of cookies."

"What about people who are new to the neighborhood?"

"We make sure they know about it. Really, it's not any trouble spreading the word." Phyllis wasn't sure why Detective Largo was so interested in the cookie exchange when the crime had taken place next door, not here.

"So you don't have an actual invitation list, or anything like that? People don't have to RSVP?"

"Not at all. It's a very informal get-together."

"Can you tell me who was here, anyway?"

Phyllis frowned. "You mean . . . everybody?"

Detective Largo nodded and said, "As many of them as you can remember, anyway."

Phyllis leaned back in the armchair where she was sitting. "Goodness. I don't know if I can come up with all the names. . . ."

"As many as you can," Detective Largo prodded.

Phyllis thought about it. She knew everyone on both sides of the street for at least three blocks, which was about the limit of the area where people considered themselves a little community within the community. She began naming them, omitting the ones she couldn't remember seeing at the cookie exchange. Not everyone was able to make it, of course. In this hectic, modern-day world, people sometimes had commitments they couldn't get out of, even for an old-fashioned pleasure like getting together with neighbors, eating cookies, and drinking punch.

When she got to the end of the list, she said, "That's all I can think of, Detective. Of course, Carolyn and Eve and Sam were here, too, but they live here."

"Sounds like quite a crowd. There must have been, what, fifty or sixty people here?"

Phyllis nodded. "At least. The house was packed. But that's the way I like it when it comes to the cookie exchange."

"So . . . you couldn't keep your eye on everybody at once, I don't imagine."

"No, but why would I want to? Maybe it's naive of me, Detective, but these people are my neighbors. I trust them."

"I'm sure you do. I just wanted to establish the fact that you couldn't be sure where everyone was all the time."

Phyllis thought about that for a second, then said, "Good heavens! You think somebody at the cookie exchange could have slipped next door without anyone noticing and murdered Agnes Simmons, then come back over here with no one being the wiser?"

Detective Largo shook her head. "I didn't say that, Mrs. Newsom."

"No, but that's the only reason I can think of why you'd want to know exactly who was here and whether or not I was able to keep up with what they were doing all the time!"

The detective's lips thinned. "It would be better if you didn't speculate about such things."

It was too late for that advice to do any good. Phyllis's mind was already racing.

She had an answer to her earlier question now. Randall Simmons *hadn't* confessed to killing his grandmother. If he had, then Detective Largo wouldn't be worried about who had been at the cookie exchange or what they had been doing. The case would have been wrapped up. Detective Largo probably wouldn't even be here.

"I never did feel like Randall would have done such a thing," Phyllis said.

"I didn't say that, either, Mrs. Newsom. Randall Simmons is still our primary suspect." Detective Largo grimaced a little, as if she realized that she shouldn't have said that. "We're just trying to make sure that no line of investigation is overlooked."

"I understand that, but . . . what possible reason would any of my neighbors have for killing poor Agnes?"

Detective Largo looked at her and said, "You tell me, Mrs. Newsom."

Phyllis couldn't. The idea that one of the people from the neighborhood could have committed murder was as foreign to her as the fact that a murder had been committed in this peaceful community. But it had been, and if Randall Simmons wasn't guilty, then the killer was still out there on the loose somewhere.

"There's still the possibility that Agnes surprised a burglar," Phyllis suggested.

"Yes, but we know that her grandson was staying up in that attic room. If Mrs. Simmons encountered a burglar, why didn't she shout to Randall for help?"

From the sound of it, Detective Largo was giving up on the idea of *not* discussing the case with her, Phyllis thought. The detective's curiosity was getting the better of her, as it always did with Phyllis.

"Maybe she didn't have time to call for help. The burglar could have choked her with his hands before he wrapped the belt from her robe around her throat, or perhaps he hit her from behind and knocked her out, like he did with me."

Detective Largo shook her head. "The autopsy ruled out both of those possibilities. There were no bruises or finger marks on her throat; just the marks from the belt. And she hadn't been struck on the head or anywhere else. There were no defensive wounds, no skin or tissue under her fingernails. Somehow the killer got hold of the belt, wrapped it around her neck, and strangled her with it without her yelling out for help. That doesn't seem like something a burglar would do, does it?"

Phyllis had to admit that it didn't. "It sounds more like Agnes knew her killer."

"Which brings us back to the people from the neighborhood . . . or her grandson." Detective Largo shrugged. "Or one of her other family members."

"But they weren't even there," Phyllis said. "They'd gone together to Fort Worth."

"Where they went to Ridgmar Mall and split up for an hour and a half while they were shopping. You can get from the west side of Fort Worth to Weatherford and back in less time than that."

"I didn't see any of the cars come back."

"They could have parked down the street, or around the block, and gone into the house through the back. Anyway, you were busy. You might not have noticed a car arriving and then leaving again a few minutes later. That's all the time it would have taken. It's just a theory, and not a very plausible one at that." Detective Largo's voice hardened. "I don't want to miss anything, though."

"It sounds like you're being very thorough," Phyllis said.

The detective's stern demeanor eased as she smiled again. "And you're very slick, aren't you, Mrs. Newsom?"

"I don't know what you mean—"

"I came here to question you, and I wound up telling you as much or more than you told me."

"I don't mean to cause any trouble. I'm sorry."

Detective Largo shook her head and waved off the apology. "No need to be. You're an intelligent woman. I get all these ideas swirling around in my head, and it helps to talk them out. I can see now how you managed to solve those other murders."

"I never set out to . . . to be a detective," Phyllis said. "I just wanted to find out what really happened."

"Same with me," Detective Largo said softly. "I'm just looking for the truth." She put away her notebook and opened the briefcase. "Now, let's get those fingerprints. If you'd get Mr. Fletcher and Mrs. Wilbarger and Mrs. Turner . . ."

Phyllis found Sam, Carolyn, and Eve in the kitchen and wondered how much of the conversation in the living room they had overheard. Most of it, she would have been willing to wager if she had been the sort of person who made bets. They wouldn't have been eavesdropping, exactly, but some of the walls in this old house were thin.

Sam was the only one who had been fingerprinted before. "Uncle Sam's got my prints," he said. "I was in the army for three years, back in the early sixties, when I was still a kid."

"Thank you, Mr. Fletcher," Detective Largo said. "These prints are just for comparison purposes. We know that you and these ladies were all inside Mrs. Simmons's house at one time or another, so we can rule out the prints we found over there that match any of yours."

"That boy didn't confess, did he?"

Detective Largo hesitated for a second, then said, "No, he didn't. In fact, on the advice of his lawyer, he's refused to make any statement."

"Doesn't mean he's guilty . . . of the murder, anyway."

"It doesn't mean he's innocent, either."

Detective Largo put away the fingerprint equipment as Phyllis, Sam, Carolyn, and Eve wiped the ink from their fingers with the special wipes she provided. The latches on the briefcase clicked shut.

"I'll be in touch if I need any more information," the detective said as she stood up. "Thank you for your cooperation, all of you. And thank you for answering my questions, Mrs. Newsom."

"I'm always glad to help," Phyllis said.

At Phyllis's request, Sam got Detective Largo's coat from the hall closet and then walked her out. As soon as the policewoman was gone, Carolyn said, "She thinks someone from the neighborhood did it! We overheard enough to realize that."

That confirmed Phyllis's guess about her friends listening from the kitchen. That was fine with her, because as Sam rejoined them after closing the front door, she said, "Detective Largo didn't come right out and say that, but I could tell she considers it a possibility."

"Well, you know the folks who live around here a whole lot better than I do," Sam said, "but after livin' here for a while, I got to say that nobody up and down the street strikes me as the murderin' sort."

"I agree," Carolyn said. "It's ridiculous. That boy did it. I hate to say it, since Agnes was his grandmother, for goodness' sake, but he's a drug dealer and a fugitive. Of course he did it. Agnes probably threatened to turn him in."

The same thought had crossed Phyllis's mind. Out of grandmotherly concern, Agnes had agreed to let Randall hide out in her attic, but after a while she had realized that she'd made a mistake by doing so. She'd tried to fix that mistake, and it had cost her her life. Everything fit, and as Detective Largo had said, it was the simplest, most likely explanation, by far.

Phyllis still had a hard time believing it, maybe because she had seen with her own eyes that murder was often not a simple matter.

"If anyone on this street had a reason to kill Agnes, it's something we don't know about," she said. "Maybe something that Agnes knew, but nobody else did."

"A secret," Eve said. "Everybody has secrets."

"I don't," Carolyn snapped. "My life is an open book."

"Yes, dear, but it hasn't been checked out in a long time, has it? Someone could have written in the margins," Eve said.

Carolyn frowned. "What?"

Phyllis moved over to the picture window, lifted a hand, and eased the curtain aside so that she could look out along the street. She turned her head, casting her gaze along the solidly built old houses with the trees in their front yards. Eve was right—everybody had secrets. There was no way of knowing what went on behind those walls, on the other side of those windows.

But you might catch a glimpse from time to time, especially if you spent your days sitting at your own window, watching, watching . . . as Agnes Simmons had done.

A shiver went through Phyllis, and it had nothing to do with the cold wind that swayed the bare branches of the trees along both sides of this nice, peaceful street.

Chapter 10

Agnes Simmons's funeral was scheduled for Tuesday afternoon. Phyllis went to the doctor's office that morning, where Walt Lee examined her and gave her a relatively clean bill of health.

"The fact that you haven't had any recurring headaches the past couple of days, or any dizziness, makes me think there aren't going to be any aftereffects from the clout on the head," he told her. "The stitches in your scalp look fine, no infection brewing there, and since they're the sort that dissolve on their own, you won't have to come back to have them removed. I want to see you again in a couple of weeks, anyway, just as a precaution. By then all the soreness in your knees should be gone, too." The doctor paused, then went on. "I hear that Agnes Simmons's grandson was arrested. Do the police think he killed her?"

"I don't really know," Phyllis said. "I guess he's what they always call 'a person of interest' in the newspapers."

"A suspect, in other words."

Phyllis shrugged. After the visit she'd had the previous day from Detective Isabel Largo, she didn't know what to think anymore.

The weather was sunny and had actually warmed somewhat. In this part of Texas it wasn't unusual to have mild weather for Christmas. Phyllis could remember plenty of holidays where Mike had been able to go outside and play with all the new toys he'd gotten as presents on Christmas morning. Somehow, though, cold and overcast would have been more appropriate for a funeral, she thought as she parked at the church that afternoon. Sam, Carolyn, and Eve were with her, and they had all ridden in Phyllis's Lincoln, even though the church was only a few blocks from the house.

Quite a few people were going into the church already, many of them from the neighborhood. Phyllis saw Lois and Blake Horton, Phil and Belinda Stephenson, Keith and Darla Payne, Oscar Gunderson, Helen Johannson, and Monte and Vickie Kimbrough, among others. Some of the neighbors probably hadn't been able to get off work, even for a funeral, something that Phyllis and her friends didn't have to worry about, being retired. Frank and Ted Simmons stood at the doors of the sanctuary, solemnly shaking hands with people as they went in. Both of them looked pale and drawn. A death in the family was always an ordeal, even one from natural causes that was expected. The violent, unexpected nature of a murder just magnified everything and made it worse.

When Phyllis reached the doors, she shook hands with Ted and Frank and murmured, "I'm so sorry."

Frank swallowed and said, "It's even worse than you know, Mrs. Newsom. The police have charged Randall with Mother's murder." He shook his head. "They were going to have to let Dallas County have him on those other charges if they didn't."

"That's terrible." Phyllis didn't know what else to say. If

Randall really was guilty, then he needed to be behind bars. But she knew that Frank didn't believe his son had committed this particular crime, no matter what else he had done.

"I don't know what we're going to do," Frank said. His voice was heavy with grief. "It's my fault, I suppose. Randall and I never did get along. I drove him to do whatever he did."

Ted said, "That's crazy and you know it, Frank. You didn't cause anything. Randall just never was any good."

Anger flared in Frank's eyes. "Don't say that," he warned his brother.

Their sister, Billie, appeared behind them and said in a soft but urgent voice, "Can't you two just let it go, at least for now? This isn't the time or place to be having this argument."

"You're right," Frank said with a sigh. "Mother deserves a proper funeral. But when it's over, I've got to get down to the courthouse. Randall is being arraigned later this afternoon."

Phyllis, Sam, Carolyn, and Eve went on into the church, leaving the Simmonses to deal with their grief and with the new worry of Randall being charged with Agnes's murder. Inside the auditorium, the organist was playing a hymn as people filed into the pews. A woman with red hair stood at the rear, handing folded programs to the mourners. She wore a neat black dress and a faint, appropriately sad smile. Phyllis took one of the programs from her and said quietly, "Hello, Jada."

Jada Gresham, the pastor's wife, said, "Hello, Phyllis. How are you? You're recovering all right from your injuries?"

Phyllis nodded. "Yes, I saw the doctor again this morning, and he said I was doing fine."

"That's wonderful. Dwight and I have been so worried about you."

"Yes, Dwight visited me while I was in the hospital and came by the house, too. He's been very comforting."

"Well, that's his job, you know, to minister to the sick and injured," Jada said. "It's a very important job."

"It surely is," Phyllis agreed. "Thank you, Jada."

She moved on, with the others following her, and found places to sit in one of the pews about two-thirds of the way to the front of the auditorium. The church wasn't going to be full. Agnes Simmons had been well liked but not widely known. Most of the people at the funeral either lived in the same neighborhood or had attended services here with her.

Someone sat down in the pew behind Phyllis and reached forward to rest a hand on her shoulder. She turned her head and saw Mike and Sarah. She smiled at them, mouthed *hello*, and patted Mike's hand. She was glad they'd been able to make it.

Phyllis found her gaze drawn to the closed coffin surrounded by flowers, resting in front of the pulpit. The longer a person lived, the more funerals they attended, she thought. She had been to too many of them in recent years, beginning with her husband, Kenny's. Sometimes she still didn't believe that he was gone. When something puzzled her, she would find herself thinking *I'm going to ask Kenny about that*. Then the realization that she would never ask him about anything again would hit her in the pit of her stomach almost like a physical blow. The same thing had happened when she lost her parents. And now friends were gone, too; friends she would never see again, never argue with, never laugh with. The pain of losing her close friend Mattie was still fresh in her mind. It helped to look at her son, so young and handsome, with his beautiful wife, both of them so full of life, and it was even better when she held her grandson and thought about how life renewed itself and rolled on and on through the years. . . .

But death was never far away, either, and it drew closer with each passing day. These funerals were vivid reminders of that. If she could get away with it, Phyllis thought, she would never go to another funeral—not even her own.

After a few more minutes, the organist brought the hymn to a close, and Dwight Gresham, who had come out and sat on one of the benches to the side of the pulpit, rose and carried his Bible to the podium. He opened the thick black book, even though he had conducted enough funerals that he probably didn't have to actually read the verses anymore because he had them memorized, and said, "In the book of Isaiah, the Lord says, 'Fear not, for I am with you; be not dismayed, for I am your God.' In the book of John, he advises us, 'Let not your heart be troubled, neither let it be afraid.' Also in John, he makes this promise to us: 'I am the resurrection and the life. He who believes in me, though he may die, he shall live.' "

Dwight looked up from the Bible and began reciting the details of Agnes Simmons's life: her birth in the town of Brock, Texas; her marriage to Johnny Lee Simmons; her three children, Frank, Theodore, and Billie; her numerous grandchildren—without mentioning any of them by name, Phyllis noticed, so that Randall wouldn't be conspicuous by either his presence or his absence on the list—and finally the date of her death, after a life of eighty-seven years, ten months, and nineteen days. Preachers usually pinned it down like that in their opening remarks about the deceased, right down to the number of days, because every day was important, Phyllis thought.

Dwight took his seat on the bench, and one of the ladies from the church got up to sing a hymn. As the last notes of the song were fading away, echoing against the stained-glass windows along both sides of the sanctuary, Dwight put his hands on his knees and pushed himself to his feet again. His face was drawn, and Phyllis could see what a strain he was under. Clearly, he had been close to Agnes, and Phyllis remembered what he'd said about bringing the videotapes of the church services to her every week. A friendship must have grown up between them.

The strain was evident in his voice, too, as he began speaking about Agnes—not preaching a sermon, really, just talking about the woman and her life and how it had touched others. Of course, those were the sorts of things heard at most funerals, about how the departed had been a good Christian and a faithful member of the church and how she had left the cares of this world behind and gone on to a better place. Dwight Gresham's voice trembled with sincerity as he said, "Above all else, Agnes Simmons loved the Lord and wanted to follow his teachings. She hated the sin . . . but loved the sinner. Whenever she saw someone straying from the paths of righteousness, she made it her goal in life to steer them back to the way they should be going . . . whether they wanted to be steered or not." A faint chuckle came from him. "Some of you saw that for yourselves, in your own lives. Agnes wanted the best for everyone she knew, and she would do whatever it took to bring that about. If there was ever anyone who fit the description of being willing to go the extra mile for someone, it was Agnes Simmons."

That was true, Phyllis thought. Agnes would even go so far as to let her grandson hide out from the law in her attic . . . but in her determination to help him wipe out his sin, would she have threatened, then, to turn him in? Everything Dwight was saying tended to make Phyllis believe there was a possibility that Agnes would have done just that.

Dwight dabbed at his eyes and went on, "Those of us who knew her will miss Agnes, especially all her family and friends. She was one of a kind." He paused, then said, "At the request of the family—and this was Agnes's wish as well, I know—there will be no graveside service. Let us pray."

The congregation bowed their heads, and when the brief

prayer was done, the organist began to play again. The funeral directors, a pair of sober, black-suited, middle-aged men, stepped forward and opened the casket so that the mourners could pass by for a final look at Agnes Simmons. This custom was one Phyllis didn't particularly care for, and her will contained specific instructions that it not be done at her funeral. But it seemed to be important to most people and was done at nearly every funeral she attended, so she stood up and dutifully passed by with the others who were sitting in the same pew when it was their turn. The line then led to the back of the sanctuary and outside, into the welcome sunshine.

Even though there would be no graveside service, many of the people lingered a few minutes on the church porch and on the lawn in front of the building, talking among themselves and waiting to say good-bye to the Simmons family. Sam said, "I don't know about you folks, but the preacher seemed a mite more upset than usual, almost like it was his own mother who'd passed away."

Phyllis nodded. "I thought so, too. I think I'll go talk to Jada and make sure Dwight's all right."

She spotted the preacher's redheaded wife at the other end of the porch and walked over to her. Jada nodded to the couple she'd been talking to and then turned to Phyllis with a solemn little smile.

"Dwight's taking Agnes's death hard, isn't he?" Phyllis asked.

"He always takes it hard when a member of the congregation passes away. You hear priests refer to the parishioners as their flock, but that's just as true for Baptists, too."

"And other denominations, I expect. Did they become close when Dwight was taking the videotapes of the services to her every week?"

Jada nodded. "That's right. He always came back talking

about how Agnes did this or Agnes said that. It was quite touching, really. Dwight's mother passed away some time ago, you know, so it was almost like Agnes became sort of his surrogate mother. I doubt if that would have ever happened if she hadn't fallen and broken her hip, though. It was after that they became close." Jada's smile disappeared and a sigh came from her lips. "That was a blessing, too, because Agnes's own family certainly wasn't as close to her as they should have been."

"I know," Phyllis said. "I hardly ever saw them visiting. Not that I watched to see who was visiting her or anything, but you can't help but notice things when you've lived in a neighborhood as long as I have."

Jada leaned closer and lowered her voice. "I really shouldn't say anything, especially on a day like today, but Agnes's children neglected her at times. She didn't want for money or anything like that; her husband left her well off. But the children never came to see her unless they needed something. Why, Dwight told me that Frank Simmons expected his mother to invest all the savings she had left in his business, so that he could keep it afloat. She told him she couldn't do that, of course."

"I don't think I even know what Frank does for a living," Phyllis said.

"He has a hardware store in Dallas. In one of the suburbs, actually, but I can't keep track of which one is which. I think it used to be successful, but a Wal-Mart went in just down the street, and of course Frank's having a hard time making it now."

Phyllis nodded. "That happens a lot, I suppose. What about Ted and Billie? Did they get along better with Agnes?"

"Well, I'm not sure. They didn't come to see her any more often, though, if that counts for anything. And there was a long period of time when Billie wouldn't even speak to her mother.

She held some sort of grudge against Agnes. I have no idea what it was about, some sort of petulance over something that happened when she was a child, maybe. But it was just recently that Billie started having anything to do with Agnes again. It's terrible when hard feelings linger like that in a family."

"I've heard it said that no one can hate quite as hard as someone who used to love," Phyllis said.

Jada frowned at her. "I suppose that might be true. I've heard about brothers who have an argument and never speak again, and parents who disown their children. If I was poor Claire Simmons and it was my son who was in jail, accused of such a horrible crime—"

Jada didn't get to finish explaining how she would feel or what she would do if she found herself in Claire's circumstances, because at that moment Claire herself emerged from the church with Frank beside her. He was as grim faced as ever as he held an arm around his wife's shoulders. Claire dabbed tears from her eyes with a handkerchief. Their other children followed them; then came Ted and his wife and children, and finally Billie and Allen Hargrove and their kids. People's conversations trailed away as everyone turned to look at the family of the murdered woman.

As the oldest son and the spokesman for the family, Frank stepped forward and raised his voice to say, "I want to thank all of you for coming today. I'm sure my mother would have been pleased to see all of you here and to know that so many people cared about her." His voice caught a little. "She'll never be forgotten."

His emotion seemed genuine. If Frank really cared that much about his mother, Phyllis thought, he should have made the effort to show it more often while she was alive. Jada had told her an old, all-too-familiar story . . . the elderly relative who's just a bother to the rest of the family, the one who sits alone while those who are younger and more vital go on about their lives. Thank God she hadn't reached that point, Phyllis told herself. She hoped she never would. She stayed busy and had good friends, but the time would come when she couldn't do as much, when those friends began to leave for one reason or another. She didn't think Mike would ever abandon her, but it was so hard to know how these things were going to turn out.

She shook herself out of that unpleasant reverie and joined the others who were shaking hands with the family and saying good-bye. Within a few minutes, she, Sam, Carolyn, and Eve were on their way back to the car, and Phyllis was glad to be able to put this funeral behind her.

"Looked like you had a good talk with the preacher's wife," Sam commented.

"Yes, Jada was telling me about how Dwight felt sorry for Agnes because of the way her family neglected her. I can believe it; I've hardly ever seen any of them over there, ever since the children got married and moved away."

Phyllis couldn't get some of the other things Jada had told her out of her head, either . . . like the way Frank had asked Agnes for money to save his business, and she had turned him down . . . and the old, bitter grudge, possibly left over from childhood, that had caused Billie to stop speaking to her mother for years. For all Phyllis knew, Ted resented his mother just as much as his brother and sister did. He certainly hadn't been any more attentive to Agnes than Frank and Billie had been.

Rapid footsteps behind them in the church parking lot made the group slow down. Mike and Sarah drew even with them. "Hello, everybody," Sarah said.

"How are you today, Mom?" Mike asked. "You were supposed to see Dr. Lee this morning, weren't you?"

"That's right, and he said I was doing just fine," Phyllis replied. She couldn't help but smile a little. She didn't have to worry about Mike neglecting her, she told herself. If anything, he was a little too protective of her. She was going to get spoiled by all the attention if he didn't watch out.

"That's good," Mike said with a nod. "I just wanted to make sure."

"Heard anything more about the boy they've got locked up?" Sam asked.

Mike shook his head. "No. I'm tempted to go talk to Detective Largo again, but I don't want to make a pest of myself."

Sarah took hold of his arm. "No, you don't want to do that," she said quickly.

"I reckon it'll all come out sooner or later," Sam said. "It's not really any of our business, anyway."

"Yeah, but I'm curious," Mike said. "I guess we all are. If I hear anything, I'll let you know."

Mike and Sarah said their good-byes and went on to their car while Phyllis and the others stopped at the Lincoln. Mike's comments had reminded Phyllis of her conversation with Detective Largo the day before, and she thought that the detective hadn't seemed fully convinced of Randall Simmons's guilt. Maybe that had been a hunch on her part, because the evidence, what there was of it, seemed to point to Randall more than anybody else. He was a fugitive from the law, he had been there in the house, and his grandmother could have represented a threat to him. . . .

But it wasn't just the people in the neighborhood who might have secrets they wanted to keep, as Detective Largo had speculated, Phyllis thought as she drove toward her home. There could be secrets inside a family, too, along with resentments and lingering wounds that had never healed. And as the detective had pointed out, the members of the Simmons family didn't really have airtight alibis for the time of Agnes's death. The words she had spoken to Jada Gresham kept going through Phyllis's brain.

No one can hate quite as hard . . . as someone who used to love. . . .

Chapter 11

$\mathcal{I}$t was three days until Christmas, Phyllis thought as she got out of bed on Wednesday morning. She had long since finished her shopping for presents; she liked to get that out of the way as early as possible. Under the tree in the living room, wrapped in bright paper, were a boxed set of John Wayne DVDs for Sam, a pair of new cookbooks for Carolyn, and a box of assorted bath oils for Eve. But there was still baking to do and other preparations to make for Christmas dinner. The thought of going to the store—which would be packed with people who *hadn't* finished their shopping early—was a little daunting, but Phyllis didn't see any way around it.

After breakfast, when she announced that she was going to Wal-Mart, Eve spoke up and asked if she could come along. "I have just a bit more shopping to do," Eve said.

Phyllis agreed, of course, and a short time later they were ready to go. Phyllis opened the garage door, got in the Lincoln with Eve, and began backing the big car toward the street. She had to actually back onto the street to leave, but that was usually no problem since there wasn't a high volume of traffic along her road.

Today, however, she had to hit the brakes suddenly as a car backed fast out of the driveway across the street and almost plowed into the Lincoln's right rear fender. Phyllis recognized the woman behind the wheel as Lois Horton. Lois didn't glance in her direction and didn't even seem aware that she had almost hit Phyllis's car. Instead Lois took off down the street at a high rate of speed, so fast that the rear of the car slewed back and forth a little.

"Oh, my!" Eve said. "Did you see that, dear? She almost hit you."

"I know," Phyllis said with a nod. The close call had left her a little shaken. She watched Lois swerve toward the middle of the street, then back toward the curb.

"Oh, no!" Eve said as Lois nearly sideswiped a car that was parked at the curb in the next block. She overcorrected as she continued on down the street, taking her half out of the middle, as the old saying went.

"Something must be wrong," Phyllis said, "some emergency, or Lois wouldn't be driving like that."

Eve said, "It looks more to me like she's as drunk as a skunk."

Phyllis thought so, too, but she had been casting about in her mind for another possible explanation. She shifted the Lincoln into drive and said, "I think I'd better follow her, just to make sure she gets where she's going all right."

Maybe it was none of her business, she thought, but as a good neighbor she considered it her duty. She and Lois Horton weren't close friends, but she had known the woman and lived across the street from her for years. Lois and her husband, Blake, had been at the cookie exchange along with just about everybody else in the neighborhood. Phyllis didn't want her to wreck her car and hurt herself—or anybody else.

How she was going to stop Lois was a question for which Phyllis didn't have an answer. All she could do was follow along and hope for the best, and maybe have a talk with Lois once she got where she was going.

After a couple of blocks, Lois turned onto South Main Street, making the turn wide and sloppy. That was the way Phyllis would have been going anyway. She stayed directly behind Lois, who headed south. Phyllis wondered if Lois was headed for Wal-Mart, too, since the big discount store was located in this direction.

That turned out to be the case. Lois managed to make it the dozen blocks or so without crashing into anyone, although she strayed far enough out of her lane a few times to cause other drivers to honk their horns at her. When she pulled into the giant parking lot in front of the store, she narrowly missed hitting a couple of cars, although in one case it wasn't her fault, because the other driver was cutting across between aisles without looking, a careless habit that always irritated Phyllis. In a crowded parking lot it was hard enough keeping an eye on everyone who was driving where they were supposed to, without having to worry about rude people taking shortcuts from one aisle to the next.

Thankfully, Lois parked rather far out, where there were several vacant spaces in a row. At this busy time of year, that meant she was a long way from the store's front doors. She stopped with her car crooked between the lines. The rear third of it was actually over the line, sticking into the next space. Phyllis parked a couple of places away.

"Definitely drunk," Eve said with a disapproving sniff.

Phyllis didn't like it, either. Like any good Baptist, she wasn't a drinker and didn't enjoy being around alcohol or people who were drinking. She wasn't the sort to tell anybody else how to live . . . but she was disappointed in Lois, anyway. It wasn't even noon yet, for goodness' sake! And worst of all was the fact that Lois had chosen to get behind the wheel and drive in her impaired condition.

Phyllis and Eve got out of the Lincoln while Lois was climbing from her car, a late-model Toyota. She slammed the door and stumbled a little as she started around the car. She fumbled with the remote control on her key ring and finally pressed the right button to lock the car. The horn gave a short beep as the locks engaged.

Then Lois stopped short as she saw Phyllis and Eve standing there. She was about forty, with dark hair lightly touched with gray, and wore oversized sunglasses.

"Hello, ladies," she said. Her voice wasn't slurred, but Phyllis thought she caught a faint whiff of alcohol on Lois's breath. Or maybe that was because she expected to smell liquor, she thought, after seeing the way that Lois was driving. Lois went on. "Come to finish your Christmas shopping?"

"We just need to pick up a few last-minute things," Phyllis said.

"Me, too. Of course, it's not actually the last minute, is it? There are still three days. But why wait, I say." Lois started around them, unsteady on her feet despite being able to keep her voice under control. Now that Phyllis thought about it, she realized that Lois's words were just a little too precise, a little too carefully spoken . . . another sign of someone who'd had too much to drink.

Phyllis put out a hand, not taking hold of Lois's arm but resting her fingers on it fairly firmly. "Lois, are you all right?" she asked.

"All right?" Lois smiled and laughed. "I'm fine. Why wouldn't I be? It's almost Christmas. The . . . the happiest time of the year."

Her voice had broken a little there at the end. Phyllis said, "I can tell that something's wrong. Why don't you sit down in my car, and we can talk about it."

"There's nothing to talk about," Lois insisted. "I told you, I'm fine. Everything's fine. *It's a winter wonderland!*"

Her voice rose to a near screech as she spoke, causing people who were nearby to look around and frown. She reached up to jerk the sunglasses off. Eve gasped as she saw the dark bruise around Lois's left eye. Phyllis managed not to show any reaction, but she felt it like a spear of sickness in her stomach.

She moved forward, reaching out to put her arms around Lois as the younger woman began to sob. The sunglasses slipped from her fingers and fell to the parking lot, luckily not shattering. Eve bent to pick them up.

Lois let Phyllis hug her for a second, then started trying to push her away. "Lemme 'lone," she said, and the precise enunciation was gone. "None o' your business. Jus' lemme 'lone."

"I'm not going to do that, Lois," Phyllis said, her own voice firm. "You're my friend, and I want to help you."

"Nothin' you can do." Tears ran down Lois's face. "Nothin' anybody can do."

Phyllis was glad that Carolyn wasn't here. If she had been, she would have wanted to go and find Blake Horton and read him the riot act, possibly dispensing a few well-placed wallops to go along with it. As it was, Phyllis was able to say, "Calm down, Lois. We'll call the police—"

Lois began shaking her head emphatically. "No. You can't!"

"Then, there's bound to be some sort of shelter where you can go—"

Again Lois interrupted her. "Forget it, Phyllis. I'm not goin' anywhere . . . 'cept into Wal-Mart to buy what I need for . . . for Christmas."

"You can't go in there like that, dear," Eve said.

Lois glared at her. "What? You mean drunk off my ass?"

"I mean your face is all red from crying. Even in Wal-Mart, a lady should always look her best, don't you think? And you're always so dignified. You don't want people to see you while you're upset."

Lois frowned. "You . . . you think I'm dignified?"

"Of course."

"Then, you don't know me very well, Eve. You don't know me at all."

"I think I do." Eve's voice was sharper now, taking on some of the same timbre it had possessed whenever one of her students challenged her authority in class. "I know you well enough to be absolutely certain that this isn't like you. Here." She opened her purse and took out a handkerchief, which she pressed into Lois's hand. "Dry those tears, and then we'll get in your car and do a little touch-up job on your makeup, and then we'll march right in there and do our shopping. We'll look so good, we'll give the old geezer at the door a heart attack, too."

"Oh, I wouldn't want to do that," Lois said as she wiped the moisture from her cheeks.

"Well, maybe we won't give him a heart attack. Just palpitations."

Lois laughed. Since Eve seemed to have things under control, or at least getting there, Phyllis stepped back. She let Eve steer Lois back into the Toyota, where she sat beside her in the front seat and talked to her as Lois calmed down. When they emerged from the vehicle ten minutes later, Lois had the sunglasses on again and seemed much steadier as she started toward the store with Eve. Phyllis wished they could have straightened up Lois's car so that it wasn't parked crooked, taking up two spaces, but she supposed that she had better leave well enough alone.

Phyllis followed them into the store. The area at the entrance where the carts were kept was almost empty, which was a good indication of how busy the place was. Christmas music came from the public address system, although Phyllis supposed that it had to be referred to as holiday music now, since even here in Weatherford political correctness had dictated that Christmas couldn't actually be called by its real name.

She pushed that thought out of her mind. She couldn't solve the problems of the world. She had to be content with doing the best she could for her family and friends. Today, though, it was Eve who had salvaged a bad situation, stepping in to somehow get poor Lois Horton halfway straightened up. Phyllis still thought it would be a good idea to call the law and report what Blake had done, but that decision should be Lois's.

Eve and Lois were actually laughing together as they shopped. From time to time Lois was still a little unsteady on her feet, but Eve was right there to help her as they made their way through the crowded aisles. Satisfied that she was no longer needed, Phyllis told them that she would be in the grocery section and pushed her cart in that direction. She was looking for a good ham, and Carolyn had given her a list of a few things she still needed for the wild rice and cranberry stuffing.

There were a lot of children in the store, most of them wide-eyed with happiness because Christmas was almost here. Some things never changed, Phyllis thought . . . and even if they did, they didn't go away entirely. She remembered how the kids in her classes, even though they were eighth graders and tried hard to be oh so mature and sophisticated, started looking forward to Christmas as soon as Thanksgiving was over.

Phyllis started at the back of the grocery section and worked her way toward the front of the store, not really hurrying because she didn't know how long Eve and Lois were going to be. The more time Lois spent in here before getting behind the wheel again, the better. Phyllis wondered if the woman would consider just being a passenger and letting Eve drive her car back home. That might be the safest way to proceed.

Phyllis was almost finished when Eve and Lois appeared. Lois was pushing a basket, and that helped to steady her. It was full of clothes and gadgets and electronics, and Phyllis didn't know who was buying what. All three women went to get in line at the busy checkouts.

Paying for what they were buying took almost as long as picking it out, as was usual at this time of year. The cashier wished them a corporate-mandated "Happy Holidays," and feeling momentarily contrary, Phyllis told her, "And Merry Christmas to you!" in a loud voice.

By the time they were headed for the cars, Phyllis was glad the ordeal was over. There might be another ordeal facing them, though. Since there was no point in postponing it, when they got to the cars she suggested, "Lois, why don't you let Eve drive you home?"

Lois shook her head. "That's not really necessary," she said. "Look, I know I was upset before . . ."

She'd been more than upset, Phyllis thought. She'd been drunk.

"But I'm perfectly capable of driving home," Lois went on. "I'm feeling much better now."

It was true that they had been inside the store for a pretty good while. But had it been long enough for Lois to completely sober up? Phyllis doubted that . . . even though they *had* been in Wal-Mart three days before Christmas, which was a pretty sobering experience in itself.

Eve caught Phyllis's eye and shook her head without Lois noticing. Phyllis took that to mean that her friend was telling her not to press the issue. Eve had spent a lot more time in the store with Lois than Phyllis had, so maybe she was a better judge of what sort of shape the younger woman was in. Phyllis decided to go along with her suggestion. She nodded and said, "All right. I'm glad to hear it. But anytime you need help, Lois . . . any sort of help . . . just remember that we're right across the street."

Lois smiled and nodded. "Thank you. That means a lot to me, Phyllis."

She loaded her purchases in the trunk of the Toyota, then closed the lid and looked at the car for a second before shaking her head and giving a rueful laugh.

"Boy, I really did a lousy job of parking, didn't I?"

Still shaking her head, she unlocked the car and climbed in.

Phyllis and Eve got the things they had bought into the Lincoln's trunk, not wasting any time about it. Phyllis wanted to follow Lois home and make sure she got there all right. Lois couldn't take offense at that; Phyllis would be going the same way regardless, since she lived across the street.

"What a horrible situation," Phyllis said as she started the car and pulled out behind Lois. "Did she tell you anything about it?"

"Not really," Eve said. "I could tell she didn't want to talk about it, so I kept the conversation on other things instead."

To Phyllis's relief, she saw that Lois seemed to be driving fairly well and not moving around too much in her lane. And she didn't stray out of it at all.

"I had no idea that she drank so much . . . or that Blake hit her. They seem like such a nice, normal couple."

"Oh, there's no such thing, dear," Eve said.

Phyllis frowned over at her. "What do you mean?"

"I mean that you never know, just by looking at how people behave outwardly, how they really live their lives. Every couple does things they wouldn't want the world to know about. It might be something serious like drinking or abuse, or it might just be something a little embarrassing, like what they do in the bedroom. But just think about the tales that children bring to school. You and I didn't encounter it so much because our students were older, but we've both heard Carolyn relate some hair-raising stories about things her second graders used to tell her about their home lives."

That was true, Phyllis thought. Children were so innocent, especially the little ones. They didn't really know they were doing anything wrong when they came to school and told their friends and their teachers about what went on at their homes. The stories ranged from the horrible and the heart wrenching all the way to the utterly bizarre and—might as well admit it, Phyllis told herself—amusing. One thing was certain, though: If you had something in your life you wanted to keep secret, it was probably wise not to let a seven- or eight-year-old know about it.

Of course, there were children that grew old fast . . . too fast. She remembered Carolyn telling her about a little girl who stopped another girl from talking about something bad her father had done. She solemnly told her that she shouldn't talk about those things, that she should keep them to herself—like she did. Carolyn had made sure the school counselor knew about both girls.

Lois made it home safely, much to Phyllis's relief. She waved across the street to Phyllis and Eve as she unloaded her purchases and carried them inside. The dark glasses hid Lois's eyes, but they couldn't hide the memory of what Phyllis had seen.

All the extra vehicles were still parked next door at the Simmons house, Phyllis noticed. She supposed that Frank, Ted, Billie, and their families had planned to stay with Agnes through Christmas, but now that Agnes was gone and the funeral was over, would they all just return to their homes, leaving the old house locked up and empty behind them? After everything that had happened, Phyllis couldn't imagine that they still wanted to stay here through Christmas.

On the other hand, Randall was still in jail here in Weatherford, and Frank and Claire probably wanted to be close to their son. It would be easier for them to stay in Agnes's house than to make the drive back and forth from Dallas every time they needed to talk to Randall's lawyer or appear in court.

Thinking about Agnes's murder made Phyllis glance suddenly across the street at the Horton house. She wouldn't have dreamed that Blake Horton was capable of giving his wife a black eye like that.

What else was Blake capable of that she never would have dreamed? Phyllis wondered.

Then she told herself that suspecting Blake Horton was crazy, absolutely crazy.

But the idea lingered in her mind anyway. There were so many dangerous secrets that Agnes, perched there in front of her window, might have been privy to. . . .

Chapter 12

"That's a big ham," Carolyn said as she looked at it sitting on the kitchen counter.

"Eighteen pounds," Phyllis said.

Sam patted his flat belly under his flannel shirt. "Plenty of good eatin', looks like."

"Don't start drooling yet—it's for Christmas dinner," Phyllis said as she opened the refrigerator and looked for a place to put the ham. She hadn't really thought this out, she told herself. There wasn't a space big enough for the ham, so she would have to rearrange some things, maybe even throw out a few, so that she could fit it in. She added, "You know that. I'm not even going to cook it until Christmas morning."

"Well, by then I'm sure gonna be ready for it," Sam said with a grin. "I'm lookin' forward to Christmas like a little kid again."

Eve said, "When you see my present, you'll feel like a kid again, dear."

Phyllis frowned as she bent to look into the refrigerator. She wasn't sure she knew what Eve meant by that. She wasn't sure she *wanted* to know.

It took her about ten minutes to make a place for the ham. When she went to pick it up from the counter, Sam stepped forward and said, "Let me handle that big fella for you." He took it from the counter and slid it neatly into the space Phyllis had made for it.

Everything else from the store was already put away, so there was nothing more to do at the moment. As Phyllis walked into the living room, her eye fell on the black box containing the videotape of the church service from the previous Sunday. She had watched it that same afternoon, after Dwight Gresham dropped it off, and she'd called the church office on Monday morning to let them know she was finished with it. She'd expected someone to pick it up that day and had set it on the little table in the foyer. Since then she'd been busy enough that she'd forgotten all about it, and she was a little surprised to notice that it was still there.

"Goodness, I thought Dwight or one of the deacons would have come by and gotten that tape by now," she commented. "It's Wednesday. They need to get it to people who are actually homebound and really need it."

"You let 'em know at the church that you were through with it?" Sam asked.

Phyllis nodded. "First thing Monday morning."

"Who'd you talk to? The preacher?"

"No, I spoke to the church secretary, but she said she'd tell Dwight. I guess he must have forgotten to come by and get it. He was busy with Agnes's funeral and all." Phyllis went to the phone, picked it up, and dialed the number of the church office from memory. It rang a couple of times before it was picked up and a familiar voice answered.

"Jada?" Phyllis said, a little surprised to hear the voice of the pastor's wife.

"That's right."

"This is Phyllis Newsom. I didn't know you worked in the church office now."

"Oh, hello, Phyllis," Jada Gresham said. "I'm just filling in because Charlaine had to be out of town today. What can I do for you?"

"I just realized I still have the videotape of last Sunday morning's service that Dwight dropped off here on Sunday afternoon for me to watch. I called Monday morning and told Charlaine that I was done with it, so I thought someone would have picked it up by now."

"You still have the tape?" Jada sounded puzzled. "Dwight told me he was going to pick it up on Monday. I suppose it slipped his mind. He was working on the funeral service for poor Agnes Simmons, and he was upset about that. He was fond of her."

"We all were," Phyllis agreed. "If you could mention it to him . . ."

"Of course."

"I don't want any of the people who watch it on a regular basis to miss seeing it."

"Don't worry about that," Jada assured her. "I'll see to it that Dwight takes care of it." She laughed. "And it's not like that's the only videotape the church owns. If everyone's not through with it by Sunday, we'll just use another one."

"All right; that's fine. Thank you, Jada."

"Anything else I can do for you? How are you getting along?"

"I'm pretty much back to normal," Phyllis said, "so I can't think of a thing."

"Well, try not to overdo it. You can't be too careful with head injuries."

Phyllis thanked her again and hung up. She said to Sam, "Honestly, you'd think I had a fractured skull or something, the way people keep worrying about me."

"That's because folks care about you," Sam said. "A lot."

She looked at him. "Really?"

"No doubt about it," he said with a nod.

Phyllis and Carolyn were in the kitchen that afternoon, getting ready to make some pies for their Christmas dinner, and Carolyn's daughter's, too, when the doorbell rang. Eve had gone out, Phyllis knew, and Sam was in the garage, puttering around at the workbench, so she said, "I'll see who that is."

"Good," Carolyn said. Her hands were covered with flour from the pie crusts she was working on. You could buy perfectly good pie crusts at the grocery store now, but Carolyn, being Carolyn, preferred the ones made from scratch.

Phyllis left the bowl of pumpkin and the spices she was about to mix with it on the counter next to the ingredients Carolyn had laid out for her chocolate pecan pies. She went to the front door, looked through the little window in it, and saw a woman she didn't recognize standing on the porch.

"Hello," she said as she opened the door. "Can I help you?"

"Mrs. Newsom?" The woman was around forty, Phyllis judged, slender in a gray wool skirt and jacket over a plain, cream-colored blouse. Her brown hair, which had a few lighter streaks in it, was pulled back in a rather severe style. Her best feature was a pair of intense green eyes that were made to seem even larger than they were by the silver-rimmed glasses she wore. She carried a briefcase in her left hand.

"Yes, I'm Phyllis Newsom, if that's who you're looking for," Phyllis replied with a nod.

"My name is Juliette Yorke, with an E. I'm an attorney."

That didn't surprise Phyllis at all. Juliette Yorke *looked* like a lawyer, and a no-nonsense one, at that. Phyllis glanced down at her shoes. Low heeled, conservative, and comfortable. Again, not a surprise.

"What can I do for you, Ms. Yorke?"

"Would it be all right if I came in and talked to you for a few minutes about the murder of Agnes Simmons?"

Phyllis stepped back. "Oh, of course. Goodness' sake, where are my manners? And just a few days before Christmas, at that! Please, come in, Ms. Yorke."

Once they were sitting in the living room, Phyllis on the sofa and Juliette Yorke in one of the armchairs, the lawyer put her knees primly together and placed the briefcase on her lap. She snapped the catches back and opened it.

"I'm representing Randall Simmons," she said, "and I'd like to record this conversation, if that's all right with you, Mrs. Newsom."

"You mean like a deposition? Shouldn't the district attorney or one of his assistants be here if you're going to do that, Ms. Yorke?"

Juliette Yorke's lips tightened a little. "Your son is a deputy sheriff, isn't that right?"

"Yes, he is."

"We met during the Dunston case. I represented Lindsey Gonzales."

"Oh, of course," Phyllis said. "I remember Mike mentioning you."

"I suppose having a relative in law enforcement is why you know about such things as depositions."

Juliette Yorke's accent, and her rather stiff demeanor, showed that she wasn't from around here, Phyllis thought. She said, "I know it probably wouldn't be a good idea to discuss the case against Randall with you, at least not without someone here from the district attorney's office. So I don't want you to record what we're saying."

The lawyer sighed, lowered the lid of her briefcase, and closed the catches. "I suppose we have nothing to talk about, then."

Phyllis didn't feel any particular liking for Juliette Yorke, but her natural hospitality prompted her to say, "Would you like something to drink while you're here? Or maybe some cookies? I hate to think that your trip over here was for nothing."

Juliette Yorke leaned forward as if she was about to get to her feet. "No, thank you," she said. But then she stopped and leaned back in the armchair instead, and her severe expression eased a bit. "Actually, I skipped lunch," she said. "A cookie sounds wonderful."

Phyllis stood up. Since she had so many cookies on hand, she'd been keeping a plate with an assortment of them on the coffee table so that people could stop by and graze on them any time they were passing through the living room. She picked up the plate and held it out to the lawyer. "Take as many as you like," she told Juliette Yorke.

The woman hesitated. "They all look so good." She pointed at one of the cookies. "What kind is that?"

"It's a gingerdoodle," Phyllis explained, glad that Juliette Yorke had picked that one. "Like a snickerdoodle, only it has ginger in it, too. It was Agnes's recipe, in fact. She got the idea after I told her about using ginger to make spicy peach cobbler a while back. Agnes wanted a cookie that was more mellow than a gingersnap but still had the taste of ginger."

As a matter of fact, Phyllis had submitted the gingerdoodle recipe to the newspaper contest for Agnes, dropping off the recipe and samples of the cookies when she left her own entry at the newspaper office.

Juliette Yorke shook her head as she picked up one of the gingerdoodles. "I'm afraid I don't know what a snickerdoodle is."

Phyllis tried to contain her surprise. "No offense, Ms. Yorke, but you must not have grown up in Texas."

"Pennsylvania," the lawyer said around the small bite of cookie she had taken. "Philadelphia." She swallowed. "But it's entirely possible they have snickerdoodles there, too. I just never baked cookies."

"Never?" Phyllis couldn't imagine spending forty years or so on this earth without ever baking a batch of cookies.

"Well . . . only the kind that come in a can in the refrigerated section of the grocery store, and not very many of those." She took another bite. "This is good."

"You've missed a lot of fun if you never made cookies. Why, I remember my mother teaching me when I was little how to mix up a batch of cookie dough and roll it out and use a cookie cutter to cut out each individual cookie. . . ." With a shake of her head, Phyllis let her voice trail away, then said, "But you didn't come here to talk about cookies, did you?"

Juliette Yorke finished the last bite, then said, "No. I came to talk about how an innocent young man is in a lot of trouble for something that he didn't do."

Aware that she probably shouldn't respond to that, knowing that Juliette Yorke was using a lawyer's wiles to draw her into talking, Phyllis said anyway, "Randall is hardly innocent. He skipped out on his bail on drug charges in Dallas County. That's not in dispute."

The younger woman shrugged. "He hasn't been found guilty on those drug charges, and certainly no case has been proven against him in the murder of his grandmother. He's supposed to be considered innocent until proven guilty. And defaulting on a bail bond is hardly in the same category as those other offenses."

"No, I suppose not," Phyllis agreed. "You're his lawyer. Has he confided in you? *Did* he kill Agnes?"

"I've entered a plea of not guilty in the matter of Mrs. Simmons's death. That's a matter of public record."

"What about the drug dealing and bail jumping?"

For a moment Juliette Yorke didn't answer, and Phyllis assumed she was following the lawyer's credo that if you never said anything, you didn't have to deny anything. But then the woman surprised her again by replying, "We're considering a plea of no contest to those charges in return for a reduced sentence."

"Then he *is* a drug dealer!"

"You don't know the whole story, Mrs. Newsom," Juliette Yorke said, "and you don't really know my client at all."

Phyllis wasn't going to lose her temper with a guest, even a lawyer, so although her voice was cool, her tone was polite as she asked, "And how long have *you* known Randall, Ms. Yorke?"

The younger woman shrugged. "I only met him a few days ago, true, but in my line of work I've learned how to size up people pretty quickly."

"I learned the same thing," Phyllis said. "I was a schoolteacher for a long, long time. I got to where I could size up a class and pick out the troublemakers, the brownnosers, and the truly good students, usually on the first day of school. Within the first week, for sure."

Juliette Yorke regarded her intently for a long moment, then nodded. "I see. And based on what you learned as a teacher, Mrs. Newsom . . . do you truly think that Randall Simmons is a murderer?"

Phyllis leaned back against the sofa. She wished that the

lawyer hadn't asked her that question. But since she wasn't in the habit of lying unless it was absolutely necessary, she said, "He doesn't really strike me as a killer, no."

"Interesting choice of words, because it's commonly assumed that the killer *did* strike you. Knocked you unconscious, in fact. How are you doing, by the way? Any aftereffects from being attacked?"

"No, I'm fine." *Except for having to answer that question.*

"You got a good look at Randall. Do you think he would hit a woman on the head, hard enough to knock her unconscious and possibly injure her severely?"

"I don't know. I suppose he's capable of it. People are usually capable of things that you wouldn't believe they'd do, if they find themselves in a bad enough situation."

Juliette Yorke nodded and said, "I know that's true."

"I suppose you see proof of that all the time in your work, if you're a defense attorney."

"Yes, of course." A faint smile touched the lawyer's lips. "I have every right to be hard and cynical, Mrs. Newsom, based on my experiences. So when I *do* believe in someone, that ought to tell you something."

"Yes, I suppose it does," Phyllis agreed. "But a good lawyer will fight just as hard for a client she doesn't believe in, won't she? That whole business about how every defendant is entitled to the best possible defense?"

"That's the way it's supposed to be. Don't think for a minute, though, that lawyers aren't just as human as anybody else. Since you insisted that this conversation be off the record, Mrs. Newsom, I don't mind telling you that sometimes lawyers *do* work harder for clients they believe to be innocent. It's just human nature."

Phyllis turned that over in her mind. Juliette Yorke was

being open and honest with her . . . or else playing on her emotions to get what she wanted. Who could tell with a lawyer?

"What is it you want from me, Ms. Yorke? Why did you really come here today?"

"I was hoping you'd tell me everything you can remember about what happened on Saturday afternoon."

"I've given my statement to the police."

Juliette Yorke nodded. "And I've read it. But I want to hear it from you, Mrs. Newsom, in your words as you remember it now."

"You're trying to get me to change my story so you can discredit me at the trial," Phyllis said with a smile.

"Not at all. But there might be details that come back to you now that you couldn't recall when you talked to the police. Or you might remember things the same way but put a different interpretation on what you remember. I really just want to get a feel for the way things were that afternoon, and you're the only one who can tell me . . . because you and the killer were the only ones there except for Agnes, and she can't speak for herself anymore. You have to speak for her."

That was nicely done, Phyllis told herself. Heartfelt and sincere, with just enough outrage in the timbre of Juliette Yorke's voice. What would it be like, she wondered, to live in a world where doing your job meant playing on the emotions of other people and probably manipulating your own emotions in the service of the client until you might not even know what you really believed?

She was glad she had been a teacher, not a lawyer.

"All right," Phyllis said. "But you're not going to get anything that you didn't already see in the police report."

She began telling about the events of Saturday afternoon. As she had predicted, she didn't recall anything new, nothing that she hadn't already told Mike and then Chief Whitmire and Detective Largo.

But as Phyllis spoke, something nagged at the back of her brain—not something she remembered, not something she was saying, but something else entirely. She couldn't pin down what it was, but she thought that whatever had set off that uneasiness, it was something Juliette Yorke had said.

And yet, as Phyllis paused and replayed the conversation in her head as best she could, there was nothing unusual there, nothing that stood out.

"Are you all right, Mrs. Newsom?" the lawyer asked with a frown.

"Yes, I'm fine," Phyllis replied. "Just trying to make sure I have everything straight."

"That's what I want."

Phyllis went back to the story, and that elusive whatever-it-was receded. She decided that she was just uncomfortable talking to the defense lawyer when she was supposed to be on the side of the prosecution.

She suddenly asked herself why she felt that way. It wasn't like Mike was building the case against Randall Simmons. She had no personal stake in this case except wanting justice for Agnes Simmons.

And if Juliette Yorke was right and Randall was innocent, that meant the real murderer was still out there somewhere, and that idea rubbed Phyllis the wrong way, and also scared her a little.

Finally, Phyllis said, "That's all. I just don't remember any more. I told you that you weren't going to learn anything new."

"Maybe not, but now I have a clearer picture of how everything looked to you. And as I pointed out, Mrs. Newsom, you're really the only witness."

"Yes, I suppose I am."

That was worrisome, too. If Randall hadn't killed his grandmother, then the murderer might get nervous about Phyllis. Was it possible that *she* might be targeted? Getting rid of her could backfire on the killer, because then it would be obvious Randall couldn't have done it while he was in custody . . . but if her death was made to look like an accident . . .

Phyllis took a deep breath. She was just trying to scare herself, and she needed to stop it. She was perfectly safe. Nothing was going to happen to her.

Juliette Yorke stood up, briefcase in hand. "Thank you for talking to me, Mrs. Newsom." She smiled. "And thank you for the cookie. It was good. Gingerdoodle, right?"

"That's right." Phyllis picked up the plate as she got to her feet, too. "Here, take a few with you."

The lawyer hesitated, then said, "Thank you," and picked up several cookies, taking another gingerdoodle, a couple of the lime snowflake sugar cookies, and one of Carolyn's pecan pie cookies. "They all look so good."

Phyllis showed her out, then stood at the door and watched as Juliette Yorke got into a late-model car parked at the curb and drove away, munching on a cookie as she did so.

Then a footstep sounded right behind Phyllis, and she jumped and gasped.

"Hey, what's wrong?" Sam asked, frowning in surprise at her reaction as she turned around quickly.

"Nothing," Phyllis said, embarrassed that she had been so startled for no good reason. "I was just talking to Randall Simmons's lawyer."

She'd been dwelling too much on the idea that the killer might want to get rid of *her*, too. She couldn't allow herself to become paranoid.

But maybe it would be a good idea if she did some more thinking about the case. The police thought they had their man, and despite Detective Largo's follow-up questions about other suspects, Phyllis didn't really expect a thorough investigation into any of the other possibilities. For her own peace of mind, if nothing else, she was going to have to look into this until she was *sure* that Randall was guilty, that no one else could have murdered Agnes Simmons. Otherwise she was going to keep looking over her shoulder in fear, and she didn't want that.

Sam's eyes narrowed as he studied her. "Something's brewin' in that head o' yours," he said. Demonstrating that he had some natural shrewdness of his own, he made a guess. "You don't think the Simmons kid did it, do you?"

"Well, he's certainly the most likely suspect, given his criminal background and the fact that he was there, hiding out from the law. . . ."

"That doesn't make him guilty."

"No," Phyllis said. "No, it doesn't. We've seen for ourselves that people can look guilty without actually doing anything wrong."

"The kid's done some stuff wrong, no doubt about that. But murderin' his own grandmother, when she'd been tryin' to help him out . . ."

"It doesn't seem likely, does it?"

Sam stared at her for a long moment, then shook his head and muttered, "Here we go again."

No, Phyllis thought. She wasn't going to investigate Agnes's murder. Not really.

But surely it wouldn't hurt anything to ask a few questions. She just wished she could figure out what Juliette Yorke had said that had made her wonder. . . .

Chapter 13

Detective work was one thing, cooking was another, and there were still those pies to bake. But when Phyllis returned to the kitchen, she found that Carolyn already had the pies in the oven. She hadn't realized that she'd talked to Juliette Yorke for so long.

"Don't worry," Carolyn said. "I followed the recipe for the pumpkin pie filling that you had lying on the counter." She paused. "I might have modified it just a little bit. . . ."

That came as no surprise to Phyllis. When it came to cooking, Carolyn always thought that her ideas were just a little bit better than Phyllis's.

Soon the aroma of the pies baking filled the house, and Phyllis had to admit that they smelled really good.

With nothing to do where the baking was concerned, she might as well start trying to figure out who else might have killed Agnes, she decided. In order to do that, she needed more information about what was going on in the neighborhood. Maybe someone had noticed something suspicious going on around Agnes's house in the days before her death. Despite the little things that seemed to indicate that Agnes had known her killer, it was still possible that the murderer was someone who broke in. Phyllis had learned from Mike that sometimes there were elements of a crime that went forever unexplained, even when the culprit confessed and there was no doubt of his or her guilt. Phyllis wanted to know if any strangers had been lurking in the neighborhood or if anything else suspicious had been going on.

And the best way to find out things you wanted to know was to ask.

Luckily, she had a good reason to go visiting, here just a few days before Christmas.

Since there were still plenty of cookies left, she put together a plate of them and covered it with clear plastic wrap. Most people wouldn't turn down cookies. Even Juliette Yorke, stiff as she was, had unbent long enough to sample a gingerdoodle.

Phyllis knew that if Sam was aware of what she was doing, he would insist on coming along with her. A part of her wanted him to come along, not only because she enjoyed his company, but also because they had proven to be a good investigative team in the past. And if there *was* still a killer on the loose, she could do a lot worse for a companion than rangy, athletic Sam Fletcher.

But Sam was still a relative newcomer to the neighborhood, and Phyllis thought that people might open up more if they were talking to just her. So she waited until he was busy in the garage again before she got the plateful of cookies and headed next door to Oscar Gunderson's house.

For many years, Oscar had worked in the personnel department of the aircraft plant over in Fort Worth, which had gone through a series of ownership and name changes. The place had been Consolidated Vultee, Convair, General Dynamics, and finally Lockheed. Oscar had retired and enjoyed a few years with his wife, Geneva, before she passed away. Since then Oscar had lived alone, friendly with his neighbors but a little reserved. Geneva had been the social member of the couple, and without her Oscar didn't have anybody around to prod him out of his shell very often.

Phyllis walked across to Oscar's front door, noticing as she did so that the weather was even warmer today than it had been yesterday. It looked like this was going to be another mild Christmas—unless this was the period of milder temperatures before another cold front blew through. . . .

Phyllis rang the doorbell and heard movement inside. No one came to the door, though, and after a moment she frowned. She knew she had heard someone walking across the room, and they'd been fairly heavy footsteps, at that.

The thought occurred to her that if Agnes *had* been killed by a burglar, the criminal could have returned to the neighborhood. That wouldn't be a very smart thing to do, but lawbreakers usually weren't noted for their intelligence. That same burglar could be inside Oscar's house right now. He could have done something to Oscar! As Phyllis stood there on the little front porch, staring at the door, she seemed to sense some sort of malevolent presence just on the other side of it, listening, waiting to strike. . . .

"Who's there?"

The gruff voice that called the question through the door was instantly familiar. Phyllis recognized it as belonging to Oscar Gunderson. She heaved a sigh of relief.

"It's just me, Oscar," she said. "Phyllis Newsom."

"Oh. Hang on just a minute."

Oscar didn't sound like he was hurt or under any sort of

duress, just busy with something. Phyllis felt a little silly now, letting her fears run away with her like that.

When Oscar opened the door a few moments later, he was wearing a robe that left his sturdy calves bare. His feet were bare as well. Some gray chest hairs poked out of the opening at his throat. He was a short, broad man with a bulldoglike face and a fringe of gray hair around his ears.

"Oh, I'm sorry," Phyllis said. "I got you out of the shower, didn't I, Oscar?" That was the most obvious explanation for his attire, although Phyllis would have sworn that she'd heard him moving around in the living room right after she rang the bell.

"No, no, not at all," he said. "What can I do for you, Phyllis?"

She lifted the plate in her hands. "I wanted to bring you some cookies, since we had so many left over from the get-together the other day. And I thought we might visit for a while. Do you have any plans for Christmas Day? You could always come over and have dinner with us. We'll have more than enough food. We always do!"

She was talking a little fast, she knew, but she hoped that he would invite her in to chat so that she could work the conversation around to Agnes's murder and find out if he had noticed anything unusual going on in the neighborhood recently.

However, Oscar wasn't showing any signs of doing that. He said, "Thanks for the invitation, but I'm driving down to Brownwood on Friday to spend the weekend with my son and his family." Oscar's son was a professor of economics at Howard Payne University. As he reached for the plate of cookies, he added, "These look great. I'll take them with me down there . . . if there are any left by then!"

As she got ready to hand over the cookies, she realized that her plan wasn't going to work. She couldn't very well snatch the cookies back and refuse to give them to him unless he allowed her to question him.

Then she glanced down, was surprised by what she saw, and said, "Your, uh, slip is showing, Oscar."

His eyes widened. He said, "What?" then jerked his head down and stared at the two or three inches of what appeared to be the lacy hem of some silk lingerie showing below the bottom of the robe. A strangled sound came from his throat.

Phyllis tried hard not to be shocked. She had to admit that for a fleeting second, seeing Oscar in a robe in the middle of the day like this, she had wondered if he had a woman in his house, even though as far as she knew, he hadn't even dated since his wife's death.

Evidently that wasn't the case.

She thought for a moment that he was going to slam the door in her face—either that or have a heart attack on the spot, if his rapidly purpling face was any indication. Then his shoulders slumped as if he were giving up. He stepped back, opened the door wider, and rumbled, "Come in for a minute. Please."

Phyllis hesitated. She didn't think she was in any danger from Oscar Gunderson, having known the man for twenty years, for goodness' sake, but obviously people were capable of all sorts of surprises, even good old Oscar. Her curiosity got the better of her, though, so she stepped into the house. He closed the door behind her.

The drapes over the front window were tightly drawn, so that no one could look in. The reason for that became understandable when Oscar loosened the belt of the robe and opened it a little, sort of like a flasher. He wasn't exposing himself, though, but rather the sleek, pale pink slip that he wore. It matched a pair of feathery slippers sitting on the floor where Oscar must have kicked them off before answering the door.

He pulled the robe closed and knotted the belt again. "You can't tell anybody about this," he said.

"Don't worry," Phyllis assured him. "It's none of my business, Oscar. None of anybody's business."

"Darned right it's not." He scrubbed a hand over his face and then sighed. "I got to admit, though, in a way it . . . it's nice to have somebody to talk to about it. Since Geneva's been gone . . ."

Phyllis didn't *want* him to talk about it with her. She was as open-minded as the next person, but there were still some things that made her uncomfortable. And at the same time, she was having to fight the impulse to giggle. She knew that would be a terrible, hurtful thing to do. . . .

But the sight of gruff, burly Oscar Gunderson standing there in a pink slip had just been so funny.

She forced that image out of her mind. Oscar was entitled to his dignity, and she had no business judging anyone. And if she did talk to him for a few minutes, maybe he would open up to her about things other than his . . . hobby.

"Did Geneva know?" she asked, making her tone as caring as she could.

"Oh, yeah." He waved her into a chair. "Sit down. Just set those cookies on the coffee table."

Phyllis sat down, and Oscar lowered himself onto the sofa opposite her, being careful to keep the robe closed—for which she was thankful.

"Geneva always knew, right from the start," he went on. "I wouldn't keep something that important from her. She helped me, in fact. It was sort of like a hobby we shared, like bird-watching or stamp collecting."

"All right," Phyllis said.

"Just don't get the idea I'm some sort o' pansy." Oscar poked a stubby finger in the air for emphasis. "I'm a hundred percent male. I just . . . I just like the feel of it. The silk's so smooth against the skin. You must know that."

Phyllis managed to nod.

"Thank God for the Internet," Oscar continued, warming to his subject now. "You can get all kinds of things in all different sizes. I tell you, back in the old days, it wasn't easy finding stuff to fit a guy like me, especially panties and girdles—"

"Oscar," Phyllis said in a weak voice.

He looked surprised, as if he hadn't realized how enthusias- tically he was going on. "Ah, hell," he said. "Now I'm making your skin crawl, I'll bet. I'm sorry, Phyllis. I didn't mean for you to find out. It's just that . . . when I dress up, it's kinda like when Geneva was still here. It makes me feel, I dunno, closer to her somehow."

Phyllis swallowed. She'd had to fight off laughter a few mo- ments earlier, but now she felt more like crying. Instead she leaned forward and said, "Oscar, I think that's exactly the way Geneva would want you to feel. You do whatever you need to do. Not that you need my permission, or anybody else's, of course."

"Thanks," he said with a nod. "I appreciate that, I really do. And I appreciate the cookies. I'll take 'em down to Brownwood and share them with my boy and his family, like I said."

Phyllis knew he expected her to get up and leave now, and goodness knows there was a part of her that wanted to, but she'd had a reason for coming over here, and she hadn't accomplished it yet. She wanted to keep him talking for a little longer.

"Does anyone else in the neighborhood know?"

"About this?" Oscar waved a hand in front of himself to in- dicate what he was wearing. "Lord, I hope not. Geneva and I al- ways kept it behind closed doors, you know."

"I suppose there are a lot of secrets, even in a nice neighborhood like this," Phyllis said, thinking about Lois Horton's drinking and the black eye she had been sporting the day before.

Oscar grunted. "Darned right there are. If there's one thing I learned working in personnel all those years, it's that people are strange. Downright weird sometimes." He chuckled. "I'm a fine one to talk, aren't I? But you must've run into that when you were teaching. There are all kinds of people in the world, and most of 'em will surprise you sooner or later."

Phyllis smiled. "Yes, I'd say that's true." Oscar seemed more relaxed now, so she went on, "In fact, I was wondering if you'd seen anything surprising around the neighborhood lately."

"You mean other than myself in the mirror?" He laughed out loud this time, then shook his head. "No, not really. I don't know anybody else's deep, dark secrets, if that's what you're getting at."

"Actually, I was thinking about Agnes's murder."

"Oh." He sobered. "Yeah. Terrible thing, just terrible. I'm not gonna say she was your stereotypical sweet little old lady, but she was okay. I'm glad they caught the guy who did it. Hard to believe it was her own grandson." He looked like he remembered something. "Say, you got clobbered that same day. How—"

"I'm doing just fine," Phyllis said before he could ask the question.

"Well, that's good. Anyway, I can't imagine a kid killing his own grandmother like that. I hear he was some kind o' druggie." Oscar shook his head. "People'll do just about anything for that damned junk, if you'll pardon my French."

"Yes, that's true. I got to worrying a little, though. . . . What if Randall Simmons *isn't* the one who killed Agnes?"

Oscar frowned. "Who else could it've been? He was staying right there in the house, right?"

"Yes, but I'm not sure he had any real motive."

"Motive." Oscar snorted. "He wanted money, and she wouldn't give it to him. Or she threatened to turn him in to the cops. That's all the motive a punk like that needs."

Unfortunately, Oscar was right. Because no one knew exactly what had gone on between Randall and Agnes, both of those scenarios were plausible—more than plausible.

"My first thought was that it must have been a burglar, or somebody like that," Phyllis said.

Oscar's brawny shoulders rose and fell. "Could've been, I suppose. I would have thought the same thing if the kid hadn't been there."

"You didn't notice any strangers in the neighborhood in the past week or two?"

"Casing the houses so they could come back later and break in, you mean?" Oscar shook his head. "Some guys from the city were working out there at the water main about a week and a half ago. I think I saw a florist's truck deliver some flowers at the Horton house. A couple of times, in fact." He smiled. "Ol' Blake must've got the wife mad at him for something."

Yes, like punching her in the eye. Phyllis doubted if having flowers delivered was going to make up for something like that. Though, as Oscar had proven today, you never really knew about people.

"The preacher stopped by the other day, and I see the Meals on Wheels guy go by, and FedEx and UPS drop off packages now and then. . . . That's about it. You know as well as I do, this is a quiet neighborhood."

Phyllis nodded. "Yes, it is." She hid her disappointment, but she had to admit to herself that Oscar hadn't been a bit of help.

She would just have to try the cookie ploy with some of the other neighbors who hadn't been at the exchange and hope that they had noticed something more important. At least she was fairly certain that she wouldn't run into anything quite as surprising as the sight of Oscar Gunderson in a lacy pink slip.

Then she realized that she shouldn't have even let herself think such a thing. That was just asking for trouble.

She stood up and said, "Well, enjoy the cookies, Oscar. It was good visiting with you."

He spread his hands. "Even with what you found out?"

"I try not to pass judgment on anyone," she told him. "And don't worry; I won't mention this to anyone, either."

"I'd appreciate that." His voice hardened. "At my age, I sure as heck don't want to wind up the laughingstock of the neighborhood."

"Of course not." Phyllis went to the door. "I hope you enjoy your trip to Brownwood."

"Thanks. And thanks again for the cookies." He slid his feet into the feathery slippers. "If you wouldn't mind letting yourself out . . ."

"Of course."

When the door was shut behind her, Phyllis blew her breath out in a long sigh. That visit with Oscar had been edifying, but certainly not in the way she had hoped.

Unless . . .

He had sounded almost angry when he said that he didn't want to be the laughingstock of the neighborhood. And he had warned her, as soon as she found out what he was doing, not to tell anyone.

Phyllis suddenly found herself wondering if she was indeed the first one, other than Oscar's late wife, Geneva, to discover his secret. All along she had thought that Agnes Simmons might have found out about something that proved to be dangerous for her.

Just how far would Oscar Gunderson have gone to keep anyone else from finding out?

"No," Phyllis whispered to herself. "That's crazy, just crazy. He wouldn't . . ."

But she never would have dreamed that he would dress up in women's lingerie, either. As Oscar himself had said, people were downright weird sometimes. Weird didn't have to mean dangerous. . . .

But as Phyllis walked toward her house and went past the front window of the Gunderson house, with its tightly drawn curtains, a little shiver of uncertainty ran through her as she thought about what was going on behind them.

Chapter 14

Phyllis wanted to recover for a while from the somewhat disconcerting conversation with Oscar before she talked to any of the other neighbors. Anyway, if she was going to use the cookie ploy again to get in the door of wherever she went next, she had to have another plate of cookies.

That was why she walked straight from Oscar's front door to hers, and when she got there, she saw Frank Simmons standing there on the porch with his hand raised and his finger poised to press the doorbell button.

"Oh, hi, Mrs. Newsom," Frank said as Phyllis came up the steps. "I was just looking for you."

"What can I do for you, Frank? And by the way, I think you can call me Phyllis. You're a grown man, not the little boy who lives next door anymore."

He smiled. "Yeah, but you know that inside of every grown man, there's still a little boy."

"Oh, I never doubted that for a second. Come on in the house."

Frank gestured toward the metal swing hanging from chains attached to the porch roof. "It's pretty warm for December. What say we sit outside and talk for a few minutes?"

Phyllis considered the suggestion and then nodded. "All right." They moved over to the swing, which was big enough for three people to sit side by side, and as they settled down on it at opposite ends, she went on, "I'm glad to see that you look like you feel a little better now than you did the last time I saw you."

"Oh, that's just an act," Frank replied with a shake of his head. "There's only so much weeping and wailing a person can do. I ran out of mine. Claire hasn't yet, though."

"I'm sorry to hear that. If there's anything I can do to help . . ."

"That's why I'm here." Frank took a deep breath. "Mrs. Newsom . . . Phyllis . . . I want to ask you to tell the police that you've thought it over, and you've decided that Randall wasn't the person who hit you in my mother's kitchen."

Phyllis frowned at him. "But that would be a lie," she said. "I don't *know* who hit me. I never saw him. And I never identified Randall as my attacker, either, for that very reason. I just don't know."

"But if you told the police that you *do* know, and it wasn't Randall—"

Phyllis shook her head. "I just can't do that. I'm sorry."

Frank sighed and passed a hand over his face. "I didn't really think you would," he said. "That's why I'm going to have to do something I didn't want to do."

Phyllis felt a shiver of fear at his words. What did he mean by that vaguely threatening statement? She wondered where Sam was, and if he would hear her if she called for help.

"I'm going to have to tell you the truth," Frank said. "All of it."

Oh. Well, that wasn't quite as threatening, although it was still confusing. The best way to clear up that confusion, Phyllis thought, was to listen to what Frank had to say.

"Go ahead," she told him. "I'm always glad to hear the truth."

Was he going to confess that *he* had killed his mother over that loan she'd refused him for his business? With Agnes dead, Frank might inherit enough money to save his store.

"You know Randall was charged with selling drugs over in Dallas?"

"Yes," Phyllis said. So this was going to be about Randall, and not a confession by Frank.

"Well, actually, it was possession with intent to sell, not actually dealing the stuff. And he had it, no doubt about that. The cops caught him red-handed. He was going to sell it, too. He was arrested before he had the chance."

"Frank, I don't see why you're telling me this."

"What you don't know is *why* he got mixed up in that mess," Frank said. "He was forced into it."

"By whom? Society?"

Frank waved a hand. "No, I never believed in all that crap. A guy named Jimmy Crowe forced him to do it."

"Did this man Crowe put a gun to Randall's head?" Phyllis couldn't contain her skepticism.

"No. Crowe put a gun to *my* head."

Phyllis stared at the man beside her on the swing.

"Not literally," Frank went on. "Just figuratively. But that was bad enough. He told Randall that he'd kill me if Randall didn't work for him. Crowe's a bad dude. He's into all kinds of shady deals over in Dallas, mostly drug related. But he's a loan shark, too, and that's how Randall got on his bad side. He borrowed money from him and then couldn't pay it back, so he was gonna have to work off the debt in Crowe's main line of business."

"How do you know all of this?"

"Randall told me. Not back when it was all going on, but just this week. He broke down while I was visiting him in jail and explained the whole thing to me." Frank shook his head. "Jail's been rough on him. Since he already jumped bail once, the judge set his bond for the murder charge at a million bucks. I don't have that, and I can't even get a bail bondsman to get him out. I don't have enough assets to make it worth the risk, just a store that's gonna go out of business soon, anyway, in a building I don't own."

"I'm sorry, Frank," Phyllis said. "But I still don't understand why Crowe would threaten you—"

"To make Randall go along with what he wanted. You see, Randall gave the money that he borrowed to me, to help with the business. I didn't want to take it, but Randall insisted. Lord, if I'd known where it came from . . ." Frank put his hands over his face and sat there for a moment before he could go on. When he was able to continue, he said, "He told me that he was working as an engineer for a computer company in north Dallas and that he'd gotten an advance on money they owed him. We hadn't talked much in recent years, and I knew he'd always been good with computers, so I believed him. Maybe I was just desperate enough to believe him. But then it didn't work out, and that money was gone, too, and I needed to pay Randall back. So I asked my mother for help." He shook his head. "But she turned me down."

Phyllis had heard that part of the story. She hadn't known it was just the tip of a particularly sordid iceberg.

"I told Randall I couldn't get the money to pay him back. I didn't have any idea it was really Crowe I'd be paying back. That was when Randall dropped out of sight for good. He tried to hide out, not from his family, but from Crowe. But the guy found him, of course, and told him that he'd have me killed unless Randall did some errands for him—like delivering a bunch of drugs that Crowe was selling to some other lowlife. Crowe said that was only fitting, since I was the one who'd wound up with the money and now couldn't pay it back." Frank shrugged. "So Randall did what he was told to do . . . and got caught at it. Then he dug himself an even deeper hole by skipping out on his bail and going into hiding. I don't know what made him think of coming over here to my mother's place. Maybe he knew she'd hide him. She was always more fond of her grandkids than she was of her own kids. I'll bet you never knew what a tyrant she was when we were little. Poor Billie cried herself to sleep nearly every night because of things that Mom said to her. Told her she was ugly and stupid and would never amount to anything. . . . Of course, she said the same things to me and Ted, but not as often as she picked on Billie. I guess she knew we were tougher and could take it better. But she sensed a weakness in Billie. . . ."

Frank's voice trailed off, and he stared straight ahead, a vacant expression on his face as if his body was here but his mind wasn't. Phyllis didn't know what to say, so she sat there silently as the man beside her struggled to escape from the trap of his memories.

Finally a little shudder went through Frank's bulky frame, and he turned his head to look at her. "You didn't know about any of that going on, did you?" he asked with a faint, sad smile.

"No," Phyllis admitted. "I'm sorry, but I didn't."

"Yeah, Mom was good at the sweet little old lady bit. And you know what? . . . After the three of us grew up and moved out and got married, she really *was* sweet most of the time, especially after we all had kids. She doted on those grandchildren. She was always after us to bring them to see her. We couldn't hardly stand to be around her, though, so we didn't visit very often. But when we did, she was like a different person. It was like none of the bad times ever happened." Frank spread his hands. "I guess some people just aren't cut out to be parents, but they can handle being grandparents okay."

Phyllis nodded, still unsure what to say. She hadn't been prepared for the sort of searing revelations she had heard from Frank Simmons, and the fact that she was hearing them while sitting in a front porch swing on a mild December day at Christmastime just made the whole experience more bizarre.

"So I'm not really surprised that she tried to help Randall," Frank continued after a moment. "Just like I wasn't surprised when she reverted back to type when I asked to borrow that money. I could see it in her eyes. . . . It was a touch of glee, just a little touch, that I really was the failure she'd always predicted I'd turn out to be."

"I've seen you for the past few days, Frank," Phyllis said. "At the funeral, and next door. You were truly grieving for her. I could tell."

"Well, of course I was. She was my mother. I loved her." A bleak chuckle came from him. "That's the problem. Some people, even when they treat you like crap, you just can't stop loving them. Even if you want to."

But there was that old saying about there being a thin line between love and hate, Phyllis thought, and those words contained a lot of truth. She had heard hatred in Frank's voice when he spoke about the way his mother had turned him down when he asked her for money. She could only imagine how he must have felt, a proud man who had accepted help from his son, only to be unable to repay that debt; forced to turn to his own mother, only to be rebuffed . . . caught between two generations, with failure on one side and rejection on the other. . . .

There was no telling what a man in that much pain might do. Just no telling at all.

"Anyway," Frank resumed, "that's the story. That's why Randall did what he did. So you see, Phyllis, he's not really a bad kid. Those drug charges aren't as bad as they look. He was just trying to protect me. The bail jumping . . . that was just a matter of being young and scared and stupid. But none of that makes him a killer. Randall would never hurt anybody, especially his grandmother. And he wouldn't have attacked you. I'm sure of it. That's why I thought . . . maybe if you knew the whole story . . . you could see your way clear to sort of help him out."

"I wish I could, Frank," Phyllis said. "I can't lie to the police, though." She paused. "And are you sure that this story about the loan shark . . . well, are you sure that it's true?"

A frown creased Frank's forehead. "Randall's too scared to be lying now. Anyway, that lawyer of his, Ms. Yorke, he told her about it, too, and she checked out that guy Jimmy Crowe with some contacts of hers in Dallas. He's as bad as Randall said he is. That's why Randall was so scared when he spotted Crowe over here in the neighborhood a few days ago. He was afraid Crowe had found him."

"Wait a minute," Phyllis said as she leaned forward. "Crowe was here in the neighborhood?"

"Yeah. Randall was watching from the attic window and saw him drive past."

"When was this?"

"Last Thursday. And then Crowe was back on Friday. But he didn't hang around, just drove along the street a few times and then disappeared, Randall said. I think he found out that Randall's grandmother lived here, and he was staking the place out in case Randall showed up. He didn't know Randall was already hiding in the attic."

"He still wants the money that he's owed," Phyllis mused.

"Yeah, that's what I figure, too."

"Do the police know about this?"

Frank shook his head. "Randall's too scared to tell them. He doesn't want Crowe to know that he ratted him out. He's afraid that he's gonna be sent to prison, and he knows that with the contacts Crowe has in the penitentiary, he'd be dead in a month or less if Crowe gave the order. Ms. Yorke's been trying to convince him to spill the whole story, but so far he won't do it."

"But you just told me."

"Yeah. It's a calculated risk, I guess you'd say. I wanted your help, Phyllis, so I figured you deserved to hear the truth."

"You've put me in a bad position," she told him, her voice a little prickly with anger. "If the police ask me whether I know anything else about Randall, I'll have to tell them what you told me."

"It wouldn't be admissible in court. It's just hearsay."

"Yes, but it would be enough to put them on Crowe's trail and maybe tie him in to the murder." Phyllis paused. "Or is that what you really want, Frank? Did you tell me all this *hoping* I would go to the police?"

Alarm leaped into his eyes. "Good grief, no! I don't want to make Crowe's grudge against Randall any worse, either. I just thought . . . oh, Lord, I didn't think. I didn't think it through far enough. I was just desperate to come up with something that might help him. Instead, I . . . I may have doomed him."

Again, he covered his face with his hands.

The whole thing would have seemed lurid and melodramatic, Phyllis thought, if it hadn't been real. Real life sometimes put soap operas to shame when it came to convolutions and emotional turmoil.

She said, "Take it easy, Frank. I'm not going to run to the police, at least not right now."

He lowered his hands and looked over at her. His eyes were wet. "You're sure?"

"I'm certain. I want some time to think about everything you've told me. Of course, if they come to me and ask me about it, I'll have no choice but to tell them the truth, as far as I know it. But they've already questioned me several times, and I don't see any reason why they'd want to ask me any more questions right now."

Frank wiped the back of his hand across his eyes. "Thank you. I can't tell you how much I appreciate that. I . . . I'm sorry I came over here and asked you to lie."

"You're at your wit's end, I know," she said with a nod. "You just want to do anything you can to help your son."

"That's right."

"Goodness knows, I'd feel the same way if Mike was in trouble."

A rueful smile appeared on Frank's face. "Mike would never get in trouble like this. He's a good kid. Always has been."

Phyllis smiled back at him. "I can't argue with that."

"So," Frank said after a moment, "what do I do now?"

"I don't know what to tell you," Phyllis replied honestly. "In one way, it seems like it would be a good idea for Randall to tell the police why he did the things he did, but if that man Crowe is really as dangerous as he seems to be, Randall would be running a risk. I know it's hard on him, being in jail and all, but it might be best to just wait right now and hope something else turns up. Juliette Yorke strikes me as a pretty sharp lawyer. She might come up with something that clears Randall without making Crowe's grudge against him even worse."

"I don't know what it would be," Frank said.

Phyllis reached over and patted his hand. "That's why people conduct investigations . . . to turn up things that might otherwise be hidden."

"I guess so. Thanks, Mrs. Newsom . . . Phyllis." He sat forward and put his hands on his knees. "I guess I'd better be going. I've taken up enough of your time."

"I'm glad you trusted me enough to tell me the truth, Frank. Even if it might cause some awkwardness in the future. We'll hope that it doesn't come to that."

"Yeah. I'm gonna hope really hard." He got to his feet, managed a weak smile and a wave, and went down the porch steps to turn toward the house next door.

When he was gone, the front door of Phyllis's house opened. She looked over and saw that Sam was standing there.

"You and Frank were sure havin' a mighty intense conversation," he said. "I didn't want to interrupt, though, and I didn't eavesdrop."

Phyllis patted the swing beside her. "Come here and sit down. I'll tell you about it."

"Don't mind if I do." As Sam came onto the porch and closed the door behind him, Phyllis caught a whiff of the cooking smells inside the house. Those pies were going to be delicious.

Sam sat down beside her, a little closer than Frank had been. "I'm not sure I should be telling you this," she began. "You could wind up in the same uncomfortable position that I'm in, knowing more than you really want to."

"You look like you shouldn't be carryin' around that burden by yourself," Sam said. "I'll take a chance."

"All right. Remember, you asked for it."

She filled him in on everything Frank had told her, starting at the beginning with Randall Simmons's connection to Jimmy

Crowe, the loan shark and drug dealer. Sam frowned slightly during the story but didn't say much, interrupting only now and then to ask a question and clarify one point or another. He shook his head sympathetically at the part of the story involving Agnes's treatment of her children when they were young.

Telling Sam all about it served a dual purpose. Phyllis knew that he had a keen mind, so she was interested in his opinions. And putting it into words herself allowed her to go over the whole thing again in her mind and make sure she had everything straight.

When she was finished, he said, "Sounds like a pretty tangled-up mess to me."

"Me, too, but a couple of things jump right out at me."

"One of 'em bein' the fact that this fella Crowe was here in the neighborhood last week?"

Phyllis nodded. Oscar Gunderson hadn't mentioned seeing any suspicious characters, and Jimmy Crowe certainly fit that description. But Oscar didn't see everything that was going on along the street, either. He was bound to have missed some things. Even Agnes, laid up with a bad hip and sitting at her window all the time, couldn't have seen everything.

"If Crowe knew that Randall's grandmother lived here," Phyllis said, "he could have decided to talk to Agnes and see if she knew where her grandson was. A man like that wouldn't hesitate to try to force information from her, and things could have gotten out of hand. . . ."

"Well, I don't know the fella, but from what I've heard, he sounds more like the type to kill an old lady than anybody else involved in this business. You said there were two things that jumped out at you. What's the second one?"

"How terrible it must have been for Frank to have to go to his mother for help, and then how she made him feel like a failure. Like he was crawling to her to beg because he couldn't take care of his own family and business."

"You think she was really that bad? I was around her some, and she always seemed pretty nice to me."

"I've heard it said that people have many different faces. That certainly seems to have been true for Agnes."

"Yeah, but bad enough that her own son would choke the life out of her?" Sam shook his head. "I don't see it. And if Frank killed her, why doesn't he just confess and get his boy off the hook for the murder?"

"At this point, the police might not believe him. They might think he was lying and giving a false confession to try to protect Randall." Phyllis sighed. "I'm afraid there's only one thing that's going to help Randall now."

"Proof that somebody else really killed his grandmother?" Sam guessed.

Phyllis nodded. "That's it. Exactly."

The question was, who was going to find that proof?

Since the police thought they had their man, the only one still looking for the killer was her, so that sort of answered that . . . didn't it?

Chapter 15

As late in the afternoon as it was, and with as much as had happened already, Phyllis didn't want to get started on anything else today. Anyway, she had plenty to think about as it was. She didn't for a second consider Oscar Gunderson a serious suspect in Agnes's murder, but for half a second . . . well, it was hard to rule him out entirely.

Jimmy Crowe, though . . . Now, there was an actual suspect. He was used to dealing with people violently, and when he wanted something, he wasn't the sort to let anything stand in his way, not even an old woman.

Of course, Phyllis reminded herself, all she had to go by were the things that Frank Simmons had told her. She didn't know Jimmy Crowe and couldn't make any real judgments about him. As far as she was aware, she had never even laid eyes on the man.

So she set the investigation aside to mull over everything she had learned so far, and to do some more planning for Christmas dinner, which was now less than seventy-two hours away. In addition to the ham and the wild rice and cranberry stuffing, other dishes would be needed.

One of Phyllis's holiday standards was a sweet potato casserole with brown sugar and whipped cream, topped with crushed pecans. It was almost sweet enough to consider it a dessert, but since the main ingredient was sweet potato, Phyllis preferred to think of it as a vegetable.

A green bean casserole was another classic. Phyllis didn't care for it, but Carolyn always made one and Phyllis usually ate a little, just to be polite. Better was Carolyn's fruit salad. While potato salad wasn't a traditional Christmas dish, Phyllis thought it would go well with the ham, so she thought about making one on Christmas morning while the ham was cooking. Even if they didn't eat it Christmas Day, it would go wonderfully with the ham for leftovers.

Scalloped potatoes might be a little more festive, though, she decided. She'd do those instead of the potato salad. And of course they would need some nice, quick yeast rolls or maybe some cheese grits. . . .

These plans were starting to go overboard on the starches, she realized. She pulled down a cookbook and started flipping through the table of contents for the vegetable section. An interesting recipe for zucchini stuffed with tomatoes and eggplant caught her eye. She found it in the cookbook, wrote down the ingredients she would need to buy, and marked the page for later. For dessert they would have the pies—and the cookies, of course. Carolyn had made both pumpkin and chocolate pecan pies for their dinner and the one at her daughter's house. Now, if they could just get all the rest done by Christmas.

It was nice to stop thinking about murder for a while and just concentrate on holiday preparations instead, but the situation forced itself back into Phyllis's attention that evening when

Mike called. Sam answered the phone and then gave it to Phyllis, telling her, "It's that boy o' yours. He sounds upset about somethin', too."

Phyllis frowned as she brought the cordless phone to her ear and asked, "Mike? What is it? Bobby's not sick, is he?"

"No, Mom, we're all fine," Mike said, "but one of my friends at the police department called me just now and told me that Randall Simmons tried to kill himself this evening."

"Oh, dear God," Phyllis exclaimed, causing Sam, Carolyn, and Eve, all of whom were in the living room with her watching a video of *White Christmas*, to look up in alarm. On the TV screen, Bing Crosby and Danny Kaye were paused in the middle of arguing about something, Kaye grabbing Crosby's arm in an attempt to elicit guilt from his old army buddy. "What happened?"

"He managed to hang himself in his cell. Evidently he swiped a plastic knife from a food tray and sharpened it until he was able to use it to rip some strips of cloth off his jail outfit. He tied them together to make a rope. He wasn't on suicide watch, so he was able to get away with it, but one of the officers found him before he choked to death."

"So he's still alive?"

"Yeah. They rushed him to the hospital, of course, and it's close by so they got there in a hurry. The guy who called me said the word is, Randall will probably survive."

"I hope so," Phyllis said. "His poor family has already been through enough."

Carolyn mouthed, *What?*

Phyllis held up a finger to tell her to wait a minute. When all the young people started using that gesture, it had annoyed her, but she had to admit that it came in handy sometimes.

"My friend knew that I was connected to the case through

you and thought I'd like to know," Mike went on. "And I was sure *you'd* want to know."

"Yes," she said. "Thank you for calling." She was about to hang up, but paused long enough to ask, "You and Sarah and Bobby are coming over here for Christmas dinner, right?"

"You bet. Wouldn't miss it."

"All right. See you then, if not before."

Phyllis thumbed the button to break the connection, then walked over to the table and returned the phone to its base. Carolyn had been patient for as long as she was going to. She asked, "For goodness' sake, *what happened?*"

"Randall Simmons tried to commit suicide by hanging himself in his cell this evening."

Sam said, "But I heard you say he's still alive?"

Phyllis nodded. "Yes. The police took him to the hospital. I don't know how badly he's hurt, but supposedly he's going to recover. I'm sure he's under police guard at the hospital, and they'll have him on suicide watch from now on."

"What a terrible thing," Eve said. "I've never understood how anyone could want to end their own life."

"Randall's scared," Phyllis said. She looked at Sam and saw that he understood what she meant. She hadn't explained everything to Carolyn and Eve the way she had to him. He knew that Randall was not only frightened because he was locked up in jail and accused of murder, but also because he had the threat of the vicious loan shark Jimmy Crowe hanging over his head, as well. Randall might have thought that if he was dead, Crowe would forget about the money he'd lost and leave the rest of his family alone. That seemed unlikely to Phyllis, but truly desperate people didn't always think straight.

"Well, I'm glad they were able to help him in time," Carolyn said, "but the ones I really feel sorry for are that boy's family.

Doesn't he know that he's putting them through hell, first with what he did to Agnes and now this?"

"I'm not convinced that Randall did anything to Agnes," Phyllis said. "In fact, from everything I've seen, there are other suspects who are just as likely to have done it, if not more so."

Carolyn gave her a shrewd look and repeated, "Suspects? You've been doing detective work again, Phyllis?"

"No, not really." Phyllis shook her head as she felt a flush warm her face. "I've just been thinking about the case. You can't blame me for being interested. I mean, it happened right next door. And I got hit on the head. I have a personal stake in seeing to it that the police get the right man."

Carolyn nodded, a smug expression on her face now. "And since you've been successful at solving murders before, why not this one, right?"

Phyllis felt like she was being challenged, and she didn't care much for it. "I just want justice to be done. Agnes may not have been the best person in the world—"

"What was wrong with Agnes? She always seemed like a sweet little old lady to me."

"You don't know everything about her. None of us do, really. Regardless of that, she didn't deserve to be killed. And I'll admit it—I just don't believe that Randall is guilty."

"Hanging himself is not the act of an innocent man."

"We don't know that. I'd say that it was the act of a scared, desperate man."

Carolyn frowned at her for a long moment, then said, "Well, just be careful; that's all I've got to say. Good grief, Phyllis, you're not Miss Marple."

"More like Nancy Drew, I'd say," Sam drawled.

Phyllis had to laugh. "I haven't been *that* young for a long time." She took her seat on the sofa again. "Anyway, I'm not going to be doing any detecting tonight. We have a movie to watch, remember?"

And at that moment, as if the videotape knew what it was doing, the movie came off pause and Bing Crosby said in exasperation, "Where'd you leave that? In your snood?"

Phyllis's sleep was restless that night. She couldn't stop thinking about Randall Simmons, and also about Randall's father, Frank, who had already been experiencing the torments of the damned over the unfortunate turns his son's life had taken. This latest incident had to have plunged Frank into an even deeper, darker pit of despair.

First thing in the morning, a welcome distraction landed on the front porch: the edition of the newspaper containing the announcement of the winner of the Christmas cookie contest. Phyllis was on her way downstairs to put on the coffee and start fixing breakfast when Carolyn appeared at the top of the stairs and hurried down.

"The paper should be here by now, shouldn't it?" she said as she passed Phyllis.

"Probably. Oh, that's right. It's Thursday, isn't it?"

She was being a little coy. She knew good and well what day it was, and knew, as well, that the results of the contest would be in this morning's paper. But she wasn't going to race Carolyn to the door. If it was so important to Carolyn that she find out first who had won, then let her go right ahead, Phyllis thought.

Anyway, it was possible that neither of them had won. There were plenty of good bakers in Weatherford besides them.

Wearing a thick robe and house shoes, Carolyn opened the door and looked back and forth on the porch. Even though the past few days had been mild, the nights were still fairly chilly, and Phyllis felt a cool wind blowing in the door. She didn't say anything, though, not wanting to spoil Carolyn's fun.

"There it is!" Carolyn said. She stepped out onto the porch and retrieved the paper from under the swing, where it had slid when it landed. She straightened and pulled the rolled-up newspaper out of its plastic wrapper. It unrolled in her hands. Her eyes scanned the front page, and an impatient look appeared on her face. "Where is it? I don't see anything about the contest!"

"Maybe it's in the second section," Phyllis suggested as she stood in the doorway in her robe, arms crossed over her chest and a smile on her face.

"Maybe." Carolyn pulled out the paper's second section and dropped the first one on the swing. Her eyes widened as she said, "Oh. Oh, my goodness."

Phyllis stepped toward her. "What is it?" She couldn't tell from Carolyn's reaction if she was pleased, or if something was wrong.

Carolyn turned the paper so that Phyllis could see the front page of the second section. There, in a large color photo, was a plate full of Carolyn's pecan pie cookies. The headline underneath the photo said WINNING COOKIE A SCRUMPTIOUS TREAT.

"Scrumptious," Carolyn read. "They said my cookies are scrumptious."

Still smiling, Phyllis said, "I can see that. Congratulations, Carolyn. You deserved to win."

She wasn't just saying that; she meant it. Carolyn's pecan pie cookies really were delicious.

"What about the runners-up?" Phyllis asked.

"I'm sure you must be in second place," Carolyn said as she studied the story that went with the photo. "No, wait; they didn't rank the runners-up. They just have four other recipes, to make a top five. But yours is one of them, Phyllis!" She pointed at the paper. "You see? Right there."

Phyllis saw her name, along with the recipe for lime snowflake sugar cookies. There was no photo, but that was all right. She was just glad the recipe was in the paper, so that other people could try it and get some enjoyment from the cookies.

Of course, it would have been nice to win . . . but considering all the blessings of family and friends she had, she didn't need it.

Carolyn brought the paper inside and called up the stairs, "Eve! Eve, come down and see who won the cookie contest!"

Still smiling, Phyllis headed into the kitchen to get started on breakfast.

Eve and Sam both congratulated Carolyn on her victory, and Carolyn was in a good mood all through breakfast, especially when it was interrupted several times by phone calls from friends who had seen the paper and wanted to congratulate her, as well. Carolyn's daughter, Sandra, called to share in her triumph, too.

Afterward, Sam volunteered to wash the dishes, as he often did, and Phyllis dried them and put them away. They could have put everything in the dishwasher and left it for later, of course, but that seemed almost like too much trouble. Besides, both of them enjoyed spending this time together. Carolyn and Eve were upstairs again, and Phyllis and Sam were alone in the kitchen.

"You're takin' defeat mighty well," he commented with his hands immersed in the soapy water.

"Oh, I don't regard it as defeat. Carolyn may have won, but I don't feel like I lost."

"One o' the runners-up, with your recipe in the paper . . . That's not bad, all right."

"That's the way I feel about it," Phyllis agreed. "Here in

Texas it's hard to beat anything connected with pecan pie . . . and Carolyn's cookies *are* awfully good."

"That they are," Sam said with a nod. "Of course, the same thing's true o' the ones you made." He rinsed the skillet Phyllis had used to scramble the eggs and then handed it to her to dry. That finished the washing, so he dried his hands as he went on, "I've been thinkin' about that Simmons kid. Tryin' to kill himself that way just made him look even more guilty."

"I know," Phyllis said as she dried the skillet. "Everyone's going to think that he did it now."

"Everybody but you," Sam said, "and maybe me."

"Oh, I'm not convinced either way. I just have . . . doubts, I guess you'd say. And that reminds me, there must have been something about it in the paper this morning."

She put the skillet away in the cabinet and then went to the living room, where Carolyn had left the newspaper after showing off the photo of the winning cookies to Sam and Eve. Phyllis picked up the first section, which was lying on the coffee table. Sure enough, there was a story below the fold headlined MURDER SUSPECT ATTEMPTS SUICIDE.

The details were the same as Mike had told her on the phone the previous evening. From the sound of it, Randall had been discovered pretty quickly, and while there was severe bruising to his throat and possible damage to his trachea, he was expected to recover fully. He had been kept overnight in the hospital under police guard but, depending on his condition, might be transferred to the county jail today, according to the story. He had been held in the city jail at the police station until now, but since he wasn't able to make bail and would be in custody for quite some time, pending indictment and trial, he needed to be in a facility better suited for long-term incarceration, Chief Ralph Whitmire was quoted as saying.

If Randall was at the county jail, that would make it easier for Mike to talk to him, Phyllis thought. Maybe Mike could confirm that story Randall had told his father and Juliette Yorke about the loan shark Jimmy Crowe. . . .

But that would mean telling Mike all about it, Phyllis realized, and then as a law enforcement officer, he would be duty bound to share the information with Detective Largo and the district attorney. No, she decided, she wasn't going to drag her son into the middle of a mess like that—not unless she had proof that Randall hadn't murdered his grandmother.

And that meant going back to asking questions.

When she was dressed in jeans and a pullover Christmas sweater, she gathered up another plate of cookies. As Sam watched her, he asked, "Goin' visitin'?"

She hadn't told him about what she'd discovered next door at Oscar Gunderson's house. She had been too embarrassed to—embarrassed for Oscar's sake, and her own. Of course, he had a right to live his own life as he saw fit, but still . . .

"I thought Helen Johannson's kids might like some cookies," she said. "They weren't here last Saturday, so they didn't get any."

"That's thoughtful of you. Don't suppose that while you're there you might ask the lady about whether or not she'd noticed any unusual goin's-on around the Simmons house before the murder?"

"If the subject comes up . . . ," Phyllis said.

"I reckon you'll be safe enough with that girl. She probably doesn't weigh more'n a hundred pounds drippin' wet. I'll come along with you, anyway, if you want."

"No, that's all right," she said as she finished tucking plastic wrap around the plate of cookies. "I think I can handle this by myself."

Of course, she'd thought the same thing about taking cookies over to Agnes's house the previous Saturday, and look how that had ended up.

But she couldn't have Sam tagging along as her bodyguard everywhere she went, she told herself. She had already called on him too much in that regard.

"I'll see you later."

"I'll be here," he told her.

Two days until Christmas, she thought as she walked along the street. *Christmas Eve Eve,* Mike had called it when he was little. Several front yards along the street sported giant inflatable snowmen and Santa Clauses. There was even a Grinch at one house. Most people used those icicle lights now, and they sparkled in the sun as they hung from eaves and porch roofs, almost as brilliant in the daylight as they were at night. Murder might have dampened the holiday spirit in the neighborhood for a while, but it was still there, symbolic of the hope that not even death could take away.

Helen Johannson lived on the next block, but right on the corner, so her house wasn't really very far from Phyllis's. It took only a couple of minutes to walk over there. The garage door was open, and Helen's compact car was inside, so Phyllis knew she was home. Helen was around twenty-seven or twenty-eight, with a daughter in first grade and a son in preschool. She worked as a hostess at the Applebee's out on the interstate and had been divorced for a couple of years. Before that, her husband had lived here, too, but he'd moved out after Helen caught him cheating on her with one of her coworkers at the restaurant, which had made for quite a bit of tension until the other woman had quit her job and moved to Granbury with Helen's ex, who got a job there driving a sand and gravel truck for the county. Life really was like a country song sometimes, Phyllis mused.

An index card taped over the doorbell button read, BELL DOESN'T WORK. PLEASE KNOCK. Phyllis wondered whether Sam ought to volunteer to come over here and fix that doorbell for Helen. She knew Kenny would have, if he'd still been alive. She knocked as the sign instructed, rapping her knuckles pretty hard against the door.

A moment later the door swung back, and Helen's six-year-old daughter, Denise, stood there smiling a gap-toothed grin up at Phyllis. Helen hurried through the foyer after her, saying, "Denise, what have I told you about not opening the door when you don't know who's there?" Then she looked up, saw Phyllis on the porch, and said through the storm door, "Oh, hi, Mrs. Newsom."

As Sam had said, Helen Johannson probably didn't weigh more than a hundred pounds. She was small but not fragile looking. Her long blond hair was so pale, it was almost white. She wore jeans and an old shirt with the tails hanging out, which made her look younger than she really was.

Phyllis smiled and held up the plate with the cookies visible through the clear plastic wrap. "I thought you and the little ones might like some of these, since you couldn't come to the cookie exchange the other day and we have plenty left over."

"That's awful nice of you." Helen opened the storm door. "Come on in. Denise, go play with Parker."

"I don't wanna play with Parker," the girl said. "He's a baby."

"He's only two years younger than you," Helen pointed out. "A little less than that, really."

"That's enough to make him a baby."

"Don't argue with me. Scoot." Helen gave her daughter a light swat on the rump to hurry her along.

"Some people would call that child abuse," Phyllis said

when Denise had disappeared into a room along the hallway. She smiled to let Helen know that she didn't fall into that category.

"Yeah, well, some people don't have any common sense. I'd never hurt my kids, but sometimes you gotta let 'em know who's boss." Helen reached out to take the cookies from Phyllis. "Don't these look good. I'm sorry we couldn't come for the cookie exchange this year, Mrs. Newsom. Parker's preschool scheduled their Christmas program for the same afternoon, and of course he had to go to that."

"Of course," Phyllis said. "I planned all along to bring you some cookies; I just hadn't gotten around to it until now." She paused. "It's been a busy week."

"Yeah, I'd say so, what with a murder right next door and all. Would you like some coffee? I don't have to be at work until one, so I've got plenty of time."

"That would be nice," Phyllis said. "Thank you."

"And you can tell me all about what happened," Helen went on. "I haven't heard any good gossip in a long time."

Well, this was working out all right, Phyllis thought. Helen wanted to talk about the exact same thing that she wanted to talk about.

They went into the kitchen, where Helen already had coffee ready. They sat down at the table with their cups, and Helen said, "Shoot. I've read about it in the paper, of course, but I want to hear it from you, Mrs. Newsom. It's almost like something you'd read in the tabloids, with a grandson hiding out in his grandmother's attic like that and then killing her. Say, you got hurt, too, didn't you? How are you doing?"

"Back to normal," Phyllis said. "No lasting effects from the attack, except that my head hurts a little where the stitches are if I happen to bump it against something."

Helen shook her head. "Wow. Getting knocked out by a murderer. You're lucky to be alive."

"I know."

"So, tell me," Helen said. "What happened?"

Phyllis didn't particularly want to go through all the details again, but she didn't see that she had any choice. Besides, if she wanted to draw any new information out of Helen, this was the best way to go about it.

"You never noticed anything unusual going on at Agnes's house before she was killed?" Phyllis asked when she was finished with the recitation. "From what I gather, Randall was there for several days before the murder."

Helen shook her head. "No, I never saw anything out of the ordinary. Of course, I wasn't looking for anything, and it's not like I live next door to the Simmons house, or right across the street."

"Well, I never noticed anything, either," Phyllis said, "but in talking to people after it happened, I've found out that several of them noticed a suspicious character hanging around the neighborhood for a few days before the murder."

Helen's eyebrows arched as her eyes opened wider. "Really? That's kind of scary. It really would be frightening if the police hadn't already caught the killer. He could still be lurking around here."

"That's what I thought," Phyllis said. "What if Randall Simmons didn't kill Agnes?"

"But the police have charged him with the murder." Helen frowned. "They wouldn't do that if they didn't know he was guilty, would they?"

"It's happened before. People have been charged with crimes they didn't commit. They've even been convicted for them."

A shiver went through Helen. "Yeah, you're right. I've read about things like that. Why would anyone want to kill a harmless old lady like Mrs. Simmons, though? I didn't know her well at all, but I can't imagine why anybody would want to hurt her."

Phyllis decided it was time to push a little harder. "Well . . . Agnes sat in front of her picture window all the time, especially since she broke her hip, watching everything that was going on in the neighborhood, and I thought maybe she saw something she shouldn't have seen, or found out something that someone wanted to keep secret—"

Before Phyllis could go on, Helen suddenly bolted to her feet. The smile was gone from her face, as was the gossipy glint in her eyes. Instead her expression was a mixture of anger and terror as she pointed toward the front of the house and gasped, "How—how dare you! Get out of my house! Get out right now!"

Chapter 16

$\mathcal{P}$hyllis was too shocked by Helen's reaction to do anything except sit there for a long moment and stare at the furious young woman. Helen continued to sputter, "You come in here and accuse me . . . I never did anything to you . . . You don't know what you're talking about!"

"Helen . . . Helen, take it easy," Phyllis said when she finally regained her voice. "Just calm down. I never said *you* killed Agnes."

Helen stood on the other side of the table, trembling and wild-eyed, and then her head jerked around as a small voice asked, "Mama . . . did you kill somebody?"

Phyllis turned her head and saw Denise and Parker, Helen's two children, standing there in the kitchen doorway, looking confused and frightened. Helen looked at them, too, and then she covered her face with her hands and slumped back into her chair as she started to sob.

Phyllis stood up and went over to the doorway, where the children watched her with wide eyes. She knelt down to put herself on their level and said in a calm, quiet voice, "Why don't you two go play in another room or watch television or something? Your mother is upset right now, but she's all right, I promise you."

"But did she kill somebody?" Denise asked again.

Phyllis reached out and hugged the little girl. "Of course not, dear. Now, you need to run along—"

The legs of the chair where Helen sat scraped against the floor as she pushed it back. "Get away from them!" she said. "Get away from my children!"

Phyllis let go of Denise and straightened to her feet. "Please, Helen, you know I'd never hurt them," she said.

"You've already hurt them! Coming in here and accusing their mother of murder! What did you think that would do to them?"

Phyllis's voice hardened with anger now as she looked at Helen's blotchy, tear-streaked face. "I never accused you of murder," she said. "You're the one who brought that up."

Helen ignored that as she turned to the children and said, "Go to your rooms—*now!*"

Parker started to cry, too, but he went with his sister as Denise pulled him away from the kitchen. They ran down the hall and disappeared into another part of the house.

Helen said coldly to Phyllis, "I told you to get out."

"Not just yet," Phyllis said. She knew she was being stubborn, but she felt almost like she'd been attacked again, and she didn't like it. "I want to know what made you fly off the handle like that. All I said was that I thought Agnes might have discovered someone's secret. . . ." She let her voice trail away as she stared at Helen for a long moment. Then she said, "You've got a secret you don't want anyone to know, don't you, Helen?"

"That's none of your business."

"No, of course not," Phyllis agreed. "But I feel like I've caused a problem for you, and if there's anything I can do to help, I want to."

"Oh, you've caused a problem, all right." Helen's voice was bitter. "My kids may never look at me the same way again."

Phyllis shook her head and said, "Don't worry about them. Children are amazingly resilient. They'll have forgotten all about this incident in a day or two, and even if they remember that it happened, it won't upset them."

Helen frowned. "You're sure?"

"I'm certain. I saw it with my son, and with the students I taught in school, too."

"Lord, I hope you're right." Helen sat down again as weariness seemed to overwhelm her. "I didn't want them to ever find out about it, but I should have known they would, sooner or later. I just thought that surely they'd be older first. . . ." She looked up at Phyllis. "You're just dying to know what I'm talking about, aren't you?"

"Like I said, it's none of my business," Phyllis replied, but she was hoping that Helen was upset enough to feel the need to talk to somebody.

Helen sighed. "You might as well sit back down. I've heard what a busybody you are. You won't be satisfied until you hear all about it."

Another surge of anger went through Phyllis at the young woman's tone and the unflattering description. She didn't think she was a busybody at all. But she wanted to know the truth; that was undeniable.

"You should have more respect for your elders," she snapped as she went around the table and sat down again.

Helen shrugged. "You're probably right. I'm just upset, like you told the kids. I'm sorry, okay?"

"Okay." Phyllis paused. "And I'm sorry I stirred up some memories that are obviously very bad."

"Oh, yeah, you could say that. . . . Maybe it *would* do some good to talk about it. Just let me make sure the kids aren't listening in. After all this uproar, I'll have to tell them *something*, but I'm not sure yet what it'll be. As long as it's not the truth."

She stood up and went down the hall. It occurred to Phyllis that Helen might not come back, but after a couple of minutes, the younger woman reappeared and took her seat at the kitchen table again. The coffee they had been drinking earlier sat cooling in the cups, forgotten. Neither woman was interested in it anymore.

"You know," Phyllis began, "it's usually a bad idea to lie to your children. You'll find that they can handle the truth most of the time. It's just a matter of finding the right way to express it."

"I'll decide what I tell my kids and what I don't. And I don't feel much like telling them that their mother killed a guy." A humorless smile touched her lips. "That's right. I'm a killer, Mrs. Newsom."

"But not a murderer," Phyllis guessed.

"Oh, no, it was ruled self-defense, justifiable homicide, whatever you want to call it. Wasn't even involuntary manslaughter. No charges were ever filed against me. I was fifteen. That was thirteen years ago."

Helen fell silent, remaining that way for so long that Phyllis thought she was going to have to prod the younger woman into speaking again. But then Helen took a deep breath and resumed the story.

"He was one of my mother's boyfriends. We lived down in south Texas, between San Antonio and Corpus Christi. My dad left when I was little, and we never saw him again. My mother tried to find somebody else. I guess she was one of those women you hear about, the kind who can't stand to be without a man, any man. So she wound up dating some real creeps."

Helen fell silent again. The faraway look in her eyes told Phyllis that she was reliving those days, and they weren't very pretty. Phyllis guessed, "This man you're talking about . . . did he make advances toward you?"

"What?" Helen seemed a little surprised, as if Phyllis's question had broken her out of her memories. "Oh. No, he never laid a hand on me."

"I just thought, from the way you said you were fifteen . . ."

Helen shook her head. "No, not at all."

"Did he abuse your mother?"

"Not the way you're thinking of. The son of a bitch was a thief. He found out where we had some extra money stashed, and he went after it. My mom caught him about to sneak out of the house with the money. She tried to stop him, and he pulled a gun." Helen paused and shook her head again. "You believe it? He was going to shoot her over a measly six hundred bucks."

"But you stopped him."

"You bet I did. He didn't see me behind him. There was a butcher knife on the kitchen counter. I picked it up and shoved it in his back as hard as I could."

Phyllis tried to suppress the shiver that ran through her. Helen's voice was almost emotionless now. She didn't seem to care that she had ended a man's life, and in a particularly gruesome fashion at that.

As if to confirm what Phyllis was thinking, Helen said, "Understand, I didn't lose any sleep over what happened. Well, not much, anyway. There were a few nights when I started thinking about all the blood, and that sort of got to me. But not as much as the way the kids acted at school. Some of them whispered about it behind my back. I was the badass girl who'd stabbed a guy to death. Some of the others thought it was cool, like I was some sort of action movie hero. But neither of those things was true. I just wanted to protect my mother, and the knife was there. The guy was a lot bigger than me, so I used what I could to stop him."

"And you had absolutely no reason to feel guilty about it," Phyllis said.

"I didn't think so. Still, even if he's a jerk, when you end a guy's life . . . when he's breathing and thinking and wanting things one minute, and then the next he's just . . . nothing . . . it's kind of hard."

"I'm sure it must be." Phyllis hoped fervently that she never found out firsthand what that was like.

"Anyway," Helen continued, "the cops and the district attorney believed my mom and me and didn't file charges against me. The man I killed had stolen from some of his girlfriends in the past, and been in other trouble with the law. A few months later we moved, since my mom knew what it was like for me at school. She has relatives in Millsap, so we came up here, and nobody knew who I was or what I'd done. The story wasn't big news. It was a fresh start, and that's just what I wanted." Helen looked across the table at Phyllis. "Now you know my secret. You think I'd kill to keep anybody else from finding out?"

For a second Phyllis couldn't tell if the younger woman was threatening her. Then she decided that Helen was genuinely curious.

"I don't think so," Phyllis said. "Did Agnes Simmons find out?"

"That's the thing. . . . I don't know. My mom still lives in Millsap. She comes over here to visit me and the kids pretty often. A few months back I accidentally got a piece of Mrs. Simmons's mail. It was stuck between a couple of big envelopes in my mailbox. I doubt if the postman ever saw it. So I took it over there to her, and my mom walked down the street with me and met Mrs. Simmons, and they hit it off pretty well. Ever since then, when Mom comes to visit me, she usually stops by and says hello to Mrs. Simmons, too."

"So she could have told her about what happened to you when you were fifteen."

Helen nodded. "Yeah, she could have. Mom likes to talk, and sometimes her mouth gets a little ahead of her brain, you know what I mean? But even if she had, it wouldn't have been that big a deal. I mean, I don't want people to know, but I wouldn't . . . *kill* anybody over it."

Phyllis didn't want to think that could be the case . . . but she remembered the violent reaction that had gripped Helen when the young woman thought she was being accused of murder. If Agnes had threatened to expose Helen's secret, perhaps to her two young children, what might Helen have done in the heat of the moment? From the way Helen talked about the incident in south Texas, clearly she was capable of acting swiftly and violently and then regarding what had happened somewhat dispassionately. The mood swings she had displayed here today might be a sign of an unstable personality.

Or they might just be the sign of a young woman with a tragedy in her past, a failed marriage, a stressful job, and two young children, Phyllis told herself. She didn't need to jump to any conclusions.

"I'm sorry," she said. She reached across the table and gripped Helen's hand, and Helen didn't pull away. "I didn't mean to upset you or your children. But I'm really not sure that Randall Simmons killed his grandmother."

"I don't know one way or the other," Helen said. "All I know is that I didn't have anything to do with it."

"Of course not." Phyllis squeezed Helen's hand and then let it go. "I'd better be going. You and Denise and Parker enjoy those cookies, now, you hear?"

Helen summoned up a smile. "All right. Thank you, Mrs. Newsom."

"Goodness, you don't have to thank me. Not after all the up-roar I caused, even if I didn't mean to."

Phyllis left, hoping that Helen would be able to think of something to tell the children that would calm their fears and make them forget that this incident had ever happened. That wasn't always quite as easy as Phyllis had made it sound when she was trying to reassure Helen. Sometimes, things stuck in the minds of children and stayed with them the rest of their lives, for both good and bad.

From the sound of it, Helen hadn't been much more than a child herself when she'd had to take that man's life in order to protect her mother. Something like that would stay with a person, too, no matter how much she tried to tamp it down in her memory, and Phyllis had to wonder what sort of effect it might have the next time that person found herself threatened some-how . . . or believed herself to be threatened, anyway. . . .

And there she went again, she realized, thinking of Helen Johannson as a suspect, when she'd already decided that she wasn't going to do that.

The thing of it was, if Randall Simmons hadn't killed his grandmother, then somebody else had to be guilty.

And it was looking more and more to Phyllis as if the killer might have come out of this very neighborhood. Even though she couldn't pin it down, she still had the feeling that someone had lied to her, somewhere along the way, and she ought to know who it was. . . .

Phyllis took cookies to several more of the neighbors during the day, and in each case she was able to draw them into talking about Agnes's murder. She didn't have to try very hard since it was still on everyone's mind. But she didn't uncover anything as shocking as the revelation from Helen Johannson's past, nor did anyone she talked to mention having seen suspicious people or activities in the neighborhood in the week or so before the murder.

Phyllis found herself wondering if Jimmy Crowe even existed. Was it possible that Randall had just made him up to try to throw suspicion on someone else?

No, she recalled, Frank had told her that Juliette Yorke had checked out Crowe through contacts of hers in Dallas. She didn't think the lawyer would lie about something that could be verified so easily. Jimmy Crowe was real, and he was probably every bit as dangerous as Randall said he was.

But that didn't prove that he had ever been here in Weatherford, did it?

Phyllis's last visit of the afternoon was to Vickie Kimbrough, who was glad for the company and eager to talk. Phyllis knew that Vickie's husband, Monte, worked long hours, and they didn't have any children, which was evidently the source of some tension between the Kimbroughs. Phyllis recalled Vickie mentioning several months earlier that she and Monte had gone for some marriage counseling at the church, which had a faith-based counseling center as one of the sidelines to its regular business of saving souls.

Vickie took the plate of cookies and said with a grin, "You know I have a sweet tooth, Phyllis. I think I'm going to eat a couple of these right now."

"Go right ahead," Phyllis told her as they sat on the sofa with the plate of cookies on the coffee table in front of them.

Vickie picked up one of Carolyn's pecan pie cookies. "I saw the picture of these in the paper this morning. They look delicious." She took a bite, chewed, and enthused, "They *are* delicious!"

"I'll tell Carolyn you said so."

"I saw them at the cookie exchange but didn't get a chance to try one before . . . well, before all that other business happened."

"Yes, that ruined the whole afternoon, didn't it?" Phyllis said, glad that Vickie had brought up the subject of the murder so that she wouldn't have to.

"Yes, but not as badly as poor Agnes's afternoon was ruined."

"No, of course not."

Vickie shivered. "I hate to think of something like that going on right across the street. I mean, her grandson hiding out there and all, and then . . . and then . . ." She shook her head. "Well, it's just hard to believe; that's all."

"I'm not sure I *do* believe it," Phyllis said.

Vickie frowned. "What do you mean? The police arrested Randall Simmons, didn't they? I know I read that in the paper, after I saw all the commotion over there the other day."

"Randall was arrested, all right, but I'm not sure I'm convinced of his guilt." That was putting it right out in the open, but Phyllis had been beating around the bush all day and was tired of it. "In the past week or two, have you seen any strangers around here, or anyone acting suspicious?"

Vickie thought about the question for a long moment before shaking her head. "I don't remember anything like that," she finally said. "I'd ask Monte, but I'm sure he wouldn't know. He's never around here enough to know what's going on in the neighborhood."

Phyllis felt a pang of sympathy for her. "He's still spending most of his time at work?"

"Yes. He was a little better about it for a while, when Dwight was counseling us, but once those sessions were over, he went right back to working all the time." Vickie gave a little laugh but didn't sound very amused. "I suppose I should be grateful that he's just working and not getting drunk or playing around with other women."

That set off a little alarm bell in the back of Phyllis's mind. She had known couples in the past where the husbands had strayed, and in almost every case, they had tried to cover up their infidelity by claiming that they were putting in long hours at their jobs. In reality, though, they had been with other women instead of at work. Phyllis wondered if Monte Kimbrough was the sort of man to do that . . . and if he was, whether Agnes Simmons might have found out about it somehow.

But she was really reaching with that idea, she told herself. Agnes had been laid up with that broken hip, and even before the injury had occurred, she hadn't gotten out all that much. She wasn't likely to have discovered that Monte Kimbrough was having an affair unless he was carrying it on right under his wife's nose, with someone here in the neighborhood.

Phyllis started to catch her breath but managed to suppress the reaction quickly enough so that Vickie didn't notice it. Maybe Monte *was* having an affair with a neighbor. Or maybe something was going on between some of the other people who lived on the street. Maybe everyone in the neighborhood was involved in some sort of floating orgy that involved them all except for Phyllis and her friends, and Agnes, of course.

She couldn't stop herself from chuckling at that crazy thought. And it *was* crazy. She was seeing murderers and motives behind every tree. Sure, the people who lived around here had their secrets. People in every neighborhood did. But that didn't mean they were killers.

Vickie looked puzzled. "What's funny, Phyllis?"

"Oh, nothing," Phyllis said. "I was just thinking about how pleased Carolyn is going to be that you liked her cookies."

"Now, which ones are yours again?"

"The lime sugar cookies that are shaped like snowflakes."

"Oh, yes, I remember. Dwight Gresham told me the other day that you'd made them and how good they were. Let me try one." Vickie picked up one of the green, snowflakelike cookies and took a bite. "Scrumptious," she said as she nodded.

Phyllis was pleased, but she decided that she wouldn't pass along that particular comment to Carolyn, who had been so pleased when the newspaper had used that very word to describe her pecan pie cookies that morning.

After chatting with Vickie for a few more minutes, Phyllis left the plate of cookies there and went back across the street. She wasn't sure whether she had done any good or not today. She'd found out something she hadn't known about Helen Johannson, but she still found it unlikely that Helen had killed Agnes Simmons. It was physically possible, of course; despite being on the small side herself, Helen was young enough and strong enough to have overpowered the frail old lady, wrapped that robe belt around her neck, and choked the life out of her. Helen wasn't so big and powerful that the struggle would have automatically left marks on Agnes's body. That was another bit of evidence pointing toward her, rather than Oscar Gunderson or Monte Kimbrough or any of the other men in the neighborhood. Still, Phyllis thought she was being unfair to Helen. Just because someone had killed once, under extenuating circumstances, didn't mean they would kill again.

She knew Sam was curious about what she might have found

out, but she didn't get a chance to talk to him alone before dinner, and she didn't want to have to explain everything to Carolyn and Eve, too. She told herself that maybe she'd have a chance to discuss the case with Sam after they had all eaten.

That didn't happen, though, because they were still at the table when someone knocked on the front door. The sound was rather urgent, as if there were a problem of some sort. Phyllis murmured, "What in the world?" as she got to her feet and started toward the front of the house. Sam, Carolyn, and Eve followed her, equally curious.

Phyllis was surprised to see Vickie Kimbrough standing there on the porch when she opened the door. Unlike a couple of hours earlier, Vickie wasn't chatty and friendly now. In the glow of the front porch light, she looked worried instead. Phyllis opened the door and asked, "Vickie, what's wrong?"

"I'm sorry to bother you, Phyllis," she said quickly. "Your son's not here, is he?"

Phyllis shook her head. "No, I haven't seen Mike all day."

"I was hoping he would be. I thought maybe he could do something about it, you know, unofficially, so the police wouldn't have to get involved. But I don't know what else to do except call them. I'm afraid somebody's going to get hurt if I don't."

"Vickie, what are you talking about?"

The woman turned and pointed directly across the street at the Horton house, where every light in the place seemed to be lit up.

"Lois and Blake," she said. "If somebody doesn't stop them, I'm afraid they're going to kill each other."

Chapter 17

"I'm not sure this is a good idea," Sam said as he approached the house, going cautiously up the front walk toward the porch of the Horton house. "Most folks don't like it when somebody interferes in their private arguments."

A crash came from inside the house, followed by another stream of loud cursing.

"Somebody has to do something," Phyllis said from right behind Sam, "and it won't help for the police to come and haul Blake off to jail."

"Might be just what the fella needs," Sam muttered.

A part of Phyllis felt the same way, but at the same time, she didn't think it would solve anything. Being arrested might just make Blake act worse when he got back home.

Carolyn, Eve, and Vickie trailed along behind them, nervously hanging back a few yards. The neighborhood was lit up more brightly than usual because of all the Christmas lights and decorations up and down both sides of the street. Over the sounds of discord coming from inside the house, Phyllis heard music playing somewhere in the night. It was somewhat discordant, too, because "Hark! The Herald Angels Sing" and "Grandma Got Run Over by a Reindeer" were competing against each other.

Signs of the season, Phyllis thought, as inside the house Lois and Blake Horton continued to scream curses at each other.

She and Sam reached the porch. Sam jabbed a finger against the doorbell button, and even though Phyllis could hear the bell ringing inside the house, Lois and Blake didn't seem to pay any attention to it. They might not even be able to hear it over all the racket they were making, Phyllis thought.

"You'd better knock," she told Sam. "Maybe that will get them to stop."

Sam raised a fist. "Maybe I ought to holler out that it's the police."

"That might get you in trouble for impersonating an officer. Better just knock as hard as you can."

He nodded and began pounding on the door. Something broke inside the house with a shattering crash, and a voice yelled, "Help! Oh, God, help!"

A shock went through Phyllis. She wouldn't have been surprised to hear Lois Horton screaming for help . . . but this terrified voice belonged to Lois's husband, Blake.

Sam glanced at Phyllis and muttered, "What the hell . . . !"

"See if the door's unlocked," she urged him. As Blake screamed again, she realized how important it was that they get in there, even if they had to break down the door.

That wasn't necessary, though, because when Sam jerked the storm door open and tried the knob on the wooden door, it turned easily. He shouldered into the room, throwing the door back as he did so. Phyllis was right behind him. Carolyn, Eve, and Vickie stood in the porch, peering anxiously into the house.

Phyllis and Sam stopped short after rushing into the Horton living room. A fireplace was on one side of the room, and Lois had a black iron poker in her hands, lifted over her head and poised to descend on Blake, who lay sprawled on the floor at her feet, blood dripping from a cut on his forehead. The shattered remains of a lamp were on the floor near him, and Phyllis supposed that the cut on Blake's head had come from a flying piece of the lamp's ceramic base.

"Lois, no!" Phyllis cried.

Lois twisted her head around to glare over her shoulder at Phyllis and Sam. "Get outta here," she warned them. Her face was contorted with rage. "He's got it comin' to him."

Phyllis didn't know if she could reason with Lois—given the state the other woman was in—but she had to try. "Maybe so, but if you kill him you'll go to jail."

"Help me," Blake sobbed from the floor. "She's gone crazy!"

That was a mistake, because it snapped Lois's attention back to him. "Shut up!" she said. "Won't even fight back, you wimpy little coward!"

That angry statement made Phyllis frown. She looked around the room and saw that a chair was overturned, there was a big gouge in the top of the coffee table, and one wall had a couple of holes in the Sheetrock. Phyllis saw some white powder clinging to the head of the poker and realized that it was Sheetrock dust from the damaged wall.

If she didn't know better, she would have said that it looked like Lois had been chasing Blake around the room, swinging that poker at him with murderous intent.

But that wasn't possible, because Blake was the abusive one. He'd given Lois a black eye. Phyllis had seen it for herself. And his mistreatment had forced Lois to seek solace in drink . . . hadn't it?

"I'll teach you to talk back to me," Lois said. She swung the poker before anyone could stop her.

Blake yelled in terror and rolled aside. The poker slammed into the floor, tearing a hole in the carpet. Blake scrambled onto his hands and knees and then lunged to his feet as Lois slashed at him again with the fireplace implement. She missed, but only by inches.

Phyllis wanted to shout at Sam and tell him to grab Lois, but if he did that, he might get hurt. Instead she made a move for Lois herself, thinking that surely the woman wouldn't hurt her.

"Get back!" Lois screeched, jabbing the poker toward Phyllis.

Sam's hand closed around Phyllis's arm and pulled her away. As Lois turned back toward Blake, Sam leaped forward and grabbed her from behind, wrapping his arms around her and pinning her arms to her sides. She cursed and struggled and tried to swing the poker up and back at Sam, but she couldn't reach him with it.

"Grab the poker!" he called to Blake. "Get it away from her!"

For a second Phyllis thought Blake was going to be too scared to act, but then he summoned up his courage with a visible effort and darted forward to wrap both hands around the poker. Lois screamed as he wrenched it out of her hands.

But then she seemed to go limp in Sam's arms. Her head lolled forward, her knees buckled, and her arms hung loosely at her sides. She groaned.

"Put her on the sofa," Blake said as he stood there with a two-handed death grip on the poker. "I think the worst of it is over now."

Lois had stopped struggling, all right, as if all the fight had suddenly gone out of her. She began to sob as Sam lowered her onto the sofa. She rolled over and buried her face in one of the cushions as she started to wail.

"What in the world?" Phyllis said.

Blake looked down at the poker in his hands and seemed surprised to see it. He took it over to the fireplace and put it in the stand, which held a second poker and some other fireplace tools. Then he turned to Phyllis and Sam and said in a shaky voice, "She must have been drinking all day. I knew as soon as I got home from work that there was going to be trouble, but I never dreamed it would be this bad. It never has been before."

Phyllis remembered how Lois had been drunk in the morning a couple of days earlier. She remembered that black eye, too, and snapped, "She's not completely to blame for this, Blake. What do you expect, the way you treat her?"

"The way I . . . ?" Blake stared at her in what appeared to be genuine confusion. "Phyllis, what are you talking about?"

"Don't try to pull that. I saw the black eye. If you looked at Lois now, I imagine you could still see it."

"Oh, my God." Blake stumbled over to an armchair and sank down into it. He put his head in his hands for a moment. When he looked up at Phyllis, grim lines were etched into his face. "I don't know if you'll believe me or not, but I swear to you I never laid a hand on Lois in anger."

Sam waved a big hand at the destruction in the room around them. "Not even durin' all this ruckus tonight?"

Blake shook his head. "I was just trying to stay out of her way and keep her from bashing my head in with that poker."

"What about that black eye Phyllis mentioned?" Sam asked with a nod toward her.

"Lois did that to herself while she was upset and carrying on a few nights ago. We have an old-fashioned four-poster bed in our bedroom, and she accidentally ran right into one of the posts."

"Are you sure that's not just a story?" Phyllis asked, still un-willing to believe him.

"We can go upstairs and I'll show you the post," Blake offered.

"That wouldn't really prove anything," Sam said.

Blake sighed. "No, I suppose not. In the absence of proof, I guess I'll have to ask you to just take my word for it." He looked intently at Phyllis. "I'd like to know, though . . . did Lois *tell* you that I'd been abusing her?"

"Well . . ." Phyllis thought back. "Now that you mention it . . . I don't think so. I saw the black eye, and I knew that Lois had been drinking. . . . I suppose I just assumed . . ."

Suddenly she saw that she could have been completely wrong in her conclusions. She still wasn't sure whether she be-lieved Blake or not, but she was starting to feel uneasy about the whole thing.

"Lois's drinking has been a problem for a long time," Blake said. "I tried to help her control it myself. I offered to get pro-fessional help, for both of us if need be. But she wouldn't have anything to do with it. She's battled depression all her life, and I guess she thought she could self-medicate with alcohol. That just made things worse."

Sam rubbed his jaw and said, "I got to admit, you sound like you're tellin' the truth."

"That's because I am," Blake replied with a trace of anger and impatience in his voice. "Lois's drinking has been getting steadily worse, but she hadn't really been violent about it until recently."

"But why . . . why would she be like that?" Phyllis asked.

Blake shook his head. "I wish I knew. If I did, maybe I could help her."

On the sofa, Lois rolled over and cried, "Quit talking about me like I'm not even in the room, damn it!" She pushed herself into a sitting position. "And don't listen to anything that weasel says! He can't be trusted. He doesn't really love me. He doesn't want to help me. I should have gone after him with a poker a long time ago! Maybe that would teach him a lesson!"

Phyllis and Sam glanced at each other. The shrill hysteria in Lois's voice pretty much confirmed what Blake had just told them.

"Blake, you have to do *something*," Phyllis said. "There are places where they deal with things like this."

He looked horrified. "I . . . I couldn't put her in a place like that. She's my *wife*."

"And I know you love her—"

"He does not!" Lois shouted. She shook her fists at them, then reached up and grabbed her hair with both hands, pulling at it and whimpering as she collapsed onto her side again.

"Let me call Mike," Phyllis said to Blake after a moment.

Blake shook his head. "I don't want the police."

"If you're gonna do something she doesn't want you to do, the law's got to be involved somehow," Sam pointed out. "You'll have to get a judge to sign off on it."

"I won't let her be arrested and put in jail," Blake said. His face was set in stubborn lines now.

"She won't be put in jail," Phyllis said. "Listen; Dwight Gresham has contacts with various treatment facilities through the counseling center at church. Let me call him and get him involved. I'm sure he's seen this sort of thing before."

Blake frowned. "Well . . . I suppose that might be all right. . . ."

Phyllis had her cell phone in her pocket. She took it out and dialed the number of the church office, knowing that it rang in the parsonage after office hours.

Thinking that it might be a good idea not to talk too much about what was going to happen in front of Lois, Phyllis stepped out onto the front porch as the phone was ringing. Carolyn, Eve, and Vickie had heard everything that was going on through the open door. Carolyn said, "I'll go in there, just in case Sam needs help."

Phyllis didn't think that was likely to happen. Lois seemed to be pretty much out of it now; the booze had finally caught up to her and knocked her flat on her back, figuratively speaking. But it wouldn't hurt for Carolyn to be there if Sam needed a hand.

A man's voice answered the call. Phyllis said, "Brother Dwight?" and when the preacher had confirmed his identity, she launched into a quick recitation of the facts.

"So we thought you might know someone at one of the treatment facilities who could help," she concluded.

"I do," Dwight said. "Is Lois calm right now?"

Phyllis looked through the window into the living room and saw that Lois was still lying on the sofa. Her eyes were closed and her mouth hung open slackly.

"Yes, she's calm," she told the preacher.

"Then I'll make a few calls first before I come over there. But I'll be there in fifteen or twenty minutes."

"I don't know if that's necessary—"

"Of course it is. Blake and Lois are part of the church, and it's my job to help them any way I can. I'll see you in a little while."

"All right. Thank you."

After Phyllis had hung up and slipped the phone back into her pocket, Vickie asked, "Is Dwight coming over here?"

Phyllis nodded. "That's right. He said he'd be here in fifteen or twenty minutes."

"Well, then, you won't need my help anymore. I'd better go." She started to turn away, then paused. "Thank you, Phyllis. When I heard all the commotion going on over here, I didn't know what to do since I was alone. Thank goodness you and your friends were able to help."

"Monte's not home tonight?"

"No. Working late again, as usual. I don't expect him home before ten or eleven o'clock."

"Two days before Christmas and he's working that late?"

Vickie shrugged and gave a bittersweet smile, as if to remind Phyllis of the discussion they'd had that afternoon.

The younger woman went next door and disappeared into her house with a wave of farewell. Phyllis and Eve went into the Horton house and found Carolyn watching Lois with an alert frown on her face while Sam and Blake sat on the other side of the room and talked together in low tones. They both looked up as she walked over to them.

"Dwight is going to make some calls and then come over here," she told Blake. "I think you can put everything into his hands. He'll know how to go about things legally."

Blake nodded. "All right. That sounds good. Thank you, Phyllis . . . and thank you for finally believing me."

Phyllis looked at Lois and shook her head sadly. "In the end, she didn't give me any choice but to believe you."

A short time later, as she held the curtain back at the picture window and watched the street, Phyllis saw a car pull up at the curb in front of the Horton house. Thinking that it was probably Dwight, she let the curtain fall closed and went to the front door, stepping out onto the porch.

Sure enough, Dwight got out of the parked car, came around the front of the vehicle, and started toward the house. At that moment, Phyllis thought she saw movement from the corner of her eye, as if someone were about to step forward from the shadows between the Horton and Kimbrough houses.

Before she could turn her attention in that direction, though, another door slammed and she looked to see that Jada Gresham had stepped out of the car. She took hold of Dwight's arm and walked with him to the porch.

"Hello, Phyllis," she said. "Isn't this just awful?"

Before Phyllis could answer what was pretty much a rhetorical question anyway, Dwight asked, "Are Lois and Blake inside?"

Phyllis nodded. "In the living room. Sam Fletcher is with them, along with my friends Carolyn and Eve."

"Thanks." He gave her a tight smile. "We'll get them through this; don't you worry."

His wife let go of him and he hurried on into the house. Jada lingered on the porch and said in a quiet voice, "Christmas is the worst time of the year, you know."

Phyllis frowned, surprised by Jada's comment. "It is?"

"I mean for things like this. Drinking, depression, mental problems of all sorts. That's why the suicide rate is higher around the holidays than any other time of year."

"Yes, I suppose so. I guess it hurts even worse to be unhappy when everybody else seems so joyous."

"Exactly," Jada said. "Dwight's made quite a study of it. He would have made an excellent psychologist or psychiatrist if he hadn't been called to the ministry. But that's very important work, too, don't you think?"

"Of course," Phyllis agreed. She knew how proud Jada was of her husband, and with good reason. No one was better liked or did more good than Dwight Gresham.

He proved that over the next hour by arranging to have

Lois placed in one of the local alcohol and drug rehabilitation centers. Phyllis thought that it was a sign of how much things had changed in the world that not only was such a facility located in Weatherford, but there was more than one of them. She remembered a time when people didn't need to go to rehab.

Actually, there were probably quite a few people who *had* needed it . . . but those treatments weren't available back then. So those unfortunates had drunk themselves to death instead, or died as hopeless drug addicts. Phyllis was a firm believer in the idea that the so-called good old days really had been better in a lot of ways . . . but she had to admit that progress had been made in some areas, too.

When the ambulance carrying Lois pulled out of the driveway and Blake followed it in his car, Phyllis stood for a moment on the front porch of the Horton house with Sam, Carolyn, Eve, Dwight, and Jada. Vickie Kimbrough hadn't returned, but Phyllis thought she might have watched the ambulance leave from inside her house. Monte's car still wasn't in the driveway. He had missed all the excitement.

Phyllis almost wished that she had.

"I guess we'd better be going," Dwight said. "I'll stay in touch with the doctors at the treatment facility and go see Lois when she's up to having visitors."

Jada smiled and nodded. "Good night, everyone."

When the preacher and his wife were gone, Carolyn said, "I hope you know that supper will be ruined by now."

"We'll throw it out," Phyllis said. "There's a pizza in the freezer that we can heat up."

"Frozen, store-bought pizza," Carolyn said. "Nothing says Christmas quite like that."

Phyllis suppressed the urge to snap at her, knowing that it

wouldn't do any good. Carolyn really wasn't as unsympathetic as she sometimes sounded. She just didn't suffer fools gladly.

Lois Horton certainly fit into that category. Phyllis happened to be of the opinion that both alcoholism and depression should be considered diseases, but at the same time, plenty of people had been known to conquer those two demons. A person couldn't give up and descend into near madness, the way Lois had done. You had to at least put up a fight.

But maybe she was being too judgmental, she told herself, never having had to deal with either of those plagues. She understood, though, why Carolyn lacked a great deal of patience with Lois. Phyllis felt sort of the same way herself.

Carolyn and Eve walked ahead as the four of them started back across the street. Phyllis found herself lingering behind, and Sam adjusted his pace to hers, although that couldn't have been easy with his long legs. Phyllis turned her head and glanced at the shadowy area between the Horton house and the Kimbrough house. The glow from the neighborhood Christmas lights made it brighter than it would have been otherwise, but the shadows under the trees were still thick enough to hide something—or someone.

"Problem?" Sam asked.

Phyllis shook her head. "No, I suppose not. I was just thinking that a lot goes on in a neighborhood that you never see unless you're looking for it."

"I'd say you're right about that. I've lived across the street from those folks for six months now, and I didn't have any idea the lady was a drunk—and a violent one, at that."

The way Lois had gone after Blake with that fireplace poker was another thing weighing on Phyllis's mind. Lois had been at the cookie exchange and she hadn't seemed to be drunk, but she'd probably had plenty of experience at covering up her condition. She could have slipped out, gone next door to Agnes's house . . . Anyone who would try to crush her own husband's skull with a poker was capable of choking an old woman to death, wasn't she?

But why? Phyllis asked herself. What motive could Lois have possibly had for murdering Agnes Simmons? Maybe Agnes had found out about Lois's drinking . . . but no one would kill somebody over that, would they?

Who knew what Lois was capable of when she was under the influence? Phyllis never would have dreamed that she would chase Blake around the room and try to kill *him*, yet obviously she had done just that.

Then there was the feeling Phyllis had about someone lurking between the houses, starting forward and then pulling back and disappearing. She didn't know who that could have been . . . or, indeed, if anyone had actually been there. As nervous as she was these days, maybe she was seeing suspicious characters everywhere she looked—a potential murderer behind every door in the neighborhood.

That was no way to be. She shook off the feeling and linked her arm with Sam's. "It was a terrible thing," she said, "but it's over. Now it'll be up to Blake to take care of his wife."

"I reckon he'll be up to it," Sam said. "When we were talkin', I got the feelin' that he really loves her. Folks will do 'most anything for somebody they love."

"That's true," Phyllis said, and a thought that she didn't particularly want leaped unbidden into her mind.

Some people will even kill for love.

Chapter 18

Christmas Eve morning dawned cloudy and considerably colder than it had been for the past few days. Phyllis had heard something on the news the night before about another cold front coming through, but she hadn't really paid that much attention to the forecast.

Her thoughts had been too full of everything that had happened earlier in the day, from her discovery of Helen Johannson's tragic and violent past, to the disturbing truth about Lois Horton being revealed, to the moment of possible paranoia on her part when she'd thought that she saw some mysterious figure lurking in the shadows. She'd been too concerned with all of that to worry too much about what the weather was going to be.

As the women sat at the table having breakfast, Sam ambled into the kitchen, looked out the window over the sink and studied the sky for a moment, and then sang in a deep voice, "Snoooooooow," just like Bing Crosby in *White Christmas*.

"It is *not* snowing," Carolyn said.

Sam grinned at her. "No, but it looks like it might. Could be we're gonna have a white Christmas after all."

"I wouldn't count on it," Phyllis told him. "They're rare around here."

"I know that. I've lived in this area all my life, too. But it happens every now and then, and to me that sky looks like it's got some snow in it."

Carolyn snorted. "I'll believe it when I see it."

"I hope it does snow," Eve said. "There's nothing much more romantic than a nice soft snowfall on Christmas Eve."

"You *would* think of it like that," Carolyn told her.

"Somebody has to, dear. Otherwise there wouldn't be any romance left in the world at all."

"Yes, well, if that were true, the world might be a better place."

Eve stared at her, aghast at the very idea. "Don't even *say* such a thing," she admonished Carolyn.

"Why not? Think about how much harm has been done in the world because of foolish romantic notions. What about the Trojan War? Even before that, and certainly ever since then, people have been fighting because of . . . of hormones! Either that or some misguided sense of honor that's a close cousin to romance. And don't get me started on all the murders that have been committed because of lust or jealousy or unrequited love. No, I think the world would be a much saner, safer place if romance would just go away." She glared around defiantly at the other three and added, "Anyway, at our age it's all a moot point, isn't it?"

For a moment there was silence in the kitchen as none of the others rose to that challenge. Finally, Eve said, "I'm not going to argue with you, dear . . . but you're wrong."

With that she rose and left the room.

Carolyn frowned and said, "I didn't mean to make her mad. I've got a right to my opinion, don't I?"

"Of course you do," Phyllis said. "But that doesn't mean the rest of us have to agree with it."

"You don't agree with me? After all the murders you've seen?"

Sam had heaped pancakes and bacon on a plate, and now as he poured himself a cup of coffee he said, "Seems to me we're due for a change o' subject here. I don't know what sort of traditions you ladies have here, since this is my first Christmas in the house, but on Christmas Eve I've always liked to drive around and look at all the lights and decorations. Didn't do it last year, but I think maybe I'd like to start again."

Phyllis thought she knew why Sam had discontinued his holiday tradition. The previous Christmas had been only a few months after his wife had passed away, and obviously he hadn't felt up to doing anything festive, especially something that he had been in the habit of doing with her.

"That sounds lovely," Phyllis said. "Usually we just have a quiet evening at home on Christmas Eve, but it might be nice to go out and see all the lights. There seem to be a lot of them this year."

"That does sound nice," Carolyn agreed in a grudging tone. "Maybe Eve will be over her snit by then and want to come along, too."

"I'm sure she would if you asked her to," Phyllis said.

"Well . . . maybe later. After she's had a chance to cool off."

Phyllis let it go at that. Carolyn could think whatever she wanted to, but Phyllis refused to believe that the world would be better off without romance. She and Kenny had had their ups and downs, of course, the same as all couples did, but over-all they'd had a long, happy marriage that Phyllis wouldn't have traded for anything in the world. And even though Kenny had been gone for several years, she still missed him and occasionally still caught herself thinking that she was going to ask him about something or tell him some funny thing that had happened to her during the day. At first, moments like that had caused her pangs of grief and loss, but by now the pain had dulled and she realized all it meant was that she would carry his memory . . . would carry *him* . . . with her forever.

And that was all right. That was the way it should be.

At the same time, just because she would always love Kenny didn't mean that there was no room in her heart for anyone else. The driving passion of youth might be gone, but there were even deeper longings that the young knew nothing about. She thought about a late-night moment she had shared with Sam Fletcher in this very kitchen a couple of months earlier, a simple moment when he had rested his hand on hers as they stood side by side at the counter. That touch, brief though it had been, had brought smiles to both of their faces, and a few times since then, when they were alone, his hand had squeezed her shoulder for a second or she had reached over and brushed her fingertips against his arm as they passed. Whatever was between them had grown slowly, and it might never progress any further than where it was right now . . . but it might, she realized, and for the first time she was willing to admit that to herself. She thought about how nice it would be to ride around with Sam, looking at Christmas lights, and a tiny shiver went through her, announcing its presence for the first time in . . . in . . . well, in she couldn't remember when!

It felt good, too.

"And when we get back," Carolyn was saying as Phyllis forced her thoughts to return to the kitchen, "we'll watch our old tape of *It's a Wonderful Life*, as usual."

"Sounds mighty fine to me," Sam agreed.

"Yes," Phyllis said. "It certainly does."

She hoped that nothing happened before tonight to ruin those plans.

Around the middle of the morning, the doorbell rang, and when Phyllis opened the door she found Blake Horton standing on the porch, his breath fogging in the cold air.

Phyllis opened the door and said, "Come in, Blake. I was wondering how you were doing this morning."

Blake smiled a little as he came into the house and Phyllis closed the door. "You mean you were wondering how Lois is doing."

"Well, that, too," Phyllis said. "But I really was wondering about you, as well."

"I'm fine—or as fine as I can get, anyway, under the circumstances. I thought you'd like to know that I saw Lois a little while ago, and she's doing better."

"Oh, I'm so glad to hear that. How long will she have to stay . . . where she is?"

"It's all right to call it rehab. That makes it sound like she might have broken a hip or something." Blake's smile took on a pained look. "She begged me to get her out of there and take her home. She said she couldn't spend Christmas locked up like that. But the doctors all agree that she still has a long way to go. She'll probably be there until after New Year's, at least."

"I'm so sorry," Phyllis told him, and meant it.

"So am I, but I keep telling myself it's for the best. If I can get her back, healthy and happy, that's the best Christmas present I could ever hope for, even if it's after Christmas by the time I get it."

"We'll be praying for Lois . . . for both of you."

Blake took a deep breath. "That's another reason I came over here, to ask if you'd pass along my appreciation to Dwight Gresham. You know that Lois and I have never been, ah, very faithful about going to church. But Dwight was right there to help us, anyway, when we needed him." Blake reached inside his coat and took out an envelope. "Could you give this to him? It's a check."

Phyllis hesitated. "I'm sure Dwight doesn't expect any sort of payment. . . ."

"It's an offering. For the church. I figured he could put the money to good use."

"Oh. Oh, of course." Phyllis took the envelope. "I'll see that he gets it."

Blake smiled and nodded. "Thanks. I'd drop it off there myself, but I'm going to stay with my brother and his family up in Gainesville until after the holiday. The doctors said I couldn't see Lois again until sometime next week."

"That's going to be hard for both of you."

"Yeah, but I keep telling myself it'll all be worth it."

"I'm sure it will," Phyllis said.

Blake said his good-byes and left. Phyllis laid the envelope with the check in it on the hall table, thinking that she probably wouldn't get to the church to give it to Dwight until sometime early the next week. That would be soon enough, she thought.

Less than an hour later, the doorbell rang again. They were getting plenty of visitors today, Phyllis told herself as she went to answer it. This time the man standing on the porch when she opened the door turned out to be the burly Frank Simmons.

"Just wanted you to know that we're all leaving, Mrs. Newsom," Frank said after Phyllis had invited him in and taken him into the living room. "Of course, you probably would have figured that out when you saw that all the cars were gone from next door."

"You're not staying until after Christmas?"

Frank's smile was sad. "Well . . . there's not really any reason to, is there?"

"Oh, I'm sorry, Frank. I didn't think—"

He lifted a hand. "No, no, that's all right. Don't worry about it, please. Sometimes it's hard for me to remember that she's gone, too. But Ted and Billie and I all talked about it, and we decided that our families would rather spend Christmas at home instead of staying here, so we'll be heading out after a while."

"How's Randall?"

Frank shrugged. "All right, I suppose. As all right as he can be, locked up in jail and charged with murder. But except for a sore throat, he's pretty much recovered from . . . what he tried to do. I talked to both Detective Largo and Ms. Yorke this morning, and they said there was no reason for me or the rest of the family to stay around right now. The grand jury won't meet until after the New Year. That's the next step, the grand jury hearing to see if Randall will be indicted for the murder."

"And he has to stay in jail until then?"

"Yeah, since we couldn't raise the bail bond for him. I've put my store up for sale, and if I can sell it, I . . . I hope to get enough to bail him out and to pay his legal bills." Frank shook his head. "But I don't know. It's hard to get much money for a failing business."

Phyllis said, "I don't want to pry into things that are none of my business, but . . . your mother's estate . . . ?"

Frank shook his head again. "Won't be settled until sometime in January, if not longer than that. And she didn't leave much except the house, which means it'll have to be sold in order to divide up the proceeds between the three of us, and there's no telling how long that'll take or how much it'll sell for."

Phyllis thought the Simmons house ought to be worth quite a bit. It was old, but it was large and solidly built and in a good state of repair, on a decent-sized lot with quite a few big old trees, close to downtown. She thought it might bring a couple of hundred thousand dollars, at least.

But as Frank had pointed out, that money would be slow in coming, and he'd indicated that when it did it would be split into three equal shares among him and his brother and sister. By then Frank's business in Dallas might have gone under entirely, if he hadn't been able to sell it. Randall would probably still be awaiting trial, which meant his legal expenses would be ongoing. Phyllis had no idea how much Juliette Yorke charged, but the woman was a lawyer. Her services wouldn't come cheap.

"Well, I hope it all works out for you," Phyllis said. "I'm sorry for everything that happened, Frank."

He gave a rueful shake of his head. "None of it was your fault. If Randall just had any sense—" He broke off and waved a hand in dismissal. "Ah, it's way too late to be wishing that now. If the boy had had any sense, he wouldn't have gotten in so much trouble to start with. Now he's gonna be convicted of murder, and he'll be lucky if he doesn't get the death penalty. I mean, his own *grandmother*, for God's sake!"

"But he didn't do it," Phyllis said.

"I don't think he did, either, but without any proof . . ." Frank shrugged helplessly.

Even though Phyllis didn't like to think about doing it, she brought up what Frank had suggested earlier. "If I told the police I was sure it wasn't Randall who hit me—"

"It wouldn't do any good now," Frank broke in. "They've got their minds made up. They'd never put you on the witness stand."

"The defense could call me as a witness."

"And the district attorney would break you down on cross-examination and make you admit that you never really saw who hit you, because that's the truth. You're just not the type of person who can lie under oath. I realize that now." He summoned up another faint smile. "But don't think I don't appreciate the offer, because I do." He put out his hand. "Well, so long."

"Good-bye, Frank," Phyllis said as she shook his hand.

As he started down the porch steps, she called after him, "We'll keep an eye on the house for you, since it'll be sitting there empty."

He paused long enough to turn and lift a hand in farewell. "Thanks."

Phyllis closed the door and shook her head. She hated to see Frank and the others go. In her mind, at least, whether she wanted to or not, she still considered them suspects in Agnes's murder. The members of the Simmons family had alibis, but not ironclad ones. And from everything Phyllis had learned about the family history, some of them had motives, too. Old grudges that had festered for years could lead to unexpected outbreaks of violence. So could the desperate need for money— and the anger at being turned down for help.

But Frank had been right about one thing—the police probably weren't looking for any other suspects now. They thought they had their man in Randall Simmons, and they would be concentrating on building a case against him, rather than seeking out other possible killers.

It wouldn't be too difficult to build that case, given Randall's criminal background and the fight he had put up when he was taken into custody. Throw in the jailhouse suicide attempt, and barring a rock-solid alibi or eyewitness testimony, a conviction was almost a certainty. The fact that Jimmy Crowe ought to be considered a suspect, along with some of the other people in the neighborhood, wouldn't even come into play.

That was unless Phyllis revealed the secrets she had uncovered and shared her suspicions with the authorities, most notably Detective Isabel Largo.

And who, exactly, did she have for suspects? Well, there was a widower who enjoyed dressing in women's clothing; a young single mother who had acted to defend her own mother; a woman who battled the twin demons of alcoholism and depression; and possibly her husband. Then there were the other members of the murdered woman's family, who had allegedly been twenty-five miles away in Fort Worth at the time of Agnes Simmons's death.

Detective Largo would probably be too polite to laugh in her face, Phyllis thought . . . but the detective would feel like doing just that, more than likely.

She could talk to Mike, though. If she laid out the whole story for him, especially the part about Jimmy Crowe, he might be able to convince Detective Largo to take those things seriously.

Nothing was going to happen about any of it until after Christmas. The fact that December twenty-fifth fell on a Saturday this year meant that everything would come to a halt for the weekend. Even today, on Christmas Eve, a lot of offices and other businesses were closed so that their employees could have a long holiday weekend. The state and federal governments were shut down, so that meant the banks were, too. No mail would be delivered today.

The stores were still open, although most of them would

close early, probably at six o'clock. Between now and then they would do a booming business, especially Wal-Mart, as last-minute shoppers descended on the place in search of gifts and food they had forgotten to buy. Phyllis had planned carefully. She had everything she needed for Christmas dinner the next day. There was no way she was joining that last-minute mob unless an actual emergency required it.

She was sitting in the living room, looking through a magazine, when Carolyn came through the hall and stopped beside the table. "What's this?" Carolyn asked as she picked up the envelope Blake Horton had left with Phyllis.

"It's a check Blake wants to give to the church, in appreciation for Dwight's help with Lois last night," Phyllis explained. "He's going out of town, so he dropped it off and asked if I'd see to it that it gets to Dwight. I told him I would, but I didn't see any point in making a special trip today, since the banks are closed anyway."

"Yes, the government will seize any excuse for a long weekend, won't it?" Carolyn said as she turned the envelope over in her hands.

"Well, Christmas isn't really an excuse. It's a good reason, as far as I'm concerned."

"I suppose so."

"Anyway, I thought I'd just take it to church with me Sunday and put in the collection plate. I don't have any idea how much the check is for, of course, but I thought that would be all right. It has Blake's name on it, so they'll know who it came from."

"I'll tell you how much it's for," Carolyn said as she switched on the overhead light in the hall. Then she held up the envelope so the glare shone through it, and squinted at it as she tried to read the numbers on the check it contained.

Phyllis started to tell her not to be so nosy, but then Carolyn lowered the envelope abruptly and turned toward her.

"You really don't know how much this check is for?"

"I don't have any idea," Phyllis said again. She guessed, "Fifty dollars? A hundred?"

"Try five thousand," Carolyn said.

Chapter 19

Phyllis was hardly aware that she set the magazine aside as she stood up and stared at Carolyn. "Five thousand dollars?" she said in disbelief.

Carolyn gestured toward the light. "Come and see for yourself."

Phyllis had never considered herself a snoop—despite the fact that she had solved several murders in the past six months—but she went over to Carolyn and took the envelope from her, anyway. Surely Carolyn had to be making a mistake about the amount on the check. She had just looked at it wrong; that's all. It was probably for fifty dollars. Phyllis held the envelope up to the light and squinted just as her friend had a moment earlier.

There was the five . . . and she made out three zeros after it . . . then a dot and two more zeros. . . .

"Oh, my Lord," Phyllis said. "It *is* five thousand dollars."

"Just like I told you," Carolyn said.

Phyllis lowered the envelope, put it back on the table, and stepped back quickly, almost like it was some sort of wild animal. "Blake didn't tell me how much it was. If he had, I would have asked him to take it on over to the church right then and there. I don't want the responsibility for that much money."

"Where did Blake get that much?" Carolyn asked. "He's an accountant, isn't he? Do you think he could have embezzled it from some of his clients? Maybe he's laundering money through the church!"

"Stop that," Phyllis said. "Blake's not an embezzler or a money launderer."

Carolyn crossed her arms over her chest. "Then where *did* the money come from?"

"I assume he makes a good living at his job. They both drive fairly new cars. And five thousand's not really *that* much, this day and age. It just seems like a lot to us because we remember when that was a year's salary."

"You could buy two good cars for that amount," Carolyn said. "Now you can't even get a very good used one for five thousand."

From the other end of the hallway, Sam asked, "What's this about five grand?"

Phyllis and Carolyn both started a little and looked around hurriedly at him. As he ambled toward them, he smiled and went on, "You ladies look a mite guilty about something. What're you up to, if you don't mind my askin'?"

"Nothing." Phyllis pointed to the envelope on the table, still not really wanting to touch it. "Blake Horton stopped by and left this check. He wanted me to give it to Dwight."

"I didn't think preachers took pay like that."

"It's an offering for the church."

"Five thousand dollars," Carolyn said.

Sam's bushy eyebrows rose slightly. "That's a lot o' money. I'm sure the church can put it to good use."

Phyllis nodded. "That's what Blake said. I just wish he hadn't entrusted it to me."

"Oh, I think you're trustworthy enough," Sam told her. "It's not like you're going to run off to Las Vegas with it or something."

Carolyn laughed. "The very idea! Phyllis in Las Vegas?" She shook her head. "No, I can't see that."

Phyllis wasn't quite sure whether to take that as a compliment or an insult. It wasn't like she didn't have a wild side. . . . Well, actually, she *didn't*, she supposed. . . . She said, "I just don't want the responsibility for that much money that belongs to somebody else." She reached a decision. "I'm going to take it over to the church now, instead of waiting until Sunday."

"Will the office be open today?" Carolyn asked.

"I don't know, but even if it's not, the parsonage is right next door." Phyllis looked at Sam. "Would you mind coming with me?"

"I was about to suggest the same thing," he said. "Lemme get my coat."

"I'll need mine, too."

"I'll guard the money," Carolyn offered. She planted herself in front of the table, arms crossed and a fierce glare on her face.

Phyllis didn't think masked bandits were liable to break down the front door and try to steal the check, but she had to admit that she would feel better if someone was keeping an eye on it while she and Sam got ready to go. She told Carolyn, "Thank you. We'll be right back."

Sam was ready by the time Phyllis had her coat on and came back downstairs. In jeans, boots, and a brown leather jacket, he looked quite rugged and masculine, she thought. He picked up the envelope from the table and asked her, "My pickup or your car?"

"Let's take your pickup," Phyllis said. "If you don't mind."

"Wouldn't have suggested it if I did." He handed her the envelope.

"Be careful," Carolyn cautioned. "There's a lot of crime this time of year."

"I don't think desperadoes will be roaming the streets between here and the church," Phyllis said. "It's only a few blocks. We could walk it if the weather wasn't so cold."

"Just be careful—that's all I'm saying."

Phyllis nodded and said, "We'll be back in a little while." This errand shouldn't take very long. She hoped not, because she planned to make the stuffed zucchini this afternoon.

Sam's pickup was at the curb. He unlocked it and they climbed in, with him holding the door for her and then closing it when she was in. Such politeness wasn't put on with Sam; it was just his nature.

When he turned on the engine, country music blared from the speakers. "Sorry," he muttered as he pushed the button that turned off the radio. "I like to crank it up when I'm by myself. I know you don't care much for that goat-ropin' music."

"I just never understood the appeal of all that honky-tonking, getting drunk, and cheating on your spouse."

"I never did any of that myself. I guess people like to listen to that broken-heart stuff so they can say, there but for the grace o' God, go I. Their own lives don't seem so bad when they hear about how bad other folks have it. That's why some people like the blues, too."

"I suppose so," Phyllis said. "I like music that makes me feel better. Why don't you turn the radio back on and see if you can find some Christmas music?"

Sam grinned. "I bet I can do that. Some of the stations around here went all Christmas, all the time, before Thanksgivin'."

The velvety notes of Mel Tormé singing "The Christmas Song" filled the pickup's cab as Sam drove toward the church. Since it was so close by, he reached it before the song was over. Phyllis felt a little disappointed. She liked Tormé's version—not quite as much as Nat King Cole's, but it was still very good.

The church offices were in a converted house next to the sanctuary. The parsonage was on the opposite side of the church. Sam parked in front of the office building, and he and Phyllis got out of the truck and went up the walk. No other vehicles were parked there. Phyllis didn't see any lights burning inside.

"Looks like they may be closed up," Sam observed.

"I was just thinking the same thing. But we can try here first, anyway."

The front door was locked when Sam tried it, and nobody responded to his knock. He turned to Phyllis and said, "Guess we'll try the parsonage."

Phyllis had already seen that there was an SUV parked in the driveway of the house where Dwight and Jada Gresham lived, so she figured someone was home. If Dwight wasn't there, she would give the check to Jada. All Phyllis cared about was that she didn't have to hang on to it until Sunday.

They walked across the lawn in front of the church and across the parsonage driveway, then followed the walk to the front door, which had a large wreath hung on it. That was the only Christmas decoration on the house, although a large manger scene was set up on the church's front lawn.

Sam rang the doorbell, and a moment later Dwight Gresham appeared, carrying a book in one hand with a finger stuck in it to mark his place. He looked surprised to see Phyllis and Sam, but he smiled at them as he said, "Hello, you two. What are you doing out on Christmas Eve?"

Phyllis held up the envelope. "We brought you something."

"A Christmas present? Really, you didn't have to—"

"It's not from us," Phyllis said. "And it's really not a Christmas present. It's from Blake Horton. An offering for the church."

Dwight frowned. "From Blake . . . ? Goodness, where are my manners? I'm keeping you folks standing out in the cold. Come in; come in." He stepped back from the doorway and used the book to motion them inside the house.

Phyllis couldn't help but glance at the volume in Dwight's hand as she and Sam stepped inside. She expected it to be a book of sermons or some other religious tome, but instead she saw it was a thriller by a popular author. Dwight saw where she was looking and chuckled as he closed the door. "Pure entertainment," he said. "Can't study the scriptures all the time, you know."

"No, of course not," Phyllis said, vaguely embarrassed that he had caught her checking out his reading material.

"Come on into the den," Dwight said as he led them down the hall. "I want to hear about this offering from Blake."

The house was spotless as usual and smelled of pine. Phyllis glanced into the living room as they passed it and saw that it looked almost like a museum display. There was no indication that anyone actually *lived* there.

The den was a little more cluttered and homey, but not much. As Dwight set his book down on a table beside a leather-covered recliner, Jada called from the kitchen, "Who was at the door, Dwight?"

"Phyllis Newsom and Sam Fletcher, dear," he replied. "They're here in the den with me."

"Oh." Jada came into the room, wiping her hands on her apron as she did so. She smiled a greeting to Phyllis and Sam and asked, "Can I get you anything? I have eggnog . . . nonalco-holic, of course."

Phyllis shook her head. "No, thanks. We won't be here but a minute. I hate to intrude on Christmas Eve, but I wanted to give this to Dwight."

She handed him the envelope Blake Horton had left at her house.

As Dwight opened it, Phyllis went on, "Blake's going out of town, and he wanted to leave this to thank you for everything you did to help with Lois."

"He didn't have to do that," Jada said as she came forward to her husband's side. "Dwight's job is to help people."

"Well, Blake thought this could do some good for the church."

Dwight let out a low whistle of surprise as he slipped the check from the envelope and looked at the amount. "I'll say it can," he said.

Jada leaned closer. "Does that say five thousand dollars?"

"It does." Dwight looked up at Phyllis. "Did you know how much this was for?"

She hesitated, then nodded and said, "Yes, that's why I brought it right over. I didn't want to have that much money lying around over Christmas."

Dwight didn't ask whether Blake had told her the amount of the check, and Phyllis didn't explain that she had learned how much it was through snooping, first Carolyn's and then her own. He said, "Well, it's not like it's cash. The check is made out to the church. Anyone who stole it would have a devil of a time cashing it . . . so to speak."

"Yes, I know, but I still didn't want anything to happen to it."

"Of course not." Dwight tucked the check back into the envelope. "Thank you, Phyllis. It was very thoughtful of you to bring this over." He tapped the envelope against his left hand. "You know, I really ought to take this over to the office and lock it up in the safe. After you've gone to this much trouble to get it to me, I don't want anything to happen to it, either."

"That sounds like a good idea, dear," Jada told him. "It can go into the bank with the regular deposit first thing Monday morning."

Dwight nodded. "That's what I'm going to do."

Phyllis said, "We'll be running along, then."

"Before you go," Jada said, "did Blake tell you how poor Lois was doing?"

"As well as can be expected, I think. She'll be in rehab for a while, and Blake's not supposed to see her again right away, so he was going to spend Christmas with some of his relatives up in Gainesville."

"That'll be good for him," Dwight said with a nod. "He can't really do anything else to help her right away, so it's probably best for him to get some distance."

"It must have been terrible for him," Jada said, "trying to cope with such erratic behavior. Still, when you're married to someone, you have to stand by them no matter what. The vows *do* say for better or for worse."

Sam said, "I don't recall 'em mentionin' anything about fire-place pokers, though."

Jada smiled. "Well . . . within reason, of course. Some things you can't forgive."

Dwight went with Phyllis and Sam into the front hallway, where he paused to open a closet door and take out a jacket. "It's been so warm this week, I haven't needed a coat since Monday," he said as he shrugged into it.

Jada had followed them into the hall. She plucked something off the shoulder of Dwight's jacket. "What in the world have you been getting into?" she asked with a laugh.

He glanced down at the bit of pink fuzz in her hand and shrugged. "Beats me. Probably came off some Christmas decoration somewhere. They're all over this year. People are really in the holiday spirit."

"Well, I'll throw this away, and you should be more careful in the future."

That was just like Jada, Phyllis thought, not wanting even a harmless bit of fuzz to fall on her floor.

"Be right back," Dwight said to his wife. He went out with Phyllis and Sam and walked with them toward the church offices. They stopped at Sam's pickup while Dwight went on to the building. "See you Sunday morning," he called over his shoulder.

"We'll be there," Phyllis said.

"Have a merry Christmas!"

"You, too," Sam called in return.

They drove off while Dwight was unlocking the front door of the office building. "Nice fella," Sam commented.

"He certainly is. And I'm glad that *he's* got to worry about taking care of that check now, not me."

"Said he was gonna put it in a safe, didn't he?"

"That's right. There's a little safe in the main office where the offerings are kept after they're collected, along with some of the church's important papers. In case of fire, you know. The property deeds and everything really important are in a safety deposit box at the bank."

"Sounds like you know a lot about it."

"I worked part-time in the office for a while after I retired from teaching," Phyllis said. "Then I decided that if I was going to be retired, I was going to be really retired. Somehow, though, I manage to stay almost as busy as I ever was."

"Solvin' murders, here, lately."

Phyllis sighed. "Not this one, I'm afraid." A thought occurred to her. She had discovered some things she hadn't had a chance to tell Sam about, so she said, "Why don't you drive around for a while, if you don't mind. I need to talk to you without Carolyn and Eve around."

"Sounds serious," Sam said with a slight frown. He turned at the next corner and drove west along a residential street, toward the old Chandor Gardens. "Shoot."

For the next few minutes, as Christmas music played softly from the pickup's radio, Phyllis filled him in on what she had discovered about some of the neighbors and laid out her suspicions, none of which were really strong enough to deserve the name. Sam listened quietly and attentively, and Phyllis concluded by saying, "I don't really know what to make of any of it. Randall Simmons is still the one most likely to have killed Agnes, but all my instincts tell me that he's innocent. At the same time, nothing points strongly enough to anyone else for me to take what I've found out to Mike or Detective Largo."

Sam nodded and said, "Oscar Gunderson, huh? Who'd'a thunk it?"

"You can't say anything about Oscar or Helen. I have to respect their privacy. I only told you because . . ."

Her voice trailed off as she realized that she confided in Sam for the same reason she had always confided in Kenny. She felt an easy trust in him, the sort of trust you only felt for someone with whom you were very close. Like a spouse or . . .

"Yeah," Sam said, his voice a little rough. "I know what you mean. Don't worry, I won't say anything to anybody about those folks. It'll be like you never told me."

"I appreciate that. But since you *do* know, what do you think? Could any of those people have killed Agnes?"

"My impulse is to say no," Sam replied. "But you remember that business last summer. I never would have guessed who committed those murders."

"No," Phyllis said. "I never would have, either."

"I wouldn't pretend to be an expert on murder, but it seems to me that most of 'em are committed by people you'd expect to be killers. By that I mean criminals, like armed robbers, and folks who are on drugs, or people who go out and get drunk and get into fights. I've heard cops say that the simplest answer, the one you'd expect to be true, is nearly always the right one."

Phyllis nodded. "Yes, I've heard Mike say that."

"But that doesn't account for *all* the murders in the world," Sam went on. "There's a small percentage where it's more complicated than that, where you've got things goin' on under the surface. That's where your secrets come in, and your folks who lash out and kill when they get pushed into a tight enough corner. Thing of it is, they're the ones who decide when things get bad enough to do something like that. The breakin' point for them might be a whole lot different than it would be for somebody else, so you can't really predict what's gonna happen."

"So what you're saying is . . . you don't know."

"That's what I'm sayin'," Sam agreed. "I just don't know."

"Neither do I," Phyllis said with a sigh. "But what I do know is that I need to get started on some of the things for dinner tomorrow, so I guess we'd better get back to the house."

"No more talk about murder?"

"That can wait," Phyllis said. "It's Christmas Eve."

Chapter 20

Phyllis stayed busy enough the rest of the afternoon that she didn't really think about Agnes Simmons's murder and all the questions that surrounded it.

Carolyn was in the kitchen, working on the corn bread for the wild rice and cranberry stuffing. Phyllis asked her, "Would I be in your way if I started the stuffed zucchini?"

Carolyn shook her head and waved her forward. "I'm almost finished here. Is there something I can do to help?" she asked as she poured the batter into two eight-inch-square pans. "I only need one of these pans for the stuffing since it also has wild rice, but I thought we could use one this evening with dinner. The recipe I used is a sweet corn bread, which should work perfectly for the stuffing. Since it has cranberries, I thought it should be a little sweet."

Carolyn popped the two pans into the oven and wiped her hands on her apron. When they weren't competing, they worked efficiently together in the kitchen. Phyllis took the zucchini and eggplant out of the refrigerator. The tomatoes and a pretty red bell pepper were sitting on the counter. She washed all of the vegetables, and Carolyn patted them dry. Phyllis trimmed the ends of the zucchini with a knife and sliced them in half lengthwise.

While Phyllis was working on the zucchini, Carolyn peeled and chopped an onion. She went ahead and chopped the whole onion, putting half into a freezer bag to be used in stews later. She also added a small bag of chopped bell pepper to the freezer after she had measured out the half cup that Phyllis needed for the recipe.

While Carolyn was working on the filling, Phyllis scooped out the centers of the zucchinis using a long, narrow spoon. She removed the seeds and pulp, leaving plenty of the flesh to support the stuffing. Every so often, she had to pick up the knife to loosen some of the pulp so she could scoop it out.

As Phyllis was finishing with the zucchini, Carolyn banged the flat side of her knife against the garlic, which made it peel easily, then put it into a press and squeezed out the minced garlic. Phyllis turned on the burner to a medium-high heat and put a sauté pan over the flame. She added olive oil to the pan, and Carolyn put the onion, pepper, and garlic mix in and kept it stirred as Phyllis peeled and chopped the eggplant. When the onion mixture became tender, she added the chopped eggplant to the pan. Carolyn added the salt and pepper.

While Carolyn gently stirred the eggplant-and-onion mixture so it would heat evenly, Phyllis chopped the tomatoes and the fresh parsley and basil. She added them to the pan, and Carolyn stirred the mixture together. It smelled heavenly.

This is where Phyllis decided to change the recipe. She quickly grated mozzarella and Parmesan and cut some bread slices into cubes. When the tomatoes and herbs had finished cooking and Carolyn took the pan off the burner, she added in the bread and cheese, and Carolyn blended it before the cheese had time to melt completely.

While the eggplant mixture cooled, they cleaned up the kitchen.

Phyllis looked through the cabinet and found the baking pan she wanted. With two cooks, sometimes the pans moved around a bit, so they weren't always in the first place you looked.

After the stuffing was cooled enough to handle, they each took a spoon and started filling the hollowed-out zucchini. It took only a few minutes to fill the twelve halves. As she was filling the last zucchini, Phyllis wondered how it would taste with corn bread instead of whole wheat bread. She was going to have to try that some day.

All the zucchini were filled and looked nice, so Phyllis brushed the tops with a light coating of olive oil. She covered the pan with plastic wrap and put it in the refrigerator, ready to pop into the oven tomorrow. While she was doing that, the timer went off for Carolyn's corn bread. She took the pans out of the oven. The corn bread in each pan was nice and golden brown. She set them on the wire racks to cool. It was pleasant, working together quietly like this, not having to think about anything but cooking.

But something was still lurking far in the back of Phyllis's mind, some sense telling her that she was right to have doubts about Randall's guilt. Somewhere, sometime during the past week, she had seen something . . . or been told something . . . or both . . . that just wasn't right. But since she had already tried going over everything she remembered and had even discussed the case with Sam, and that hadn't worked, it was time for another tactic—time to push all the questions aside and concentrate on something else, in hopes that the answers she sought would come to her.

It was a good idea, but it didn't yield any dividends. By the time she was finished with her cooking for the day and supper had come and gone, she wasn't any closer to those answers than she had been before.

After an early supper, everyone bundled up and the four of them loaded into Phyllis's car, which was the largest and most comfortable vehicle. "Are you sure it's not going to snow?" Phyllis asked Sam as she got behind the wheel. "I don't like to drive on snow or ice."

"Weatherman said there might be a few flurries later tonight," Sam drawled. "He wasn't predictin' any accumulation, though."

"It'll all melt when it hits the ground," Carolyn said confidently from the backseat. "You wait and see."

Phyllis had told Sam to sit up front and help her navigate. Eve wasn't happy about being stuck in the back with Carolyn, Phyllis could tell, but she didn't put up a fuss about it. Eve would have much preferred having Sam with her in the backseat.

Phyllis knew her way around Weatherford, having lived there practically her entire life, but the town had grown in recent years, and she didn't see as well at night as she once had, so it was good having more than one pair of eyes watching the road. Sam was methodical in laying out a grid in his mind so they could cover all the ground they wanted to. And he knew the best neighborhoods for Christmas lights, too, since he and his wife had always come down here from Poolville to carry out their Christmas Eve tradition.

The brilliant, elaborate displays of lights and decorations made Eve forget her resentment over Sam being in the front seat of the Lincoln. Carolyn lost her usual reserve and was almost giddy with excitement. Everyone joined in the oohs and aahs as Phyllis cruised through the brightly illuminated neighborhoods. As they passed one particularly impressive display, Sam chuckled and said, "I'll bet they can see that one from space."

Phyllis had Christmas music on the radio. As Sam had said, it wasn't hard to find a station playing it at this time of year. Even the ones that hadn't gone all Christmas, all the time, weeks earlier were now in their twenty-four-hour window of nothing but Christmas music that would conclude at six o'clock on the evening of Christmas Day. It was a special time, a time when all the cares of the world seemed to recede, and people paused in their busy lives to realize what was really important to them . . . their families, their friends, their faith.

And for that hour or so as they drove around, Phyllis didn't even think about murder.

At last it was time to head home. Everyone had seen enough lights. As Phyllis pulled onto the block where she and the others lived, she frowned as she saw a car parked at the curb in front of the house.

"That's Mike's car," she said. "I hope nothing's wrong."

As she turned into the driveway, she saw her son getting up from the front porch swing, where he had been sitting. He was bundled in a heavy coat, and his breath fogged in front of his face as he walked over to the garage. Phyllis stopped the car and got out quickly.

"Hi, Mom," Mike said from the open garage door.

"Mike, what's wrong?" she asked.

"Wrong? Nothing. Not a thing, as far as I know."

"Sarah and Bobby are all right?"

"Yeah."

"Well, why in the world aren't you at home with them on Christmas Eve, then?" Phyllis demanded.

Mike grinned. "That's where I'm headed. I had to work

today; just got off duty a little while ago. I thought I'd stop by here first and wish you and everybody else a merry Christmas."

Phyllis relaxed. "Goodness, you scared me. I thought something had happened."

"Nope. Just being a considerate son."

She laughed. "Well, that's good, I guess. merry Christmas to you, too."

Sam, Carolyn, and Eve joined her in wishing Mike a merry Christmas, and then Eve said, "Why don't you come inside and have a cup of hot cocoa with us? We're going to watch *It's a Wonderful Life*."

"That sounds mighty tempting, Miz Turner, but I've got a wife and boy waiting on me. . . ." Mike hesitated. "I can't stay for the movie, but that hot cocoa sounds too good to turn down."

"It won't take long to get it ready," Phyllis told him. "I'll even fix it for you to take with you, if you want."

"Okay. Sounds good, Mom; thanks."

They all went inside through the kitchen. Sam said, "I'll hang your coats up, ladies, so you can get started on that cocoa."

He and Mike went on into the living room, Sam with three coats draped over his arm, while Phyllis and Carolyn got out a pan, measuring utensils, milk, sugar, vanilla, and cocoa. Eve went into the living room, saying, "I'll warm up the television."

"Yes, she likes to warm things up, all right," Carolyn commented when Eve was gone. "She would have warmed up the backseat if Sam had been back there, I'll bet."

Phyllis didn't admit that she'd had the same thought. She busied herself with preparing the cocoa. She measured the water into the pan and put it on the burner, setting the flame to medium. As the water started to heat, she added the sugar and cocoa. A moment later Carolyn said, "I'll be right back," and headed upstairs. Phyllis figured she was going to the bathroom.

Sam wandered into the kitchen and looked surprised when he saw Phyllis by herself at the stove, stirring the chocolate mixture. "Left it to you, did they?" he asked as he leaned a hip against the counter.

"Carolyn will be back in a minute, and, well, you know Eve. She's not much of one for working in the kitchen. Anyway, it's not like it's that difficult to make hot chocolate. Where's Mike?"

"Callin' Sarah to let her know that he'll be there in a little while. We were talkin' and I told him about us drivin' around to look at Christmas lights, and I think he's gonna suggest that they do that when he gets home. It's still early enough."

"Bobby will go to sleep in the car if they do," Phyllis said with a smile. "But that's not a bad way to spend Christmas Eve. I read somewhere that nothing makes a child feel more secure than sleeping in the backseat of a car when his parents are going somewhere at night."

Sam chuckled. "I think that was in *Peanuts*. Seems like Linus said it, but it might've been Charlie Brown. Whichever one it was, there's a lot o' wisdom there."

A moment of companionable silence passed. Phyllis added the milk to the pan, stirred the mixture, then said, "It was awfully nice, driving around like that and seeing all those lights."

"My wife and I always enjoyed it. Last time we went was year before last. She'd already been diagnosed and had some radiation and chemo, so she didn't feel just top-notch. But she wanted to go anyway, wouldn't hear of stayin' at home. She wrapped a scarf around her head so it wouldn't get cold—her hair was pretty much gone by then, you know—and off we went." Sam smiled. "She was like a little kid, laughin' and point-in' out all the decorations, just carryin' on and havin' a fine old time, like always. Got so's I had a hard time drivin' because just watchin' her and listenin' to her made me so misty-eyed. You wouldn't think it, what with her bein' sick and all, and already gettin' worn out from fightin' that stuff, but that was one of our best Christmases. One of the best times we ever had together, in fact." Sam shook his head. "By the next Christmas, she was gone." He looked around. "Your, uh, hot chocolate's fixin' to boil over, looks like."

Phyllis said, "Oh!" and looked down at the stove. She took the pan off the burner and turned off the flame. She had to blink rapidly to see as she added the vanilla, because her eyes were full of tears. She wanted to say something to Sam, but she had no idea what. This was the most he had ever opened up to her about his late wife and her struggle with cancer, and while she hurt for his loss, she was also glad that he felt close enough to her to talk to her about it.

Before she could say anything, though, Eve called from the living room, "Phyllis, I can't find *It's a Wonderful Life*."

Phyllis took a deep breath to calm her emotions and called back, "It's on the shelves with the other tapes."

"Well, I don't see it."

"Oh, all right, hang on." She quickly poured the hot chocolate into five cups, then looked at Sam. "I'd better go find that tape for her. The cocoa probably ought to cool a little anyway. It, uh, got a little too hot."

"I'll go help you look," Sam offered. "Sometimes two sets of eyes are better'n one."

They went out to the living room, where they found Eve standing in front of a large set of built-in bookshelves, a couple of which now held DVDs and videotapes instead of books. Most of the movies they watched these days were on DVD, but they still had quite a few older videotapes. The machine hooked up to the TV was a combination VCR/DVD player and recorder.

Phyllis thought she knew right where the tape of *It's a Wonderful Life* was located on the shelves, and sure enough, it was there. She reached to get it and then turned to hand it to Eve.

Her grip on the tape tightened, though, as something seemed to break loose in her brain. For a second she was barely aware of where she was. All she could focus on was the videotape in her hand. For days now she had felt like someone was lying to her, but she had never been able to figure out who or why.

Now, suddenly, she knew who, although why was still a mystery. And that knowledge stunned her so much, she couldn't think of anything else.

"Well, are you going to let me put it in the machine or not?" Eve asked as she tugged on the tape.

Her words finally penetrated the thoughts swirling in Phyllis's brain. She let go of the tape without saying anything, and Eve turned away to insert it in the VCR, not even noticing the look on Phyllis's face.

Sam saw it, however, and reached over to grasp Phyllis's arm. "Something just came to you, didn't it?" he asked. "What is it?"

Before Phyllis could say anything, Carolyn and Mike came into the living room from different directions, Carolyn from the kitchen and Mike from the front hallway. Mike asked, "How's that cocoa coming along, Mom? I really need to get going—"

"Phyllis," Carolyn said, interrupting Mike, which wasn't like her. She had an agitated, worried look on her face. "Didn't all the Simmonses go home earlier today?"

Phyllis looked at her, still feeling a little breathless from what she had just figured out. "Yes," she said. "Yes, they all left."

"Well, either some of them came back, or somebody else is in there," Carolyn said, "because I just saw a light moving around in the Simmons house."

Mike frowned and said, "You're sure about that, Miz Wilbarger?"

"I'm certain," Carolyn said, and the firmness of her voice showed that she had no doubt about what she was saying. "I saw it from one of the upstairs windows. Not only that, the light was shining through one of those ventilators on the end of the house, under the eaves. You know, like it was coming from that attic room where Randall Simmons was hiding."

Phyllis looked at Sam and blurted, "Jimmy Crowe!"

"Who?" Mike asked.

Now she had gone and done it, Phyllis thought. The authorities didn't know yet about Jimmy Crowe and his connection with the case. But it was too late to call the words back now, and she knew from the intent look on her son's face that Mike wouldn't be satisfied until he had the whole story.

Besides, it had to be Crowe skulking around over there in Agnes's house. He would have read in the papers about Randall's arrest and about how Randall had hidden in the attic of his grandmother's house. Crowe was probably up there searching the place to see if Randall had hidden any money there—or anything that might be incriminating to Crowe. With this being Christmas Eve, he might think this was the perfect time to break in, when everyone would be busy with their own holiday celebrations and not paying any attention to the supposedly empty Simmons house.

He would have gotten away with it, too, if not for Carolyn's observant nature—which was a polite way of saying that she was nosy, of course, but right now Phyllis didn't care about that.

Those thoughts flashed through her head, and then she said, "Mike, there's no time to explain right now, but I promise that I'll tell you all about it if you call for help and make sure the man in Agnes's house doesn't get away."

"I was gonna do that anyway," Mike said as he pulled his cell phone from the pocket of his coat. He turned toward the front door. "All of you stay here."

"What are you going to do?" Phyllis called after him. "You can call from in here."

"I need to get outside and keep an eye on the place, in case the guy tries to get away before the PD shows up." He unbuttoned his coat, and as it swung open, Phyllis saw the gun holstered on his hip.

"Mike, you can't try to arrest that man alone. He's dangerous!"

"Don't worry," he said over his shoulder as he started out of the house. "I'll wait for backup."

But as Phyllis looked around at Sam, Carolyn, and Eve, she had the awful feeling that Mike *wouldn't* wait if Crowe tried to get away.

She had just sent her son out into the night to face a man who might well be a killer.

Mike didn't call 911. He dialed the direct line of the police department dispatcher instead, identified himself, and reported a possible burglary in progress. The dispatcher said he'd have a unit rolling toward the address right away, with no lights or sirens to spook the guy in the Simmons house.

Mike closed the phone and slipped it back in his pocket. With his hand on the butt of his gun, he walked across the lawn in front of the Simmons house and went up onto the porch. He eased the screen door open and tried the knob of the wooden door. It was locked and didn't appear to have been tampered with. That meant the intruder had gotten in some other way, probably through the back door, or possibly a window.

Leaving the porch, Mike walked to the side of the house and looked up toward the roof. He could barely see the screened and louvered opening under the eaves. There was one at each end of the house for ventilation in the attic. He didn't see any light there now, but he found it hard to believe that Mrs. Wilbarger had just imagined it. She wasn't the imaginative type, and she certainly wasn't the sort to cry wolf.

Mike went about halfway along the side of the house, next to the hedge that separated the properties, then stopped again to listen. He slipped a small but powerful flashlight out of his pocket and held it in his left hand. Since it was Christmas Eve, there wasn't much traffic on the roads, so the night was quiet. He heard very faint music coming from somebody's house, or one of the churches, or maybe even some carolers getting in a few last-minute Christmas songs. But he didn't hear anything suspicious. . . .

Then something thudded at the rear of the house.

It sounded like a foot had inadvertently kicked something in the darkness. A moment later he heard the scrape of shoe leather against the ground. Mrs. Wilbarger had been right— someone had been inside the Simmons house and was now trying to slip away into the night. Whether the guy had found what he was looking for or had given up, Mike didn't know. But he intended to find out.

A dark shape moved around the rear corner of the house. Mike drew his pistol as he leveled the flashlight in his other hand. Since the Weatherford police weren't on the scene yet, he would have to take the burglar into custody himself. His thumb pressed the button on the flashlight.

The brilliant beam shot out and pinned the man, who stopped short, freezing between the house and the hedge with one hand raised in an instinctive effort to block the sudden glare from his eyes. Mike shouted, "Police! Get down on the ground—*now!*"

The man didn't get down. Instead he broke out of the momentary trance brought on by the dazzling light, whirled around, and ran.

"Stop!" Mike yelled, but the man didn't. The corner of the house was only a few steps away. Mike realized that he should have let the guy get a little closer before he turned the light on. Too late for that now, though. The man whipped around the corner and disappeared.

Mike went after him but stopped before he reached the back of the house. Charging blindly around corners was a good way for a cop to get killed. He pressed his back against the wall and listened again.

A garbage can crashed and clattered. The fugitive had reached the alley that ran behind the houses along the street. Mike darted around the corner and broke into a run after him.

The bobbing lance of light picked up the fleeing burglar. He was about forty feet away. "Stop or I'll shoot!" Mike shouted. But he knew he wasn't going to fire his weapon under these circumstances, and evidently so did the guy he was chasing, because the man never slowed down. He pounded along the alley and ducked around an old van that was parked back there.

Mike holstered his pistol in hopes that would help him run faster. His heart thumped heavily in his chest. He had been involved in foot pursuits like this before, and he didn't like them, especially at night. There were too many places for a suspect to hide, too many places from which a desperate man might launch an ambush against an officer who was pursuing him.

That thought had barely crossed Mike's mind when his quarry lunged out of the shadows alongside the old van, crashed into him, and knocked him off his feet.

Chapter 21

"I'm going out there," Phyllis said as she started toward the front door.

Carolyn caught hold of her arm, and Sam moved to get between her and the door. "Don't be insane," Carolyn said. "You can't do anything to help Mike."

"It's my fault he's out there maybe facing a killer," Phyllis said. Fear grew inside her until it all but filled her.

"Yeah, and he's trained to handle situations like that," Sam told her. "He'll be all right, Phyllis. You raised him to be smart and levelheaded. He won't do anything foolish."

"But if anything happened to him, and it was my fault—"

"I'll go," Sam said.

Immediately, a new fear surged up inside Phyllis. "No, you can't."

"Better me than you. If somebody has to go—"

"No, you're right." Phyllis forced herself to take a deep breath. "Mike is very capable. He'll be just fine, and I'm sure that the police will be here any minute now—"

She might have been able to keep on being reasonable about it, although that would have been hard, if at that moment she hadn't heard her son shout for someone to stop. A moment later Mike yelled again, from farther back on the property.

"Oh, dear Lord!" Phyllis gasped as she turned and ran for the back door.

None of the others were quick enough to stop her this time. She dashed through the kitchen and out the door into the back yard.

The hedge that divided the properties ran all the way to the rear alley. Running footsteps sounded on the other side of the hedge and then in the alley itself. Heedless of the cold, Phyllis headed in that direction, but she had taken only a few steps before Sam caught up to her and stopped her by grabbing both of her arms. As he pulled her to a halt, he said, "Blast it, Phyllis, you don't know what you're gettin' into—"

The sound of a collision came from the alley, followed by grunts and curses. Phyllis struggled to get loose from Sam's grip as Carolyn and Eve came up behind them. Both of the women were panting from the exertion of running out of the house and across the backyard.

Sam pushed Phyllis toward them and snapped, "Hang on to her!" Then he let go and turned to run into the alley, disappearing around the hedge.

"Sam, no!" Phyllis called after him.

But the darkness had already swallowed him.

Mike found himself on the bottom, pinned to the ground by the weight of the other man, who was considerably bigger than he was. The guy had his left hand clamped around Mike's throat. The fingers dug in cruelly, like iron bars. The man lifted his other arm, and his raised fist was poised to come crashing down into Mike's face.

Instead there was a huge clang of metal and the guy toppled to the side, letting go of Mike's throat. The upraised fist never fell. Mike wasn't sure what had happened, but he rolled over and scrambled after the man anyway. His head was spinning from being choked, but his instincts and training still worked. He landed with a knee in the middle of the guy's back, grabbed one of his arms, and snapped a cuff around that wrist before the man knew what was going on. He seemed to be half-stunned now and wasn't putting up much of a fight. Mike dug his knee into the small of the guy's back and managed to get hold of the other arm as it flailed around. He brought it back and down and found the other cuff. It locked into place with a satisfying *snick*.

"You get him?"

That was Sam Fletcher's voice, Mike realized as he pushed himself to his feet and dragged air into his lungs. The flashlight he had dropped when the suspect tackled him lay a few feet away, still burning, with its beam pointing down the alley. Mike stepped over to it and picked it up. He turned the light toward Sam. The glare revealed the rangy older man standing there with a metal garbage can in his hands. The can had a huge dent in the side of it.

"That . . . that's what you hit him with?" Mike asked.

"Yeah. I saw the two of you fightin', and I could tell the other guy was on top, so I grabbed the first thing I could find and whaled the tar out of him." Sam hefted the garbage can. "Worked pretty good, too."

Mike couldn't help but chuckle. "It sure did. You shouldn't have gotten involved, though, Mr. Fletcher. It was too dangerous."

"Are you kiddin'? You know what your mama'd do to me if I stood by and let that fella choke you? Now *that* would'a been dangerous."

"It's pretty dark back here," Mike said as he drew his gun

and covered the handcuffed suspect. "How did you know he was on top and not me?"

"There's a little bit o' light. Enough to shine on that dome o' his."

Mike turned the flashlight beam toward the suspect. Sure enough, the guy was as bald as an egg. There hadn't really been time to notice that during the brief confrontation at the side of the house. The suspect wasn't that old, in his late thirties or early forties, Mike judged, but he'd either lost his hair at an early age or else shaved it all off. It didn't really matter either way. What was important was that he was in custody.

"Is this . . . What was the name Mom said? Jimmy Crowe?"

Sam shook his head and said, "I wouldn't know. I never laid eyes on the fella before."

More voices sounded nearby. A couple of uniformed officers carrying flashlights came into the alley from the backyard of the Simmons house, followed by Phyllis, Carolyn, and Eve. With all those lights, the alley was brightly illuminated. Phyllis hurried over to Mike, who holstered his gun. He identified himself to the Weatherford officers and told them briefly what had happened. They hauled the suspect to his feet, and one of them said, "We'll find out who he is. Don't go anywhere, Deputy."

"Don't worry about that," Mike assured them. "I'll be around." Then he turned to his mother, who hugged him tightly.

"Are you all right?" Phyllis asked.

"Yeah, I'm fine. Banged up a little, but it's nothing to worry about . . . thanks to Mr. Fletcher. I wouldn't have caught the guy without his help."

Phyllis let go of Mike and turned to Sam, hugging him, too. "Thank you," she whispered.

Sam looked embarrassed as he said, "All I did was wallop the fella with a garbage can."

Mike extended a hand. "Well, I appreciate it."

"So do I," Phyllis said as Mike and Sam shook hands.

Then Mike nodded toward the street and said, "Let's go talk to the officers. And Mom . . . I want to hear all about Jimmy Crowe."

Detective Isabel Largo didn't seem too happy about being taken away from her family on Christmas Eve, and Phyllis couldn't blame her for that. She listened patiently as Phyllis explained for the third time about Jimmy Crowe and his connection to the case. She had already told Mike all about it, and then the two officers who had Crowe in custody in the backseat of their car. Crowe had had his driver's license on him, so he hadn't bothered trying to deny who he was.

Phyllis felt a little like she was betraying the confidence of Frank Simmons and Juliette Yorke, but now that Crowe's involvement was out in the open, she didn't see any point in keeping what she knew a secret. Anyway, it was all hearsay. Detective Largo would have to confirm everything with Randall. What was more important, at least in the short run, was that the police would now have to consider Crowe a suspect in Agnes's murder. He had broken into the house once—tonight, through the rear door—and he certainly could have done it before that, like on the previous Saturday, when Agnes was killed.

The problem, Phyllis thought, was that Crowe really had no connection to the thing she had figured out earlier this evening. She still didn't know how *that* fit in, if indeed it did.

But maybe Crowe would confess to killing Agnes, and all of that would be moot. Phyllis hoped it would turn out that way.

When Phyllis was through telling Detective Largo what she

knew, the woman closed her notebook and stood up. "I'll go talk to Crowe now," she said. She gave Phyllis a stern look and added, "You really should have come to me and told me about this before now."

"I didn't know if any of it was even true," Phyllis said.

"Neither do I . . . but I plan on finding out."

When Detective Largo had left the house, Phyllis looked over at Mike and asked, "Did I really do wrong?"

"Well . . . you should have told me about it, anyway."

"I was afraid the information might wind up hurting Randall, and I was already convinced that he didn't kill Agnes. Besides, I don't like to betray confidences." Phyllis paused. "Will this make the police consider Crowe a suspect in Agnes's murder, or will they just use it to make their case against Randall stronger?"

Mike shrugged and shook his head. "I don't know. That'll be up to Detective Largo and Chief Whitmire and the district attorney, I suppose. I'll say this, though . . . After tangling with the guy, I don't have a big problem with the theory that he might have strangled Miz Simmons."

There was a major problem with that theory, as Detective Largo explained when she came back into the house a half hour or so later. "Crowe's not talking about what happened tonight," she said. "He claims he was never inside the house. He doesn't have a good explanation for what he was doing in the backyard or why he ran, but he's going to try to brazen his way through that part of it, anyway. I'm hoping we'll find some fingerprints or other evidence to put him inside the house. When I asked him about last Saturday, however, he was more than willing to talk."

"Let me guess," Mike said. "He has an alibi for the time of Mrs. Simmons's murder."

Detective Largo nodded. "And a pretty strong one at that. He was locked up in the Dallas County jail. He was picked up on some outstanding warrants that morning and didn't bond out until after six o'clock Saturday evening. I called Dallas and checked on that myself, and his story holds up."

"So he couldn't have killed Miz Simmons."

"Not a chance," Detective Largo said.

Phyllis knew what that old expression about having the wind knocked out of your sails meant. That was exactly the way she felt now. Once Jimmy Crowe had been caught breaking into the Simmons house, she was sure that he would turn out to be guilty of the murder, too. Clearly, that wasn't going to happen.

So she was almost back where she had started, with the possibility that either Randall Simmons or someone from the neighborhood had committed the crime.

Except . . .

She knew something now that she hadn't known before. She didn't know what it all meant, mind you. She didn't even know whether it was connected to Agnes's murder.

But someone had lied to her, and she wanted to know why. Until she knew that, she wasn't going to say anything to Mike or to Detective Largo. The chance that she might ruin an innocent person's life was too great. There was probably a perfectly reasonable explanation for everything.

Either way, she was going to find out.

"Well, after all that excitement, sitting and watching a movie on TV is going to seem pretty tame," Carolyn said after Mike, Detective Largo, and the rest of the police were gone, taking Jimmy Crowe with them. The drug dealer/loan shark/burglar was going to be spending this Christmas in jail.

"Actually, I can't watch *It's a Wonderful Life* right now,"

Phyllis said. "There's something else I have to do. I have to go out for a while."

Carolyn and Eve stared at her in surprise. "On Christmas *Eve*?" Carolyn asked.

Phyllis nodded. "I'm sorry. I shouldn't be gone long."

"If you need something else for dinner tomorrow, you're too late. All the stores will be closed."

"This isn't for dinner," Phyllis said. She looked at Sam. "Would you mind coming with me?"

"Figured I would," he replied without hesitation.

"Well, this has just been the *oddest* Christmas Eve ever," Eve commented.

Phyllis couldn't argue with that. She was afraid that the odd part wasn't over yet, either.

She and Sam got their coats, and as she shrugged into hers, she froze momentarily and then gave a shake of her head. Now that the dam in her brain was broken, more facts were pouring through. Another possible connection between two things she had seen, several days apart, jumped out at her. Again, they might not mean anything, but the coincidences were piling up. When they did that, chances were that they *weren't* coincidences at all.

Sam suggested that they take his pickup, and Phyllis agreed. As they stepped outside, he said, "I figured from the way you looked a while ago, you had some things to think about on the way to wherever we're goin', so it's best I handle the drivin'."

"Thank you, Sam. You've come to know me pretty well, haven't you?"

"Well enough to know you've figured out who killed Agnes Simmons," he said.

"No, not necessarily. But I have some questions that need to be answered."

"Tonight? On Christmas Eve?"

Phyllis nodded. "I don't think I could sleep or enjoy Christmas without knowing the truth."

As Sam started the truck's engine, he asked, "You reckon we'd better call Mike and ask him to meet us wherever we're goin'? I'd hate to ruin the evenin' for him more than it's already been ruined, but if we're goin' to see a killer . . ."

"I'm sure I'm wrong about everything," Phyllis said. "There has to be an explanation for the things I saw. I'm not going to ruin someone's life just because I'm confused about a few things."

Sam hesitated, then nodded. "All right. I reckon I trust you. You usually know what you're doin'."

Phyllis hoped that Sam's trust was justified. But more than anything else right now, she hoped that she was just a crazy old woman who had leaped to some false conclusions.

"Look at that," Sam said as he pointed to a wet spot on the windshield. "It's finally started to snow."

As he flicked the headlights on, Phyllis saw that was true. Big fluffy snowflakes were visible as they swirled down gracefully through the cones of light.

"Where to?" Sam asked.

"The church," Phyllis said. "The parsonage, actually."

Sam looked over at her in surprise and said, "The parsonage?"

Phyllis nodded. "That's right. I have to ask Dwight about something."

After a moment, Sam nodded and put the pickup in gear. They drove off into the lightly falling snow.

It took only a few minutes to reach the church and the parsonage. The office building and the sanctuary were dark, of course, except for the spotlights that illuminated the cross on the front of the church and the manger scene on the lawn, and those were set up on timers. Quite a few lights were burning inside the parsonage, however, including strings of brightly colored bulbs on the tree that was visible through the picture window. The curtains were drawn back so that the Christmas tree could be seen from the street.

Sam parked in the driveway. As he and Phyllis got out of the pickup, Phyllis noted that the snow was falling more heavily now, but as Carolyn had predicted, it seemed to be melting as soon as it hit the ground. The temperature just wasn't quite cold enough for the flakes to freeze. Still, it made a beautiful evening that much lovelier. The snowfall and the Christmas lights and the manger scene all combined to create a tableau that looked like it ought to be on a picture postcard.

But as always, ugliness could be lurking behind beauty. It was wise to never forget that, Phyllis thought, depressing, but wise.

"I hope you know what you're doin'," Sam said quietly as they went up to the door.

"I hope I don't," Phyllis said.

Then she rang the doorbell.

She supposed that Dwight and Jada weren't expecting any company this late in the evening on Christmas Eve. It took several moments for someone to come to the door. When it finally swung back, Dwight stood there with a puzzled look on his face, peering out at them through the glass of the storm door, which he opened immediately.

"Phyllis, Sam," he said, "I didn't expect to see you again until Sunday. What can I do for you?"

"I need to ask you some questions, Dwight," Phyllis said.

"Sure, come on in—"

"Actually, I was thinking maybe we could talk out here," she suggested.

That puzzled Dwight even more, if his deepening frown

was any indication of his reaction. "I guess so. Let me get my coat." He looked past Phyllis and Sam and added, "Hey, it's snowing."

"This won't take long," Phyllis said.

Dwight closed the storm door and took a step back to get his coat from the hall closet. Jada must have asked him who was there, because he turned and called loudly enough for them to hear through the glass, "Phyllis Newsom and Sam Fletcher need to talk to me for a minute."

Phyllis heard Jada's response. "Them again?"

Dwight didn't say anything to that. He shrugged into his coat, stepped outside, and closed both doors behind him. "Now, what's this about?" he asked, and the faint note of impatience in his voice indicated that even his easygoing nature found this intrusion on Christmas Eve to be a little irritating.

"I just need to know a couple of things," Phyllis said.

"Shoot."

"Are you having an affair with Vickie Kimbrough?"

Phyllis had all her attention fixed on Dwight's face, which she could see plainly in the glow that spilled over from the spotlights on the manger scene, but she assumed that Sam was staring at her in surprise.

Dwight wasn't. He stiffened, his eyes opening wider, but he didn't seem terribly shocked by the question.

"What in the world makes you think that?" he asked.

Instead of answering, Phyllis pointed out, "You're not denying it."

"Why should I bother denying something so ridiculous? I'm a happily married man." Definite anger roughened Dwight's voice as he went on, "I'm Vickie's pastor, not her lover. Why would you even ask such a question, Phyllis?"

"Earlier today you had a bit of pink fuzz on your coat, a coat you hadn't worn since Monday, you said. On Monday, Vickie was wearing a pink sweater with the same sort of fuzz on it. A piece of it could have easily gotten stuck on your coat if you were, say, hugging her."

Dwight's eyes narrowed. "That's observant of you, but hardly conclusive of anything. There could be dozens of fuzzy pink sweaters in Weatherford. Maybe even hundreds. For all you know, my own wife could have one."

Phyllis shook her head and said, "With her red hair, Jada would never wear a pink sweater."

"That still doesn't mean anything," Dwight said as he plunged his hands into his coat pockets. "Why in the world would a little bit of fuzz make you believe something so crazy as me having an affair with Vickie Kimbrough?"

"Because that would explain why you lied to me about the videotapes."

For the first time, the confused, annoyed veneer that Dwight was putting up cracked slightly, as he said, "V-videotapes?"

Phyllis nodded. "That's right. You told me you brought video-tapes of the church services by Agnes Simmons's house every week so that she could watch them. But that's impossible. Agnes didn't have a VCR. She wouldn't have known how to use one even if she did. She hated modern technology. She wouldn't even have a microwave oven in her kitchen. Called it a newfan-gled gadget and didn't want any part of it. She felt the same way about video equipment. Her TV is thirty years old, and there's nothing on top of it except a lace doily and some pictures and knickknacks."

"Well, you . . . you must be mistaken," Dwight said, and now he was visibly shaken. "She had to be watching the tapes on something, because I took them by there every week—"

"No, that was just your story to explain why your car was in the neighborhood so often, in case anyone ever noticed it," Phyllis said. During her teaching career, she had seen enough children caught in lies to recognize the signs in Dwight, so she forged ahead with her theory. "You and Vickie started having an affair when you were counseling Vickie and Monte about the problems they were having because they couldn't have children. I doubt if it was your idea. But Vickie was vulnerable because of those problems, and because Monte is so emotionally distant and hardly ever home, and, well, these things happen."

"Not to me," Dwight said, but his denial rang hollow. "Not to me."

"You went to see her one last time on Monday," Phyllis went on. "You told Jada you were going to pick up the church service videotape from me, but actually you went to Vickie's house to tell her that the two of you couldn't see each other anymore, at least not for a while. All the commotion that Agnes's murder stirred up would make it too risky for you to come to her house. I'm not sure why the two of you didn't just meet elsewhere—"

"Because she wouldn't," Dwight snapped, his voice ragged with strain. He looked like he had been punched in the belly now. He lifted his hands to his face and covered it, so that his words were muffled as he said, "It had to be there. It had to be there in their own bed, or she wouldn't be getting back at him enough."

Phyllis was breathing hard, almost overcome by a mixture of shock and disappointment and even a little anger. She had known Dwight Gresham for years, had considered him a good man. She had hoped that he would deny the affair with Vickie and convince her that he was telling the truth. She had never wanted to be wrong so much in her life, but he had crumpled

under her accusations—and under his own guilt, she thought—
and confirmed her worst suspicions.

Only they weren't the worst at all, Phyllis realized as something else clicked together in her mind. She gasped, and Sam
put a hand on her arm as if to steady her.

"Oh, Dwight," she said, "what you'd already done was bad
enough. Why did you have to kill Agnes, too?"

Chapter 22

S am couldn't contain himself any longer when he heard that. He exclaimed, "Phyllis, you can't mean that!"

But Dwight's head had jerked up, his hands fell away from his face, and he stared at her with an awful certainty in his eyes. He struggled to force words out and finally said, "How . . . how did you know?"

"The cookies," Phyllis said.

"Cookies?" Sam repeated, still sounding shocked.

She nodded. "Vickie knew that the lime snowflake cookies were mine. She said that you told her about them a few days earlier. She slipped there, admitting that she'd even talked to you, but I didn't notice it then. It didn't occur to me that you shouldn't have known who baked those cookies, either, because when you mentioned them to Vickie, the recipe hadn't been in the paper yet. The only way you could have known was if you'd found out some other way. Agnes told you while you were making small talk with her, before you killed her. I'd just been over there and brought her a plate of cookies, and I mentioned which ones were mine."

Dwight started shaking his head. "Why would I want to kill a harmless old woman like Agnes Simmons?"

"Because she *wasn't* harmless, not to you." And not to most of the members of her family, Phyllis thought. "She found out somehow about what was going on between you and Vickie, and she threatened to tell Jada. That's what I'm guessing happened, anyway."

"You're basing all this on a *cookie*?" Dwight's voice shook. "Vickie was at the cookie exchange. She could have found out which ones you made there."

"She could have," Phyllis said, "but it hadn't even been discussed yet when I discovered Agnes's body and then was attacked." She sighed and shook her head. "You didn't have to hit me like that, Dwight. You could have really hurt me."

"That's right," Sam said, an angry growl coming into his voice. His hands balled into fists. He seemed to be convinced now that Phyllis was right about the preacher. "Killin' that old lady was bad enough, but you shouldn't have hit Phyllis, mister."

The last vestiges of Dwight's stubborn denial faded away. He sagged against one of the posts that supported the porch roof and lifted a shaking hand to rub at his temples. "You're right," he said. "Oh, dear Lord, you're right. What have I done? Phyllis, I . . . I'm so sorry. I shouldn't have hit you. I was in agony, worrying that I'd killed you, too." With a visible effort, he straightened. "Why don't you call your son, or that Detective Largo? I'll tell them everything, how I strangled Agnes and then attacked you and—"

"*Noooo!*"

The screeching, heartrending cry made all of them jump. As they turned toward the end of the porch, Jada Gresham came out of the shadows there. She must have gone out the back door and come around the house to eavesdrop on what was being said on the parsonage porch, Phyllis thought, and there was no telling how much she had heard. She took a few halting steps toward them, in front of the picture window, so that the twinkling light from the bulbs on the Christmas tree played over her stricken face.

Phyllis lifted a hand toward the younger woman. "Jada, I'm so sorry—"

"Not as sorry as you're going to be!" Jada cried.

Then she leaped forward, her hand rising, and the brightly colored lights reflected on the broad blade of the butcher knife she clutched.

Phyllis was shocked, frozen in place. Sam was behind her, unable to get between her and Jada in time. But Dwight shouted, "Jada, no!" and leaped forward, throwing himself in front of Phyllis as Jada thrust the knife out. He grunted and staggered back a step as the blade went into his body.

Jada screamed, let go of the knife, and turned to run, dashing across the front yard toward the church. Sam went after her, grabbing her and wrestling her to a halt in front of the manger scene. Jada fell to her knees as sobs racked her. "Dwight!" she cried. "Oh, Dwight, I'm sorry! All I ever meant to do was protect you! You . . . you had to carry on your good work. . . ."

Meanwhile, Phyllis had gotten her arms around Dwight and helped him sit down with his back against one of the porch posts. He was breathing harshly and had his hands pressed to his midsection. He looked up at her and said, "Phyllis, I . . . I'm sorry."

"It was her, wasn't it?" Phyllis said, still shaken from the look of insane hatred in Jada's eyes as the younger woman lunged forward with the knife. "I had that part of it wrong. *She* killed Agnes."

Dwight might have still tried to deny it, but at that moment he slumped to the side. Phyllis thought for a horrible second that he was dead, but then she pressed her fingers to his neck and found an erratic but fairly strong pulse. She pulled her cell phone from her pocket and punched in 911.

Then, as she waited for the operator to answer, she turned and looked at Sam standing over a sobbing Jada in front of the manger scene. Snowflakes still danced and swirled from the skies, surrounding them. The temperature must have dropped a little, because a few of the flakes were starting to stick now, creating a light dusting of white on the grass.

Maybe it was going to be one of those rare white Christmases after all.

"We never got around to going out and looking at lights," Mike said an hour or so later as he sat in the living room of Phyllis's house. Phyllis, Sam, Carolyn, and Eve were all there, too.

"I'm sorry," Phyllis said. "I guess I should have just let Detective Largo handle everything instead of calling you, too."

"No, no, I wanted to know what was going on." Mike gave her a stern look. "In less than a week, you've been knocked out by a renegade preacher and then attacked by a crazy woman with a knife. You're gonna have to start being more careful, Mom."

"I promise you, none of it was my idea," Phyllis said. "And at least I wasn't stabbed. Poor Dwight."

"Poor Dwight, nothin'," Sam said. "The fella hit you on the head. Could've hurt you real bad. Don't forget about that."

Phyllis shuddered. "I won't. I'm afraid I won't forget about any of this for a long time." She looked at Mike. "You're sure the doctors said that he's going to live?"

"That's the report I got," he said with a nod. "He passed out because he lost quite a bit of blood, but the knife missed all the vital organs. He'll be fine to stand trial for attempted murder and being an accessory after the fact, plus whatever else the DA can find to charge him with. Obstruction of justice, maybe."

"I don't think he was really trying to kill me," Phyllis said. She still had a hard time believing that she was saying such things about someone she had considered such a fine man.

But maybe it was dangerous to think that way, she reminded herself, to blind yourself to someone's flaws because of the good they did. Jada Gresham had committed murder because she believed her husband did such important work that not only did she forgive him for his affair with Vickie Kimbrough, but she also thought he had to be protected from having that affair brought out into the open.

"Let me get this straight," Carolyn said. "They *both* confessed to killing Agnes Simmons?"

Mike nodded. "Yeah, but Mrs. Gresham's story holds together a lot better. The preacher was just trying to protect his wife when he said that he did it. That's what I think, anyway." He leaned forward in the armchair where he was sitting and clasped his hands together between his knees. "Mrs. Gresham said she told Mrs. Simmons she wanted to take a closer look at some fancy stitching on that robe belt. Mrs. Simmons gave it to her to look at, without knowing that she was handing over her own murder weapon. Mrs. Gresham got behind her, looped the belt around her neck, and . . ." Mike shrugged. "Sorry. Didn't mean to get so graphic."

"All because of an affair?" Eve said. "Goodness, in this day and age that doesn't seem like something worth killing over."

"But Dwight is a minister," Phyllis pointed out. "If it became public knowledge that he was having an affair with a member of his congregation, and that it started while he was counseling the woman and her husband . . . well, the church would have had no choice but to let him go, if he didn't resign in shame."

"And that meant he wouldn't be able to help people anymore," Mike said. "Mrs. Gresham kept coming back to that again and again in her statement. She seems to honestly believe that he does so much good, she had to forgive him. She told him he had to break it off with Mrs. Kimbrough, though, and she wasn't happy when she found out that he'd still been seeing her. After all, she'd killed Mrs. Simmons to keep her from telling anybody else about the affair."

"Agnes was the one who told Jada?" Carolyn asked.

"Yeah. Mrs. Gresham happened to be visiting Mrs. Simmons one day, and she said something about her husband bringing those church videotapes for her to watch. Mrs. Simmons said he never brought tapes to her, that she didn't even have a VCR. That made Mrs. Simmons suspicious, so she started keeping an eye out for the preacher. Sure enough, it wasn't long before she spotted him sneaking into the Kimbrough house when Mr. Kimbrough wasn't home. She drew her own conclusions from that—accurately, as it turns out—and called Jada Gresham, told her to come over last Saturday afternoon. Mr. Gresham knew from the way his wife was acting that something was wrong, so he followed her over there and came in the back door while Mrs. Gresham was talking to Mrs. Simmons in the living room. Mrs. Simmons wanted her and Mrs. Gresham to go to the deacons and tell them what Mr. Gresham was up to. She insisted they had to, and nothing Mrs. Gresham said could change her mind, even when she told the old lady that she forgave him for cheating on her. Mrs. Simmons said it had to come out."

Remembering some of the things she had heard about the way Agnes had treated her family, Phyllis could believe that.

Agnes had had a vicious streak in her, there was no getting around that fact.

"Mr. Gresham claims he came in then and killed Mrs. Simmons," Mike went on, "but the evidence doesn't support that. I think he'll break down and tell the truth sooner or later."

Sam said, "Either way, I reckon the charges against young Randall Simmons will be dropped?"

"The murder charge will. He's still in trouble for jumping bail over in Dallas County, not to mention the original charges against him there. But at least he won't be facing the death penalty anymore."

Phyllis was glad to hear that. It was time the Simmons family got some good news for a change.

"Dwight must have panicked when he saw what Jada had done," she said. "He was probably trying to hustle her out of there when I came in. I'll bet she was in the kitchen, too, when I walked in there and he knocked me out."

"Yeah, that's what he says happened," Mike agreed, "but how did you know it was him who hit you and not Mrs. Gresham?"

"If it had been Jada," Phyllis said, "she probably wouldn't have stopped until I was dead."

Mike thought about that for a second and then gave a grim nod. "Yeah. I think you're probably right."

Carolyn shook her head in seeming amazement and said, "She loved him enough to not only forgive him but also to kill for him. That's hard to believe."

"She loved the Lord that much, and she thought that Dwight was doing the Lord's work," Phyllis said. "I think she had put him on a pedestal for so long that she couldn't really believe it, even when she was confronted with the evidence that he was just as human and fallible as anybody. Anyway, think about her house and the way she dressed and everything else about her."

"What about it?" Mike asked.

"It had to be perfect," Phyllis said. "Everything had to be perfect. And when it wasn't . . . she would do whatever she had to in order to make it that way again."

A solemn silence descended over the room, broken after several long moments by Eve saying, "You know, I don't think I feel much like watching *It's a Wonderful Life* anymore."

Mike put his hands on his knees and pushed himself to his feet. "Well, I'm going home and spending what's left of Christmas Eve with my wife and son, and I'm not even gonna think about murder again until I have to."

Sam stood up as well and clapped a hand on the younger man's shoulder. "That's a mighty sensible way to look at it, if you ask me." He turned to Phyllis, Carolyn, and Eve. "And I think we ought to go ahead and watch the movie. There's always bad things happenin' all over the world, but Christmas is still Christmas. It's got a magic all its own, and one part of it is that it helps you forget for a while about those bad things and remember the good."

Phyllis felt her spirits lifting a little. "Sam's right," she said. "We should try to salvage as much of our Christmas as we can."

"But it's late," Carolyn objected.

Sam grinned. "I reckon we'll all turn in early enough so that we won't keep Santa from showin' up."

Mike grimaced and said, "Oh, man. I almost forgot. Santa's still got to assemble a tricycle tonight! I better get going." He hugged Phyllis, kissed her cheek, shook hands with Sam, and then impulsively hugged Carolyn and Eve, too. "Good night, everybody," he called as he went out. "And merry Christmas!"

"Merry Christmas," Phyllis whispered after him.

· · ·

She was up early the next morning. There was a lot to do to get ready for Christmas dinner. Phyllis turned the oven on and took out the ham. She removed the plastic and rinsed the ham in the sink, then placed the meat in a large, shallow roasting pan.

She dug through the drawer of utensils and found her meat syringe, and then opened the bottle of cola. It was a little difficult to fill the syringe with the drink because it kept foaming up and little of the cola would go into the syringe. After a few trials and errors, Phyllis discovered the best way of filling the syringe and injected the cola into the ham over and over. When she had as much of it in the ham as she could get, she basted the ham with what was left in the bottle.

If it had been a regular day, she would have left it at that, but she felt like the ham needed to look better, so she opened a can of pineapple rings. With toothpicks, she stuck pineapple rings on the top and sides of the ham. She sprinkled brown sugar on the rings and the ham. Again with toothpicks, she placed a cherry inside each pineapple ring and then stuck some cloves in the pineapple rings. She covered the pan with aluminum foil and put it in the oven.

Carolyn joined her in the kitchen just a few minutes later, and for a couple of hours both women were very busy, before the late risers, Sam and Eve, came downstairs. Phyllis thought Sam looked adorable in his pajamas and robe, with his hair still a little rumpled from sleep, like a little boy, especially when he looked at the pile of presents under the tree in the living room, grinned, and said, "Santa's been here, all right."

"All those presents were there before," Carolyn pointed out.

"Yeah, but the milk and cookies are gone."

"What milk and cookies?"

Sam tapped the side of his nose, winked at her, and said, "Exactly."

Carolyn rolled her eyes, shook her head, and went back to the kitchen, muttering something about men who never grew up.

"I've got the coffee on, and there are pancakes and bacon for breakfast," Phyllis told Sam and Eve. "We'll have the tree after we eat, if that's all right."

"Fine with me," Sam said. He took a deep breath. "That coffee smells mighty good."

Phyllis went to the front window and looked out for a moment before returning to the kitchen. She had been so busy all morning, she hadn't really paid any attention to what things looked like outside. She had to smile when she saw the thin layer of snow on the ground. In some parts of the country, this would barely qualify as a white Christmas, she supposed, but for Texas it wasn't bad at all. And the sight of the snow made her feel even better about being inside a warm, snug house with her friends.

The morning passed leisurely, with all of them gathering in the kitchen to eat breakfast and then adjourning to the living room to open presents. Everyone was pleased with their gifts, especially Sam, who grinned at the stack of DVDs and books and said, "This'll keep me busy for a while."

Then it was time for Phyllis and Carolyn to get back to the kitchen and continue working on the preparations for the Christmas feast. Carolyn chopped all the fruit for the salad while Phyllis mixed the dough for the dinner rolls. Carolyn put the salad in the refrigerator as Phyllis covered the bowl of bread dough and placed it in a warm place to rise. Phyllis checked on the ham, which had been cooking since early that morning, and announced that dinner would be around one o'clock . . . two at the latest.

Mike, Sarah, and Bobby arrived late in the morning, smiling and bundled up against the cold. Bobby chattered away about all the presents Santa had brought him, including a shiny new tricycle that he loved so much he'd had to bring it with him. He rode it up and down the front walk while Mike and Sam kept an eye on him and Sarah pitched in to help with the last-minute chores in the kitchen. The sweet potato casserole and the scalloped potatoes went into the oven with the ham for the last hour, even though the cooking temperature for the vegetables was a little different from that for the meat. They would just cook the side dishes for a little longer than the recipes called for.

Carolyn started making her green bean casserole. She explained to the others that she had a new recipe using fresh green beans and mushrooms rather than the canned ones. She showed them the recipe she had written down on a card. Phyllis thought it sounded like it would taste better than the old recipe. She definitely would be putting some on her plate.

The women worked together, talking about family and friends. It seemed like no time at all had passed when the green bean casserole was assembled and the ham had finished cooking. Phyllis took the baked ham out of the oven and placed it on the counter to cool a little before slicing. It was time to crank up the heat on the oven and warm up all the dishes made ahead of time.

A little after one o'clock, Eve set the table while Phyllis took the golden brown dinner rolls out of the oven. Carolyn and Sarah started putting various dishes on the table. There were so many bowls and platters, it took careful placement to get all the food in the middle of the table.

When everyone sat down to eat at about one thirty, the dining room table was full. Phyllis looked around at the smiling, happy faces and thought that more than the table was full.

Her heart was, too.

It was as fine a meal as she could remember, even if she did say so herself. The ham was so tender that it practically fell off the bone, and the cola gave it a wonderful sweet taste, but not too sweet. The wild rice and cranberry stuffing was perfect, and the sweet potato casserole delicious, as were all the other side dishes. By the time they had finished eating, they were all stuffed. Carolyn said, "My goodness, I'm so full, I can't even eat any dessert."

"Well, I've been accused of havin' a hollow leg," Sam said, "but I think I could do with a piece of pumpkin pie. Just not too big of one. I'll have to try the chocolate pecan pie a little later," he added with a smile.

"Same here," Mike said.

After the leftovers had been put away and the dishes had been rinsed and put in the dishwasher—Mike and Sam volunteering to take care of that chore—Carolyn took the extra pies and left to spend the rest of the day at her daughter's house. Eve, yawning, said that she was going upstairs to take a nap. Mike, Sarah, and Bobby sat down on the sofa in the living room so that Bobby could watch an animated Christmas movie on TV, and within half an hour all three of them were sound asleep, with Bobby snugly nestled between his parents.

Phyllis walked out to the kitchen to make sure nothing that needed to be done had been neglected. Sam strolled after her, and when he saw the plate of cookies sitting on the counter, he reached out to get one of them.

"You can't *possibly* still be hungry," Phyllis said as he took a bite of the lime snowflake sugar cookie.

"Well, I'm not starvin'," Sam admitted. He propped a hip against the counter. "But these are mighty good cookies. Hard to pass 'em up." He took another bite, then said, "Life's taught me that if you pass up too many good things, then *they* start to pass *you* by."

"I suppose that's true," Phyllis said as she leaned back beside him. "A person only gets so many opportunities in life."

Sam took the last bite of cookie in his hand. "Yep."

"Sam . . ." She started to turn toward him.

But he was already turning toward her, and his arms went around her and his lips met hers, and as he kissed her she tasted the sweet crystals of sugar from the cookie that still clung to his mouth.

Then she rested her head against his chest and his hand lay on her back, and he whispered, "Merry Christmas, Phyllis."

She smiled as she remembered something that went all the way back to her childhood. Each Christmas, she had paused to wonder what the *next* Christmas would be like, to think about all the things that might happen between now and then.

"Merry Christmas, Sam," she whispered, and thought that for the first time in a long while, she was really looking forward to finding out what the next year would bring.

Recipes

Lime Snowflake Cookies

¾ cup butter or margarine, softened
1 cup granulated sugar
1 teaspoon key lime juice
1 egg
2 cups all-purpose flour
1½ teaspoons baking powder
¼ teaspoon baking soda

If your butter is not softened, place it in a microwavable bowl and heat just until soft. Mix sugar with butter; then add lime juice. Break egg into bowl containing sugar mixture. Whip slightly to distribute egg white and yolk. Stir until mixture is evenly moist. Sift together and add the three dry ingredients. Stir by hand until a dough forms. Wrap in waxed paper and chill in refrigerator, about 1 hour until firm.

Heat oven to 350 degrees F.

Roll chilled dough out until flat and ¼ inch thick. Use cookie cutters to make shapes. If you don't have a snowflake cookie cutter, you can cut freehand with a knife to make each cookie a little different. Dust with granulated sugar to make the cookies sparkle.

Bake cookies for 10 to 12 minutes, or until edges just begin to turn light golden brown. Do not for overbake. Cool 1 minute, and then remove from cookie sheet and place on a rack to cool completely.

Makes about 4 dozen cookies, depending on the size of the cookie cutters.

Pecan Pie Cookies

Cookies
3 large eggs
¾ cup (1½ sticks) margarine or butter, softened
¾ cup granulated sugar
1 teaspoon vanilla extract
¼ teaspoon salt
3 cups all-purpose flour

Filling
1 large egg
¼ cup sugar
Small pinch salt
⅓ cup dark corn syrup
1 tablespoon melted butter
1 cup pecan halves

Preheat oven to 350 degrees F.

Grease or put parchment paper on large cookie sheet.

For cookies, in large bowl, beat 3 eggs lightly. Add margarine, sugar, vanilla, and salt. Beat with mixer at medium speed until completely mixed, scraping the sides of the bowl frequently. Add flour and stir until blended. Cover bowl with plastic wrap and put in refrigerator while making filling.

For filling, in microwavable bowl, beat egg with sugar, salt, dark corn syrup, and melted butter until well blended. Microwave filling on high for 3 minutes.

Take cookie dough out of refrigerator. Dough should be slightly stiff. Using a tablespoon, place cookies 2 inches apart on prepared cookie sheet. With thumb, make an indentation in the center of each dough ball large enough for filling and pecan. Fill each indentation with a rounded ¼ teaspoon of filling. Top each cookie with a pecan half.

Bake until lightly golden, 16 minutes. Transfer cookies to wire rack to cool.

Makes about 4 dozen cookies.

Sam's Fudgy Peanut Butter Cookies

Cookies
2 cups granulated sugar
½ cup evaporated milk
4 tablespoons cocoa
4 tablespoons butter or margarine
1 teaspoon vanilla extract
2½ cups quick-cooking oats

Filling
¼ cup peanut butter
¼ cup white corn syrup

Combine sugar, milk, cocoa, and butter in a medium saucepan. Bring to a boil over medium heat, stirring constantly; boil for 1 minute. Remove from heat; stir in vanilla. Add oatmeal and stir to blend thoroughly.

Drop by teaspoonfuls onto waxed paper. Make a well in each cookie with a spoon. The dough hardens rapidly, so work quickly.

Combine peanut butter and corn syrup in a small saucepan. Bring to a boil over medium heat, stirring constantly. Boil for 1 minute. Fill each cookie indention with a dollop of peanut butter–syrup mixture.

Cool cookies on wax paper until they harden.

Makes about 4 dozen cookies.

Gingerdoodle Cookies

1 tablespoon granulated sugar
1 teaspoon ground cinnamon
1 tablespoon ground ginger
1 cup shortening
1½ cups granulated sugar
2 eggs
1 teaspoon vanilla extract
2¾ cups all-purpose flour
1 teaspoon baking soda
½ teaspoon salt
2 teaspoons cream of tartar

Preheat oven to 400 degrees F.

In a shallow bowl, combine 1 tablespoon sugar, cinnamon, and ginger; set aside. Cream shortening; gradually add 1½ cups sugar, beating well. Add eggs; beat well. Stir in vanilla.

In a separate bowl, sift together flour, soda, salt, and cream of tartar. Add sifted ingredients to creamed mixture; stir until well blended.

Shape dough into 1-inch balls, and roll in cinnamon-ginger-sugar mixture. Place cookies 2 inches apart on lightly greased baking sheets.

Bake cookies for 6 minutes or until lightly browned. Remove to wire racks to cool.

Makes about 4 dozen cookies.

Chocolate Pecan Pie

$^1\!/_3$ cup butter, melted
$^1\!/_3$ cup unsweetened cocoa powder
$^2\!/_3$ cup white sugar
$^1\!/_2$ teaspoon salt
1 cup light corn syrup
1 teaspoon vanilla
3 eggs
1 cup pecan halves
1 9-inch unbaked pie crust

Preheat oven to 375 degrees F.

Melt butter in microwave. Mix cocoa powder and sugar with butter. Add salt, corn syrup, and vanilla. Beat in eggs; then stir in pecan halves. Pour mixture into pie shell. Cover crust edge with strips of aluminum foil, or a crust shield. Pie rises as it bakes, but will fall back down as it cools.

Bake until set, 35 to 40 minutes. Allow pie to cool before serving.

Serves 8.

Pumpkin Pie

1½ cups pumpkin puree
1 can (12 fluid ounces) evaporated milk
2 eggs
¾ cup granulated sugar
1 tablespoon all-purpose flour
½ teaspoon salt
2 teaspoons vanilla extract
1 teaspoon pumpkin pie spice
1 9-inch unbaked pie crust

Preheat oven to 450 degrees F.

In a large bowl, combine pumpkin, evaporated milk, eggs, sugar, flour, salt, vanilla, and pumpkin pie spice. Pour filling into pie shell. Cover the sides of the crust with foil before baking to keep it from burning.

Bake for 20 minutes at 450 degrees F; then turn oven temperature down to 350 degrees F and continue baking 40 more minutes or until a knife inserted in center comes out clean. Cool completely on a wire rack before serving.

Serves 8.

Stuffed Zucchini

2 tablespoons olive (not virgin) oil
½ medium yellow onion, diced
1 tablespoon minced garlic
½ cup diced red bell pepper
1 cup peeled and diced eggplant
Salt
Pepper
1 tablespoon chopped basil
2 tablespoons minced fresh parsley
1 cup diced tomatoes
1 cup grated mozzarella cheese
¼ cup grated Parmesan cheese
3 slices whole wheat bread, cubed
4 6- to 8-inch zucchinis, whole

Heat olive oil in a sauté pan over medium-high heat. Add onion, garlic, and bell pepper, and sauté until tender (about 3 minutes), stirring frequently.

Add the eggplant, season lightly with salt and pepper, and continue to cook for 10 more minutes.

Add the herbs and tomatoes and cook for 3 to 5 minutes more.

Add mozzarella and Parmesan cheese and bread cubes; then remove from the heat and allow to cool.

While the stuffing cooks, prepare the zucchini. Wash them well and slice them in half lengthwise.

Hollow out the center of the zucchini. You can use a spoon to scoop out the seeds and pulp. Leave at least ¼ inch of flesh. If the pulp and seeds won't come out easily, use a knife.

When the zucchini halves have been hollowed out and the mixture has cooled enough, spoon the stuffing mixture into them so each one is fairly full.

Place the zucchini in a baking dish and bake at 400 degrees F for 10 to 15 minutes, or until the flesh of the zucchini is cooked. Test for doneness by poking with a toothpick.

Note: If you prepared this recipe ahead of time, cook a little longer at 325 degrees F, until zucchini is cooked and stuffing is heated through.

Cut into ½-inch slices, holding the slices together, then transfer each zucchini half together to a serving dish.

Serves 8.

Corn Bread

1½ cups all-purpose flour
⅓ cup sugar
½ cup yellow cornmeal
1 tablespoon baking powder
½ teaspoon salt
1¼ cups milk
2 eggs, lightly beaten
⅓ cup vegetable oil
3 tablespoons butter or margarine, melted

Preheat oven to 350 degrees F.

Grease an 8-inch-square baking pan.

Combine flour, sugar, cornmeal, baking powder, and salt in a medium bowl. Combine milk, eggs, vegetable oil, and butter in a small bowl; mix well. Add to flour mixture; stir just until blended. Pour into prepared baking pan.

Bake for 35 minutes or until wooden toothpick inserted in center comes out clean.

Serves 8.

Wild Rice and Cranberry Corn Bread Stuffing

¼ cup (½ stick) butter, divided
1 cup chopped red onion
½ cup chopped celery
5 cups chicken stock
1¼ cups uncooked wild rice
1¼ cups uncooked brown rice
1½ cups dried cranberries
1 teaspoon dried thyme
1 teaspoon dried marjoram
2 cups crumbled corn bread
¼ cup chopped fresh parsley
Salt and pepper, to taste

Preheat oven to 350 degrees F.

Melt 2 tablespoons butter in large skillet over medium heat. Add red onion and celery, and sauté until soft, about 4 to 5 minutes. Remove from heat and set aside.

Bring stock to a boil in a large saucepan. Add wild rice and bring to a boil. Reduce heat to low, cover, and simmer 30 minutes.

Stir in brown rice, cover, and simmer until liquid is almost absorbed, about 15 minutes.

Stir in cranberries, thyme, marjoram, red onion and celery mixture, and remaining butter. Cover and simmer 3 minutes. Stir in corn bread and parsley. Salt and pepper to taste.

continued . . .

Butter a 9 × 13-inch baking dish. Transfer stuffing to baking dish and cover with buttered aluminum foil. Bake until heated through, about 10 to 15 minutes.

Serves 12.

Cola Ham

1 18-pound cured ham
1 16-ounce bottle cola
Canned pineapple rings
Brown sugar
Maraschino cherries
Cloves

Preheat oven to 325 degrees F.

Place ham in shallow roasting pan. Poke a few holes in the ham down to the bone, or if you have one of those syringes for meat solutions, inject coke from out of a fresh bottle directly into the meat. Put as much of the cola into the ham as you can. Baste the ham with remaining cola.

With toothpicks, stick pineapple rings on the top and sides of the ham. Sprinkle brown sugar on the rings. With toothpicks, place a cherry inside each pineapple ring, and then stick some cloves in the pineapple rings. Cover and bake for 15 to 18 minutes per pound of ham, or until the ham reaches an internal temperature of 140 degrees F, basting with cola several times during cooking.

Note: The pineapple, brown sugar, cherries, and cloves are to dress up this ham for the holiday. You can use just the ham and cola to get a very nice baked ham. The cola makes it so tender, it will fall off the bone.

Serves 24 to 30.

Dinner Rolls

1 package dry yeast
¾ cup warm water (110 to 115 degrees F)
¼ cup sugar
1 teaspoon salt
2¼ cups flour, divided
1 egg
¼ cup butter (softened)

Dissolve yeast in warm water. Using mixer on low speed, add sugar, salt, and half of the flour. Beat well, add egg and butter, and continue mixing while adding remaining flour.

Cover bowl with a cloth, and let dough rise in a warm place for 40 to 50 minutes.

Stir down batter. Using ice cream scoop, drop scoopfuls in greased muffin tins. Let rise for about an hour, until double in size.

Bake in a hot oven (400 degrees F) for 15 minutes or until golden brown.

Makes 1 dozen rolls.

Peachy Keen Salad

Salad
1 can pineapple chunks
(if you use fresh pineapple, you will also need 1 small 6-oz. can of pineapple juice for dressing)
5 peaches, peeled, pitted, and sliced
1 pound strawberries, rinsed, hulled, and sliced
½ pound seedless green grapes
½ pound seedless red grapes
3 bananas, peeled and sliced
¼ cup granulated sugar

Dressing
Juice of one small lime
½ cup pineapple juice

Drain can of pineapple, and save juice for dressing. Combine chopped and sliced fruits in a large serving bowl; toss gently. Sprinkle with sugar. Combine dressing ingredients in a small bowl. Pour dressing mixture over fruit and toss gently to combine.

Cover and chill the fruit salad thoroughly before serving.

Serves 20.

Sweet Potato Casserole

Sweet Potatoes

2 cans (29 ounces each) sweet potatoes,
packed in light syrup, drained
¾ cup evaporated milk
½ cup packed brown sugar
2 large eggs
2 tablespoons butter or margarine, melted
¾ teaspoon pumpkin pie spice
½ teaspoon salt

Topping

3 tablespoons brown sugar
⅓ cup finely chopped pecans
1 cup flaked coconut
¼ cup melted butter

Preheat oven to 350 degrees F.

Lightly grease a 3-quart casserole.

For the sweet potatoes, place sweet potatoes, evaporated milk, brown sugar, eggs, butter, pumpkin pie spice, and salt in food processor or blender. Blend until smooth. Pour into prepared casserole dish.

For the topping, in a small bowl, mix brown sugar, chopped nuts, coconut, and melted butter; sprinkle over casserole.

Bake for 40 to 45 minutes or until golden brown.

Serves 12.

Scalloped Potatoes

6 potatoes, peeled and cut into ⅛-inch slices
Salt and white pepper to taste
2 cups half-and-half
1 tablespoon dried mustard
1 teaspoon cornstarch
1 teaspoon onion powder
2 tablespoons butter
⅓ cup grated Parmesan cheese

Preheat oven to 350 degrees F.

Layer sliced potatoes in a 9 × 13-inch glass baking dish. Season with salt and white pepper. Combine half-and-half, mustard, cornstarch, onion powder, and butter in heavy saucepan, and heat until it starts to thicken. Pour over potatoes.

Cover and bake for 1 hour. Remove cover and top with Parmesan cheese. Bake uncovered 30 minutes longer or until cheese is golden brown and potatoes are tender. Serve immediately.

Serves 8.

Fresh Green Bean Casserole

Beans

2 quarts water

1 tablespoon salt

1 pound fresh green beans, ends snapped, broken into bite-sized pieces

Mushrooms and Sauce

8 ounces baby portabello or white button mushrooms

1 tablespoon unsalted butter

1 tablespoon minced garlic

Salt and pepper to taste

1½ tablespoons flour

¾ cup chicken stock

¾ cup half-and-half

Topping

1 slice dry whole grain bread (you can use any bread)

1 tablespoon unsalted butter

Salt and pepper to taste

½ of a 2.8-ounce can of french fried onions

Bring the water to a boil in a large pot. Add the salt and beans to the boiling water. Cover and cook for 6 minutes. The beans will be bright green. Fill a large bowl with ice water. Drain beans in a colander, and then plunge it into the bowl of ice water to stop the cooking. Drain beans thoroughly.

Clean the mushrooms thoroughly, breaking off and discarding the stems. Break the mushroom tops into pieces (slicing will change the texture). Melt the butter in a skillet. Add the mushrooms, garlic, salt, and pepper. Cook, stirring often, until mushrooms begin to soften, about 6 minutes. Stir in flour, and cook another minute. Add the chicken stock, and bring to a simmer. Add the half-and-half, and simmer until sauce thickens, 10 to 15 minutes. Taste and adjust seasonings. Stir in cooked beans.

Preheat oven to 425 degrees F.

Transfer bean mixture to a greased baking dish.

In a food processor, process the bread, butter, and seasonings in about 10 quick pulses. Sprinkle mixture over casserole. Sprinkle on the onions last.

Note: You can put the onions over only half the casserole if you have family members that really don't like onions. This casserole is good even without the french fried onions.

Bake for 15 minutes.

Serves 8.

Phyllis's Favorite Hot Cocoa

¼ cup unsweetened cocoa powder
½ cup granulated sugar
⅓ cup hot water
4 cups milk
½ teaspoon vanilla extract

Mix cocoa, sugar, and water in a saucepan over medium heat. Stir constantly until mixture boils. Continue to cook and stir for 1 minute after mixture starts boiling.

Stir in the milk. Heat, but do not boil. Remove from heat and add vanilla; blend well. Serve at once.

Serves 4.

About the Author

Photo by James Reasoner

Livia J. Washburn has been a professional writer for more than twenty years. She received the Private Eye Writers of America Shamus Award and the American Mystery Award for her first mystery, *Wild Night*, written under her maiden name, L. J. Washburn, and was nominated for a Spur Award by the Western Writers of America for a novel written with her husband, James Reasoner. She lives in a small town in Texas with her husband, two daughters, and two dogs. Her Web site is at www.liviawashburn.com, and you can e-mail her livia@flash.net.

Ready for another trip to Weatherford, Texas?
Read on for an excerpt from

Murder by the Slice

Available in stores or at penguin.com.

The sun blazed down on the sidewalk in front of the Wal-Mart located in Weatherford, Texas. Phyllis Newsom was glad she had worn a hat to shade her head. Unfortunately, that didn't help the part of her sitting on the uncomfortable metal folding chair.

According to the calendar autumn had started, but that didn't mean the weather had begun to cool off. That was still a month away, maybe even longer. For now, it was still hot—Texas hot.

From the chair beside Phyllis's, Eve Turner waved at someone she knew and called, "Hello there, dear. Would you like to buy a cake or some cookies and help out the Retired Teachers Association Scholarship Fund?"

The man she had spoken to looked a little uncomfortable, as well he might since his wife was with him. Eve had probably had one or more of their children in her English class when she was still teaching, and knowing Eve, she had flirted shamelessly with the man at every school function the parents attended. As she smiled brightly at the man, he said, "Ah, maybe when we come out."

His wife just tightened her grip on his arm and kept walking.

Phyllis wasn't surprised by Eve's failure to sell anything. She had been out here for nearly an hour with Eve, Carolyn Wilbarger, and Sam Fletcher, the four of them sitting behind a folding table filled with cakes and plates of cookies, and they'd sold very little. The cookies were holding up fine, but the icing on the cakes was starting to melt against the clear plastic wrap that covered them.

Phyllis glanced up at the sun. It would move around the building so that they would be in the shade in another hour or so, but it was going to be a long hour until then.

She was as enthusiastic a member of the Retired Teachers Association as anyone—she had spent almost her entire adult life teaching, after all—but she wished she hadn't let herself be talked into helping man this bake sale table.

It was awfully difficult to say no to Dolly Williamson, the retired superintendent of the school district and the head of the RTA. Besides, the scholarship fund needed to be built up again. Each year the association awarded college scholarships to two deserving students who were the children of educators. The amount of those scholarships depended entirely on how much money the association could raise during the year.

The fall bake sale was the first major fund-raiser each year. Dolly had persuaded Carolyn to help with it, and from there it was inevitable that Phyllis, Eve, and Sam would be drawn in, as well. The four of them shared the big house that Phyllis had lived in for years with her late husband, Kenny, and they were good friends.

One thing you could say about Wal-Mart: The place didn't lack for customers, especially on a sunny Saturday afternoon. A steady stream of people had gone in and out of the store since Phyllis and the others had set up their table and chairs and hung the signs Phyllis had printed on the computer announcing what the bake sale was for. A few of them stopped and bought cookies on their way back to their cars. Phyllis didn't think they had sold a single cake.

In a way, she could understand why. It cost so much to live these days that most folks really had to watch what they spent. But it was for a good cause, and the prices weren't really that bad.

A pickup drove by with country music blasting through its open windows. It was followed a few minutes later by another pickup with loud rap music coming from it. Phyllis was always a little amused by the sight of young white men in snap-button shirts and cowboy hats listening to rap, but it was becoming more common.

She saw an attractive woman in her thirties emerge from the store and start toward the bake sale table with a couple of elementary-aged children in tow, a boy and a girl. The woman had shoulder-length light brown hair and wore blue jeans and a T-shirt with LOVING ELEMENTARY printed on it. Phyllis knew that wasn't a declaration of affection but rather a reference to Oliver Loving Elementary School, one of several elementary schools in the Weatherford School District. It was named for the famous rancher and cattleman who had been the inspiration for one of the characters in *Lonesome Dove,* either Gus or Call; Phyllis never could remember which. Loving was buried here in Weatherford.

The woman had a somewhat harried look about her—shopping at Wal-Mart with a couple of kids would do that—but she smiled pleasantly as she came up to the table and said, "Hello, Carolyn."

"Marie, it's good to see you," Carolyn said. "How's Russ?"

"Oh, all right, I guess."

Carolyn turned to Phyllis and asked, "Do you know Marie Tyler?"

"I don't believe so," Phyllis said.

Carolyn performed the introductions, adding, "And that's Amber and Aaron. Marie and her husband, Russ, go to the same church I do."

"It's nice to meet you, Marie," Phyllis said.

"You, too." Marie turned back to Carolyn and went on. "You know I'm on the PTO board at the school."

"No, I didn't know that, but I'm not surprised."

"Yeah, I'm the fund-raising chairperson. You know what that means at this time of year."

"The carnival," Phyllis and Carolyn and Eve all said at the same time.

Marie nodded. "That's right."

Sam leaned back in his chair, propped a foot on the other leg's somewhat knobby knee, and said with a smile, "Coachin' at the high school, I never had much to do with the elementary carnivals, except one year when they decided to put on a donkey basketball game in conjunction with it." He shook his head. "Before that was over, I sure wished I'd never agreed to let those donkeys in my gym."

"Well, we're not going to have any donkey basketball games," Marie said, "although we may have a pony ride. But it'll be outside on the playground."

Phyllis had taught junior high history, but she had been involved in several elementary school carnivals when her son, Mike, was that age. She had been a member of what was then called the PTA—the Parent-Teacher Association—at the school he'd attended. These days it was called the Parent-Teacher Organization, but pretty much only the name had changed. The group was still composed mostly of parents and run by a board of half a dozen or so volunteers, almost always women. It was very rare to find a man willing to be on a PTO board. Finding enough volunteer moms to take care of everything was a big enough chore.

The PTO spent most of the year raising funds. The money was spent on things the school needed that weren't included in the budget, such as copy machines, extra books for the library, and playground equipment. One of the major fund-raisers was the school carnival, usually held sometime during October. In the old days, they had often been tied in with Halloween, but of course such things were forbidden now. They had to be called fall carnivals or harvest festivals or something noncontroversial like that.

The classic school carnival was set up on the playground, with open booths around the edges, which were formed by bales of hay or sketchy wooden frameworks. Each homeroom in the school was responsible for one of the booths, where games designed to appeal to young children were played, such as ring toss, throwing a baseball at stacks of milk bottles, and "fishing" in wading pools filled with sand and little prizes. Other games that required more room were conducted out in the middle of the playground. There were also face-painting and temporary tattoo booths and sometimes dunking booths, pony rides, miniature trains, "bounce houses," and anything else the PTO board could scrounge up to make a little money. There was no charge to attend the carnival, but to take part in any of the games required a fifty-cent ticket at each booth. Kids raced from booth to booth, clutching strings of tickets and the prizes they had already won. Inside the school, in the gymnasium and the cafeteria, other activities would take place, such as entertainment by local musicians and dancers, and there was a snack bar selling cold drinks, hot dogs, nachos, and candy.

And there was usually a bake sale, too, Phyllis suddenly remembered, which was why it came as no surprise to her when Marie Tyler said, "I could really use some help, Carolyn, and from the looks of this, you and your friends have a lot of experience with bake sales."

"Oh, I don't know . . . ," Carolyn said, as Phyllis was silently pleading, *Don't get us involved in this. Please, Carolyn.*

Marie leaned closer to the table and lowered her voice to a conspiratorial volume. "It would mean a lot to me if I could find somebody willing to take over the bake sale. There's just so much involved in putting on one of these carnivals, and to tell you the truth, Shannon's really been on my ass lately about getting it all done."

Phyllis tried not to let her lips tighten in disapproval at Marie's crude language. She didn't like to be judgmental, and she knew perfectly well that this was a different day and age from the one in which she had grown up. But it still bothered her to hear a lady talk like that, especially in front of little ones.

Carolyn looked over at her and asked, "What do you think, Phyllis?"

I think you're trying to pass the buck to me and make me be the bad guy, Phyllis thought. But she said, "We pretty much have our plates full with the Retired Teachers Association—"

Before she could actually say no, another woman walked up to the table. She was older and heavyset, and the brightly colored dress she wore made her look even bigger. Her hair was dyed a startling shade of black. She said in a booming voice, "Hello, ladies. And you, too, of course, Sam."

"Howdy, Dolly," he said with a nod. "Good to see you again."

"Marie, how are you?" Dolly Williamson said as she put her arms around Marie and gave her a hug. Phyllis wasn't surprised that Dolly knew who Marie was. The former superintendent was still so plugged in to the school district that she probably knew all the PTO board members from every campus.

"I'm fine, Mrs. Williamson," Marie said. "I was just trying to recruit Carolyn and her friends to run the bake sale for the carnival at Loving."

"Why, I think that's a wonderful idea!" Dolly beamed at the four people behind the table. "I know you'll all do a fine job."

"Wait a minute," Phyllis began, but she had a sinking feeling that it was already too late. Once Dolly got an idea in her head, she was the original unstoppable force.

"After all," Dolly went on as if she hadn't heard Phyllis, "you're doing so well here."

"Haven't sold much," Sam said.

"You will, you will. Everything looks so good." Dolly turned back to Marie. "This was lucky for you, my dear. Now you can concentrate on the rest of your job."

"I know," Marie said. She gave Phyllis and the others a smile and added, "Thank you, guys, so much."

Phyllis felt like pointing out that she wasn't a "guy," and neither were Carolyn and Eve. But there was no point in worrying about such things now, she told herself. What mattered was that she had been roped into helping with the carnival bake sale, along with her friends. They might have been able to withstand the pressure from Marie, but once Dolly had walked up and found out what was going on, they were lost.

Dolly gave Marie another hug and waved a pudgy hand at the others, then went into the store. Marie said, "I'll give you a call, Carolyn, and let you know all the details you'll need to know. Thanks again."

Carolyn nodded and smiled weakly. "You're welcome."

"This'll help keep Shannon from giving me so much shi— I mean, trouble." Marie waved and added, "Bye, guys," as she led her kids into the parking lot and headed for the family SUV.

Carolyn turned to the others and said, "I'm sorry. I don't know what happened."

"Dolly happened," Sam said. He chuckled. "Sort of like a force of nature, isn't she? Doesn't have to stay around very long, but when she rolls through, she brings changes."

"Well, maybe it'll be fun," Carolyn said. "It might be, you never know. And we *do* have experience at putting on bake sales."

Eve said, "Perhaps you do, dear. I was never really the domestic type." She smiled over at Sam, with whom she had been flirting ever since he had rented a room from Phyllis and moved into the big old house on the tree-shaded street a few blocks from the courthouse square. "Which isn't to say that I couldn't still learn if I needed to. If the right man came along and asked the right question . . ."

Sam called to a family going into the store, "You folks want to buy some cookies?"

Phyllis leaned over to Carolyn and asked, "Who's this Shannon that Marie was talking about?"

"Shannon Dunston," Carolyn replied. "She's the president of the PTO board at Loving. And from what I hear, she runs things with an iron fist, as the old saying goes."

"That's odd. Usually you try to get people to do things by being nice to them, especially when you're relying on volunteers."

"That's not the way Shannon looks at it. Although I shouldn't say that, since I don't really know her. I'm just going by what I've heard."

"Well, maybe with our help, she'll get off Marie's, uh, posterior." Phyllis looked at the other three. "Right . . . guys?"